Moonlit Woods
By Brandy I. Timmons

Book Development Resources

2006 North Redwood Rd.

Salt Lake City, UT 84116

brandytimmons@bdrqazz.com

This book is a book of fiction. Names, characters, places, and incidents are either the product of the author's imagination or are used fictitiously. Any resemblance to actual persons, living or dead, business establishments, events, or locales is entirely coincidental.

ISBN 978-1-946987-08-2

Cover art by Austin Beckstrom

First Edition, 2020

Part Two of the Children of Kaespars Book Series

10 9 8 7 6 5 4 3 2 1

To those who walk by the light of the full moon,

you are not alone.

TABLE OF CONTENTS

1 CLARA WARREN 7

2 THE LODGE 15

3 RUNNING WITH THE PACK 27

4 A TERRIBLE TRUTH 40

5 THE LONE WOLF 51

6 THE FIRST MEETING 68

7 UPROAR 80

8 ACCUSATIONS AND ULTIMATUMS 91

9 INTERNAL DILEMMA 106

10 THE PACK 120

11 STUMPED 132

12 LOYALTIES 145

13 BIG, BAD WOLVES 157

14 PREVENTATIVE MEASURES 170

INTERLUDES 181

15 DATE NIGHT DISTRACTION 199

16 RANSOM CALL 212

17 FINDING NELSON 222

18 JOINING FORCES 233

19 FOR SARA 242

20 THE SILVER BULLET 264

21 NEW RESOLVE 274

22 TO THE FUTURE 286

TO MY READERS 292

ACKNOWLEDGEMENTS 293

ABOUT THE AUTHOR 294

BOOK SUMMARY 295

CHILDREN OF KAESPARS 296

DON'T MISS THE REST OF THE SERIES 297

1 Clara Warren

The brief stench of sunscreen and a gagging mixture of rotting eggs, cabbage, and mothballs on the dawn's breeze made her nose itch. Clara stopped tossing clothes haphazardly on her futon bed and sniffed again. The extreme smell hung on the morning breeze slipping in the cracked-open window, and it was growing stronger.

A vampire was near her apartment.

She slunk to her window and crouched out of sight. The wolf in her mind whined for a fight, to chase down the invading bloodsucker. With the full moon so close, it had more power and her entire body ached to transform.

Shifting her weight, Clara could see just enough to peer through the bottom of the closed blinds. The early morning rays slipped through the thin slots, and she squinted to make sense of the small figure approaching the entrance to her old apartment complex.

The man on the steps had to be the vampire, yet the bulging backpack and dark hoodie looked familiar, as did the man's gait. A heavier breeze pushed through the window opening, bouncing the blinds into her face.

He still smelled human? The scents of decay and sunscreen weren't as powerful as she was used to, and she recognized the clove-scented aftershave mixed with coffee grounds and lavender. The scent of coffee was feeble, at least a day old.

The man glanced up at her window as he opened the lobby door. She recognized his face instantly: it was Sean Butler, her newish boyfriend.

And he smelled like a vampire.

Clara jumped to her feet and ran to her door. It didn't take long in her tiny studio apartment, yet she breathed heavily as she waited to hear Sean's steps down the hall.

She'd smelled the decay and sunscreen before at Café Compendium where Sean worked. It'd been stronger lately, but the café used to be a witch's shop before it turned into a bookstore and café. Supernatural visitors weren't uncommon, even if they didn't know it was a witch's fading presence that attracted them there. If Sean had checked out books for a vampire, the revolting scents would stick to his clothes. She hated it, but when he brewed fresh coffee, the vampire whiffs were drowned out for a while. She always ordered coffee first thing at the shop when she was there to study.

Her phone buzzed from her nightstand as she waited at the door, and Clara pivoted, not sure what to do. Sean smelled like a vampire, and her brother was going to pick her up within an hour to give her a ride to the pack's full moon retreat. Benjamin didn't know about Sean yet, and him meeting her boyfriend when he smelled of the enemy would be disastrous.

Why did he smell like a vampire?

The elevator dinged softly, and the hallway carpet muffled rushed footsteps. There wasn't time to check her phone now—hopefully Benjamin wasn't saying he was running early. He was always punctual, so he wasn't running late.

At the first heavy knock, Clara threw open the door and hugged Sean. His neck smelled human, a musty flesh scent mixed with salt and oils, but the vampire stench clung to his hoodie and backpack. It was stronger than the occasional whiff at the café—was he actively spending time with one? Or at least one his friends was and smell was rubbing off on him. Normally Sean liked talking about his friends, but lately his humor had drained away and been replaced by bitterness when he mentioned them, especially Thomas. Hopefully it was one of them mixed up in the vampire world, not Sean.

"Clara?"

She released him and pulled him inside where the hallway's orange light didn't assault their eyes and add a sickly tinge to their skin. Yet inside, Sean didn't look any better. The bags under his eyes were much thicker, and he had a new gauntness in his cheeks. There was also no glimmer of his usual laughter that had made her want to talk with him when they first met. Something was plaguing him—probably the vampire who was making him stink.

She wrinkled her nose, but the musty mothball and rotting eggs smell didn't relent. Hiding her disgust with a smile, she asked, "Hey, what's up?"

Sean returned her smile, but his was wan and unconvincing.

"Hey, Clara," he said, slipping his backpack off his shoulder. "I'm sorry for not calling first. I didn't know where else to go. Mind if I stay a bit?"

"Of course not," Clara said, but her heart raced in her throat. She didn't have time to visit. Her packing was unfinished and Benjamin was going to arrive soon.

Sean grimaced as he stepped around her and plopped down on her futon bed on top of her clean clothes she wanted to pack. Shit. She couldn't pack them now, not when they smelled like a vampire. She'd have to replace them with some of her old

9

clothes deep from within her closet, something untouched by the smell Sean carried and didn't make her look like a 20-year-old from the wrong decade.

She followed him, setting his backpack on the floor as she sat down next to him. A toothbrush still in its package stuck out of one of the pockets. He must have left his apartment in a hurry and not gone back, stocking up on any forgotten items at the store. Whatever was going on was serious.

"Sean, are you ok?" Clara asked.

Sean nodded, then shook his head after further consideration.

"I messed up," he said.

"What do you mean?"

Clara watched him cautiously, scanning for the slightest change in expression. There was already a wealth of information offered up by his posture. His shoulders were slumped, caving in toward his chest, and his head was bowed in defeat.

"Um," he said. Whatever words were fighting to escape had been met with resistance. Sean fell silent.

"Sean?"

"I just walked out on Thomas. And my sister. And everyone."

There it was. That was the change she'd been looking for. Sean's brow furrowed as he talked. The wound was still fresh.

"Why?"

Both of them had a steady group of friends who were more than family to each other. It was something she liked about Sean, that he was willing to fight for them. If he was leaving them, something bigger had happened than she originally thought. Vampire problems were never small.

"Because I'm stupid," Sean said.

"Not a real answer."

Sean barely chuckled then lifted his head and smiled.

"Because I'm selfish and bad under pressure," he said. "How's that for an answer?"

"Still not good enough. Not if you're going to be knocking on my door before we're normally awake."

She left him on the futon and made instant coffee. It didn't cover the smell quite as well as the café's brews, but it helped. Sean looked a little more at ease with a steaming mug in his hands, and after a few sips, he opened up.

"Thomas just went through a pretty big change in his life. I mean, a huge change. Pretty much the biggest humanly possible."

Oh no.

"Or inhumanly," Sean added as an afterthought.

Shit.

"He's had a rough few weeks and really needed support, you know? I did pretty ok for a while. I'm not too good at feelings, but we've remained close friends even when he got insanely busy with med school a few years ago." His shoulders tensed, but he kept talking. "Things just got a little messed up and I couldn't take it. He's being such a prick right now."

"He's probably feeling a little insecure," Clara said warily. The hot mug warmed her hands, but she wasn't drinking. Nothing else mattered except Sean's words and how much the coffee smell could cover up his presence when Benjamin arrived in half an hour. "Big change, right?"

"Yeah." Sean sighed. "I know I'm overreacting, but I just couldn't keep it in control. I can't be around him right now."

"Time is the best medicine for cases like this. Just don't go see him." Could she convince him to put some space between him and his friend's vampire crisis?

"The problem is, all our other friends are staying with him, too," Sean said.

"They're taking his side?"

"No, they're literally staying with him," Sean said. He finished his coffee and set the mug down on the closest bedside table. "Artemis got attacked the other day, so we've all been staying with Thomas's new boss, just to be sure."

Clara laughed with a deceptively lighthearted tone. This was getting worse. "Just to be sure of what? Did you get sucked into the mafia or something?"

"Yeah, I wish."

Sean's expression was so grim. Clara stopped her thinly veiled laughter. Time to try a different approach. She was running out of time and she needed him to tell her if Thomas was really a vampire.

"I'm glad Artemis is safe. She's a lovely person, and I'd hate for anything to happen to her. But what about you? Do you feel unsafe?"

Sean shrugged and slowly rubbed his eyes, his face obscured by his large hands. "Not sure what I feel, anymore. Clara, I can't go back. Not yet. Would you mind if I crashed here for a couple of days?"

Dammit. He'd avoided revealing the truth. Clara glanced at her phone. She didn't have time to cajole it out of him, and she needed to start all over on her packing.

Sighing, she leaned in and kissed Sean's cheek.

"Sure, babe," she said, running her fingers through his hair. "I have to leave town for a couple of days, though. Family thing. My brother is picking me up in a few minutes; I was just packing. You can crash here until I get back though."

She would have stayed if it had been any other time of the month; she couldn't run rampant as a wolf in her apartment, not with Sean there.

"No," he said, pulling away and heading toward the door. "I didn't mean to impose or anything. I'll find somewhere else."

"Sit down," Clara said in exasperation as she jumped after him. "You can stay here. I'll just be out for a few days. I can give you the key, and you can stay as long as you want."

Sean paused as he studied her face. He looked exhausted, his eyes boring into her own dark brown ones.

"Are you sure?"

"No worries," Clara said. "If you decide to leave before I get back, just leave my key with the super downstairs."

A relieved smile flickered on Sean's face as he collapsed back onto the couch.

"Thanks, Clara," he said. "I really owe you."

"No such thing. Now shut up. I have to pack."

"Yes ma'am." Sean grinned.

He washed their mugs in the small sink as she grabbed new clothes from the back of her closet and shoved them in an old backpack. They smelled musty, which was what she was going for. Maybe she'd have time for a quick shower before her brother showed. There was nothing she could do for her hair: it was too curly and frizzy to wash and comb in five minutes. But with enough dry shampoo and hair spray, Benjamin shouldn't be able to smell anything from Sean's visit.

Sean's vampire news couldn't come at a worse time. If he'd talked to her even yesterday, she'd have been able to do something. Now she could only worry during the long trip out to the forest with her brother.

Her phone buzzed as she climbed in the shower. Benjamin always sent her a message when he was less than 10 minutes away. The shower would have to wait. She dressed in clean clothes and sprayed as much floral scented body mist as she could stand on her clothes and neck and grabbed the matching lotion for her backpack. She was going to need a good story on what scent she was covering up or Benjamin would be suspicious.

When her phone buzzed again, Clara kissed Sean and dashed out the door, rubbing lotion on her hands as her backpack threatened to fall off her shoulder.

There wasn't anything she could do for Sean right now except offer him a hide out. He'd fallen in with a bad crowd. This Thomas Spencer, Sean's friend, must have been turned into a vampire, and she was a werewolf about to be faced with the full moon.

Clara was in trouble.

2 THE LODGE

As expected, Benjamin's restored car idled with the headlights on in front of the lobby entrance, and he was half out of the driver's door when she slipped out the main doors. He waved when they made eye contact.

"I was just about to come up," he called, his nose already scrunching as if he could smell her too-heavy floral scent through the thick exhaust from his car.

Benjamin Warren, Clara's younger brother, didn't look like her anymore with his nose turned up, a repulsed expression plastered across his face. Otherwise, they shared the same angular features and athletic builds—Clara from the strict exercise routine she kept and Benjamin from the hours he spent stomping through the surrounding forests for his job with the city's parks and recreation department. Benjamin's skin was a little lighter than hers, taking more after their mother than Clara did, and the curls on his head were a little looser.

He climbed back in his car and rolled down all the windows as she approached, and she had to fight down the urge to complain. She thought she smelled, too. Just not vampire bad.

She slipped into the passenger seat of Benjamin's car, hoping his usual nutty coffee smell would dull her heavy perfume, and slammed the door behind her. Benjamin eyed her suspiciously.

"What the hell are you covering up? You never wear this much perfume."

"I broke the bottle trying to rush this morning and didn't have time to change."

"Probably true, but god that's strong. Are you sure you aren't covering something up? No one would blame you if you lost control a day early and attacked someone."

Clara shook her head and glared at him. He wasn't funny.

Benjamin growled and shifted into drive. "I'm going to dump you in a pond before I give you your coffee."

"If you do, I'll drag your car in with me." He always brought her coffee. He knew how much she liked his brew, and she'd slept in more than once on the mornings he'd come to pick her up.

"Whatever. Your cup is in the back like always." He waited for her to unbuckle and reach around her seat to retrieve her massive tumbler before he started driving. "Are you ready for this, besides your god-awful smell?"

"Ready as I ever am," Clara said, grateful he was letting it drop. The tumbler warmed her hands, and the heavy caramel and nutty steam flooded her sinuses. "Did you remember to bring your potion?"

"The potions cost about as much as a small country," Benjamin said, rolling his eyes. "Course I remembered to bring it."

As Benjamin pulled into the increasing traffic, Clara checked to make sure she still had hers and that it was bundled safe. Benjamin hadn't been kidding about the price. She'd dropped a small fortune on the potion over the years. Sometimes she hated how much she'd spent on them, but she despised the alternative. Such was the life of a modern werewolf.

The wolf that lurked inside Clara's mind never really went away. It was always there, waiting for a moment of weakness in her mental defenses so that it could leap into action. When the wolf inside escaped during the full moon, it took a hefty price to cage it again: a vampire heart.

With the Crone's potion, the werewolves could hunt and devour animals rather than vampires to become human again. Without the potion or a vampire heart, werewolves were stuck as a wolf until they could obtain one.

It wasn't easy.

Though there was always a growing population of vampires in the world, a single werewolf killed at least twelve a year. A pack of six werewolves could easily deplete a medium-sized city's vampire population in a few years. Or faster if the tick population was small.

As if the scarcity of vampires wasn't enough, vampires were stronger than werewolves, though werewolves were faster. It made hunting them difficult.

The greatest perk a werewolf had was its sense of smell. They could smell a being's nature, so they always knew if someone was human, werewolf, vampire, or something completely different. That way, a werewolf could mark a target weeks in advance and stalk it until the time the curse called for vampire blood.

The potion had changed everything for them. They didn't have to live nomadic lives and could enjoy being human again. But the Crone did not run a charity; she charged a steep price for her monthly potions.

The car crunched as one of its tires fell into a pothole, and Clara hugged her backpack as she grumbled. The last half hour of the drive would rattle the car until their jaws hurt. Benjamin glanced at Clara's bag before turning onto a dirt road leading into the forest, probably a good twenty miles out of town.

"Probably should have secured your potion in the back with mine."

Normally she did, but she'd been too concerned with hiding Sean's vampire smell and forgot.

Clara leaned into the open window, breathing in the heavy aromas of pine and moist dirt. Normally she enjoyed her stays at the Lodge, outside of the werewolf hunt, and looked forward to seeing her pack members.

The Lodge was a massive log cabin built decades ago as a haven for the pack each full moon. It was a little over an hour's drive from the city outskirts and was secluded in the middle of a large forest, providing all modern comforts except internet.

Clara saw the Lodge as a home away from home, though memories tainted some of its happiness. She'd been good friends with its owner, Rudy, who left a few years ago after losing his temper and accidentally shifting into his wolf form in a blind rage. It had been bad, the kind of transformation that the news called a freak accident because a giant wolf had appeared out of nowhere in a crowded area and mauled several people, killing two.

Rudy hadn't been able to handle the guilt and vanished after that. Some of the pack wanted to remain hopeful that he was still out there somewhere, learning how to move on. At this point, though, that was likely just wishful thinking. Clara couldn't give up hope that he'd return, though.

The car dropped as Benjamin creeped through a pothole half the size of the road, banging Clara into the side window. She growled as she rubbed her ear and sat back in her seat. The forest was denser here, and the dirt road narrower and more potholed. She recognized a large tree with a split in the trunk, half the tree dead from a long-ago lightning strike. The Lodge would be around the next corner.

Benjamin took the last corner slowly, drifting to the left to avoid a fallen branch on the right side of the road. As he steered the car straight, the trees revealed a spacious field of tall grasses and wildflowers with the Lodge tucked in the back near the trees on the left side.

The Lodge was an impressive two stories with a loft above the main living area that held an additional two rooms. A high, vaulted roof framed a wall of windows facing the forest and open field. A wooden deck wrapped around the entire building, with a massive hot tub installed in the back. Two people bounced into the window from the inside, wrestling with cues in hand. Clara snorted, wondering who was playing pool this time. The Lodge had gone through dozens of cues and a few tables from the many overheated matches over the years, often fueled by the constantly full minibar. There were always repairs needed after each full moon, and the members of the pack took turns staying behind and repairing the damages. They also rotated arriving a few days early to restock the kitchen and minibar and clean the house before everyone else turned up. Six cars were already parked were the grass was shortest and run over from nearly a half a century of use. Clara recognized every one of them, and a brief sense of calm settled on her otherwise agitated shoulders. She was home.

Benjamin pulled next to an old, battered truck and put the car into park.

"Well, we're here," he said. "Time to get this over with."

"Oh, don't be so grim," Clara said, rolling her eyes as she exited the car and grabbed her backpack. "Would it hurt you to try having fun for once?"

Somehow she'd try to have fun, too. She didn't really want the pack asking questions.

"We aren't here to have fun. We're here to make sure we don't hurt anyone."

They'd had this argument before. There was just no helping Benjamin. He was determined to be a grump. It wasn't without reason, but it did make dealing with him difficult sometimes. And she didn't need another thing to worry about and be frustrated over.

"At the very least, make sure you eat with the rest of us, will you?" Clara asked. "The pack has done a lot for us. It would be better not to alienate them."

"Yeah thanks, Mom. I will."

Clara didn't rise to his jab. She had a quick temper, like most werewolves, so she tried to avoid his needling. She wasn't always successful.

Benjamin led the way through the parked cars and wind-swept grass, walking into the Lodge without knocking. The spacious living room was already filled with about twenty people. They all paused and hollered when the Warren siblings stepped inside.

"Hey! Look what the wolf dragged in," a thick Scottish accent called from the minibar.

Standing at five and a half feet tall and nearly as broad, Donald looked more like a boar than a wolf. Even when he transformed into his wolf form, his shoulders were disproportionate to the rest of his sleek body. As the oldest werewolf in the city, he'd heard just about every joke possible about his porcine figure and hardly even snarled at the mention of it anymore.

Donald acted as a sort of shepherd to the pack and had been a close friend to the Warrens since they moved to Colesbrooke. Though the local pack snubbed the idea of having an official Alpha, Donald was the closest they had.

"Hi, Donald," Clara said, trying to sound cheerful.

Benjamin didn't even try. He just grunted by way of greeting.

"And we're all happy to see you, Benjamin," Donald said, grinning at Benjamin's dark attitude.

"Lighten up, Benji," Clara muttered. Then she raised her voice again to address Donald. "Are we in the usual rooms?"

"Aye, you are, lass," he replied. "But the Von Grimmel brothers are coming this time, so Benjamin will be in the basement with them."

"I'll help carry your stuff," a voice piped up from the back of the room. Clara was filled with an overwhelming sense of affection as Chelsea's cropped, brown hair poked up above everyone's heads. She smiled broadly when their eyes met. "I need some stuff from my room anyway."

She vaulted over the back of the sofa where she'd been standing and bounced over to Clara and Benjamin. She was sporting a faded old Led Zeppelin t-shirt and ragged jeans.

"Hey, Chels!" Clara said. "I didn't know you were here. Who'd you come with?"

"Nate." She said, pulling Clara's bag away from her shoulders. "That's it? Normally you bring more."

"I slept in," Clara lied. "You know how Benji is. I'm just glad I had enough time to pack something."

Chelsea sniffed the air then winked. "You didn't bring more of that perfume, did you?"

"Nope. I spilled it as I was leaving. I don't think I'll buy it again after smelling like this all morning." The floral scent wasn't as heavy after the car ride with the window down and basking in the coffee aroma, but it was still a little much.

Chelsea laughed and led them down a flight of rickety old stairs to the basement. There was nothing much down here but room after room filled with beds and two small bathrooms. The Lodge had beds for twenty-four people, and the rest of the pack used sleeping bags in the oversized living room. If everyone came, it was comfortable even if it was packed. Rooms were given according to seniority in the pack, with younger pack members rotating in and out of the leftover rooms and sleeping bags.

It was a good system. There were only about fifteen consistent pack members with the rest coming and going as they pleased. Werewolves liked to wander as they saw fit, and many were in and out of Colesbrooke depending on the time of year. Older werewolves were particularly prone to wandering as they'd often made their fortune early on, using smart investments to replenish their funds so they could travel indefinitely. Clara wasn't there yet, and she was certain the Crone was raising her prices faster than inflation. A lot of younger wolves were struggling to build their fortunes, but Clara didn't mind. She wasn't sure she wanted to leave. The pack was her family and she wasn't in a hurry to leave them behind.

"Alright, so this is where you're staying this time, Benji," Chelsea said.

Benjamin winced at her use of his nickname. He squeezed past Chelsea and into the room, which had two sets of bunk beds against the walls.

"The Von Grimmel brothers aren't here yet, so you get to choose where you want to sleep," Chelsea added.

"Thanks," Benjamin said, claiming one of the bottom bunks.

He set down his pack and immediately dug through it to pull out a book.

Chelsea left him to read and rolled her eyes. As Clara followed her friend out, she paused in the doorway. "Don't forget what I said about meals."

Benjamin waved in response but didn't look up from his book.

"He never changes, does he?" Chelsea asked in a low voice further down the hall.

"You know how stubborn he is. He doesn't let anyone in. Lost too many people, you know?"

Chelsea nodded. It was something all werewolves understood. "It'd probably be easy for a lot of us to end up like that. Guess we're just lucky."

"Yeah, lucky," Clara said absentmindedly. "But what's going on with Nate? Why'd you ride up with him?"

Chelsea giggled and opened the door to the last room in the hall where she and Clara usually occupied with a couple of other female pack members. "I forgot you didn't know. You've been off the grid for the past couple of weeks. Nate and I have sort of been hanging out."

"Are you serious? Do you think you'll... you know." Clara asked as she took her backpack and slid past her friend.

"Dunno. For now I'm just kind of rolling with it. I don't move as fast as you. How's that going, anyway? What was his name again? Sean?"

Luckily, Clara had her back turned when Chelsea asked about Sean. Guilt tightened in her chest from trying to forget her worry, and she carefully arranged her backpack on her usual top bunk before answering.

"It's going really well," Clara said, trying to sound excited. She and Chelsea had been friends since Chelsea joined the pack thirty years ago. It was going to be just as hard to hide Sean's vampire problems from her as from Benjamin. "I'm going to miss him while I'm here."

"Oooh. Think you'll ever tell him about your hairy little secret?" Chelsea asked in a hushed tone. "Then maybe he'll come, and you wouldn't have to be away for so long."

She needed to tell him, to explain. She needed to do it weeks ago, but she hadn't known he was going to tangle with the bloodsuckers. Hopefully it wouldn't be too late, and it wouldn't be too much of a shock for him after whatever happened with Thomas and the vampires.

"Yeah, maybe eventually. I'm not sure. I want to, but . . ."

"You should talk to Vic and Izzy about it when they get here. I bet they've got some great advice."

"Just don't say anything to Benji about it," Clara warned. "I want to figure it out for myself before he knows I'm even considering it."

"Of course."

Clara and Chelsea stayed in the room, chatting for another half an hour as their two other roommates dropped off their bags. Clara managed to steer the conversation back to Chelsea and Nate, and it felt good to catch up with her friend. The tension remained in her shoulders, but her smile didn't feel as forced when they headed back to the growing crowd upstairs.

Lunch was a boisterous affair. Once most everyone had eaten, little competitions started breaking out all around the room. Members of the pack engaged in games of pool, cards, and wrestling matches. The scene was reminiscent to what their city hangout, the Den, was like during the rest of the month, minus the blaring tv in the background. The werewolves were a rowdy bunch, but Clara liked them that way. They made everything feel so alive.

The games continued through dinner, accompanied by casual drinking and more typical squabbling. Even Benjamin had joined in for a few drinks, though he stuck to the corners out of the way of any brawlers. Clara was battling Chelsea in a close game of air hockey when a hand clapped down on her shoulders, making her jump and nearly smack Donald with her red paddle.

"God, Donald," Clara hissed. "Don't do that."

Donald chuckled. "Sorry, lass. Didn't mean to startle you. Just have something I want to talk to you about."

"Oh?" Had Donald heard something about Sean? Did he know she was dating an ally of the vampires?

"We've got quite a few people here today," Donald said, looking across the room and waving Chelsea away. She dropped her paddle and pouted, but she was all smiles when she purposely bumped into Nate. "More than we've had in a few months."

"We always have more this time of year," Clara said.

Donald nodded. "Usually that's fine, but this time is different."

"What do you mean?"

Donald glanced around them to make sure the closest pack members were busy with their own games and competitions. Satisfied, he leaned in close and kept his voice low.

"I don't mean to alarm you, but I've been hearing rumors of wolves running around these parts. Might be a new pack, might not. If it is, we don't know what they'll be like. They might be just passing through; they might be looking to expand their territory."

The hairs on her arms and neck rose as the wolf's predatory instinct flared. "If they're trying to run us out, they've bitten off more than they can chew."

"No," Donald said, shaking his head. "I'm not saying I don't think we could take them, but supernatural wars take a hefty toll. Best to avoid them when possible. Especially two at a time."

A werewolf territory spat at the same time as a vampire turf war couldn't be good, even for a city as populated as Colesbrooke.

"Then what do you want me to do?"

"I need extra pairs of eyes while we're hunting. I can hold down the fort long enough for you and a few others to make your kill, but after you do it, you'll have to override your wolf's mind but stay in the lupine form. Help me control the chaos."

Clara gulped. Usually the wolf remained in control after she made her kill, but it always wandered back to the Lodge where she'd wake up sprawled somewhere in the grass in human form. It took time to wrestle back control during the full moon, and she was happy with her current results.

"What if I can't?"

"Don't worry." Donald grinned. "It's not hard. The wolf's belly will be full, and it'll be tired. You'll slip in easily. Once everyone has fed, you can lock it up."

"I'm really not sure—"

"You'll be fine," Donald assured her. "It's easy and will feel natural to you."

"If you say so." She still wasn't convinced.

"That's a good lass." Donald clapped her shoulder again. "I've talked to Vic, Izzy, and the Von Grimmel brothers about it too. I think between the six of us, we'll be alright."

"But why me?"

Donald barked a peal of harsh laughter. "Why? Because I trust you! You've been a real help to the pack, Clara, a real help. It's about time you took on more responsibility after forty years, don't you think? I wouldn't ask this of you if I didn't think you could handle it."

"And what about the newcomers?" Clara asked.

"As long as they don't bother us, I don't care. I think I'll go join your brother at the bar. G'night, pup."

Clara waved and stared at the lonely puck on the table, her hands heavy on the table's edge. Donald's new assignment could not have come at a worse time. Control over the beast was highly dependent on a stable mentality, and right now, Clara's mind was in turmoil.

But now was not the time for doubt. Like Donald said, he wouldn't have asked her for help if he didn't think she could handle it. Donald had faith in her.

At least that made one of them.

3 RUNNING WITH THE PACK

Light drinking and games did not calm Clara's nerves over the next two days. The knot in her stomach ruined boisterous meals, and the casual supernatural gossip only made her more antsy. Several members of her pack were suspicious that the increased strange homicides and attacks were a result of the vampire war, and a few had drunkenly debated if the Colesbrooke supernatural treaty between vampires and werewolves had been broken. Waiting to talk to Sean was agony, and she'd never noticed the lack of cellphone service until this trip.

On the third day, almost everyone felt the same nervous agitation plaguing Clara. Tonight was the full moon, and most of the pack disliked having to hunt.

There were people at the bar before breakfast, and the number only grew throughout the day. Around lunch, Clara and Chelsea slipped into the woods for a walk to escape the oppressive mood. Benjamin had stopped showing up for meals, choosing to sneak into the kitchen for food once the pack was engaged elsewhere and read books in his room.

Every minute that ticked by left them quieter than the last until finally, at sunset, the Lodge was almost silent.

With the moon rising within the hour, it was time to move. The pack worked together like a well-oiled machine, having done all this a million times over. As the sun began to slip beneath the horizon, they all went to their rooms. Clara and her roommates took their clothes off and folded them on their beds. The other members of the pack were doing the same in their respective rooms. Transforming with clothes on would leave them in tatters, so the pack disrobed at the Lodge.

Next, Clara reached into her bag and withdrew the potion she'd bought earlier that month. Her roommates did the same, and together they opened their bottles and threw back their heads, drinking the potion in a few large gulps.

Clara shuddered as the liquid touched her tongue. It was heavy and vile and filled her veins with fire. The taste did not last long and was replaced by a slight buzzing sensation that would stay until she calmed the wolf after transformation.

When she was done, Clara led the way back into the living area of the Lodge. It used to be uncomfortable for her to be around so many people with nothing to hide her body, but after forty years these people were a part of her now. It was no more embarrassing to be with them than to be alone.

Once everyone had gathered, Donald spoke briefly.

"As always, we will do this as quickly and efficiently as possible. Things have been a little tense in the area lately, so be extra cautious. Try to stay with the pack and we will make sure everyone gets fed. Stray, and we won't be able to guarantee that. Any questions?"

Donald glared around the room. When no one answered, he waved toward the door.

"Then move out."

The pack filed out of the Lodge, the only sound a chorus of repetitive *smacks* from dollar store flipflops that some wore if they didn't like walking barefoot. Clara had her own orange pair she'd grabbed from a stash purchased last year at an end of summer sale. They followed a narrow trail behind the house into the trees, traveling as far away from the Lodge as possible before they were forced to start their hunt.

The trees and foliage were dense, and the sun no longer peeked through the pockets of sky between the branches and new leaves. Yet no one turned on flashlights; they carried nothing with them and could see a smidge better in the dark lighting than average humans. Everything was still dim, but at least Clara could see enough to avoid large tree roots and invading branches.

In the middle of the forest, they would not see the moon reach its zenith, but all werewolves could feel the curse inside growing more eager and desperate with each passing minute, and the potions' buzzing was growing stronger with the wolves inside. The knot in Clara's stomach twisted even tighter, and nausea made it difficult to follow Chelsea in front of her.

She just had to survive another full moon and she could get back to Sean. All she had to do was stay strong and help her pack.

She could do this. Donald believed in her, and he wouldn't have asked her if he didn't think she could do it. Clara repeated this to herself over and over until she almost believed it.

This would be natural. She just had to hunt, eat, and stay in form. Hunt, eat, stay in form. Hunt, eat—

Benjamin materialized beside her.

"You ok?" he whispered.

"Peachy."

She'd explained to Benjamin her assignment yesterday, and he hadn't taken the news well. He was worried, paranoid something would happen. It hadn't helped her nerves.

"Benji, stay with the pack tonight." She paused to search his eyes, but his expression was cloaked in the forest's darkness. "Please. If Donald's worried, we should be, too."

Benjamin nodded and pushed forward.

"Ben—"

"I'll stick close." His words were rushed, but they were still a promise.

Clara sighed, grateful for at least one less thing to worry about. The knot in her stomach didn't relax.

"Thanks, Benji."

Half an hour later the potion's now intense buzzing sensation nearly overwhelmed her focus. She'd transform soon. Donald left the trail and walked into a small clearing, the pack following him.

They circled around the clearing, still silent. The full moon glowed above them against the dark blue sky. Not long now.

Anticipation hummed in the air as the werewolves looked to the sky as one. Between that and the buzzing she felt, Clara felt she was trapped on a violin string, being played as a fiddle by the hand of fate. Any second now, the curse would activate.

Her heart pounded in her chest as the beginning tore through her. The wolf pulsed through her veins, desperate to break free. It howled in her mind, drowning out all external sound and the heavy buzzing. She closed her eyes. All that existed was Clara and the beast.

Horror began to poison her thoughts as the wolf gained control. If it wasn't the full moon, she'd be fighting as desperately as she could. But now there was no point. The beast would win. Fighting only made it worse but doing nothing was terrifying.

Fire lanced through her bones as her body structure began to morph: her jaw elongated, her limbs reconfigured themselves, and her spine snapped and popped as it reshaped itself.

Then rage filled her mind, and the wolf was free.

From somewhere in the middle of the pack, Donald howled. His cry resonated deep within her and Clara responded with her own. She was followed by another wolf, and another, until the clearing was filled with the symphony of thirty wolves' songs.

In the center was Donald, still half human. He would maintain his hybrid form until half the pack had eaten. He howled one more time, and then they were off.

Animalistic joy pulsed through Clara as she ran. The clearing was heavy with the scent of a deer herd, and together with her brothers and sisters, Clara raced toward them. The moonlight fueled the curse's power, granting her additional strength and stamina. She could sprint for an hour before she needed a short break, and she could trot the entire night without tiring. No normal prey stood a chance against her and her pack.

They were closing in on the deer. A few members of the pack broke off and sped up, circling around the herd to guide it back toward the main pack. Clara surged ahead. This was what she lived for. This was what it meant to be a wolf. The thrill of the hunt seized her, and nothing else mattered.

Her quarry was in sight.

In a dozen bounds, she was on top of it. Clara's haunches bunched and she sprang forward while the beast inside howled with pleasure. The buzzing of the potion was growing unbearable at the proximity of her prey.

The deer tried to bolt out of the way, but it was too late. Her teeth sank into its hind leg. The animal's terror smelled sweet, and it fueled the wolf.

With a surge of strength, Clara yanked backward on the deer's leg, sending it flying. The deer crashed into the ground and she was on it in a second.

Clara's vision blurred with a red haze. She could no longer see what the wolf was doing. She'd been forced out, and the wolf was in complete control. All she could feel was the jolting buzz from the potion. It could hardly be called a buzz anymore.; it rattled her bones with the force of an earthquake.

And then there was nothing.

The wolf was content, and Clara could see again. The deer lay dead before her, its carcass ripped open. A bloody cavity exposed where its heart had been. The wolf had succeeded. The curse was appeased.

This lull in the wolf's aggression was usually when Clara coaxed it back to the Lodge, but Donald's request remained with her, though her memory of him asking was foggy. Nothing else beyond the wolf matter mattered, but she knew she had to stay.

Slipping into the gap left open by the wolf from its feeding, Clara took control of the wolf form. Just like Donald had said, it was natural to her, as if her mind preferred the lupine form.

It took a moment for Clara to grow accustomed to the sensation of being in control. Everything seemed more vibrant. The smells in the air painted the scene with a hundred different stories, and she could trace with ease the paths of the creatures that had visited this part of the woods.

Rising steadily higher in the air was the scent of blood.

Clara was not the only one to have found her prey.

All around her, members of the pack were finishing their meals and trotting back toward the Lodge. Clara watched with interest, her ears perked.

Chelsea loped past her. Clara ran with her for a moment, but Chelsea did not respond. The beast was in control. Clara stopped, watching her friend go. It was strange, being aware of her surroundings when everyone around her was not.

Another two wolves passed Clara, but she ignored them. She had to find the rest of the pack.

The underbrush offered little resistance to Clara's wolf form. She was larger than a normal wolf, and the tight sinews in her legs propelled her forward with incredible speed.

The scent of a small group of wolves hung in the air in front of her. They smelled of distraction and a blind rage. Clara sped up.

The night air rushed through Clara's fur as she ran, cooling her. Three wolves sprinted without caution, following one of the million scents around them. Clara sniffed the air, looking for any hint of a trail for her pack mates to follow that wasn't so far away from the rest of the pack.

There. A small den of foxes only a few yards away.

Clara raced to catch up with the wolves, power and speed rushing through her with a wild exhilaration. She had to remain focused or she'd be pushed out from the wolf's mind.

The three wolves snarled at her, saliva hanging from their lips. They were losing control. If Clara didn't do something, they would run for miles.

She snapped at the wolves' heels, forcing them to pay attention. Her pack mates slowed, turning toward her. She growled, hoping to command them. Their hackles relaxed, and they fell in line to follow her back to the den of foxes. When they reached the den, the three wolves attacked, digging into the earth to drag out their victims. Clara turned away. She'd done her job, and she could now smell another group of wandering wolves.

This group was larger than the last, but they were not moving fast. Clara loped through the forest, weaving in and out of trees. The moon filtered through the leaves creating little pools of silver light cascading over the underbrush. She was going to want to do this again.

The distance between Clara and the other group of werewolves was closing fast. Occasionally, she could see another of her pack through a gap in the trees in the distance. They were all heading back to the Lodge. At one point she passed Vic and Izzy herding a group of six.

As Clara ran and hunted for her pack members, Clara's inner wolf grew impatient. It had been driven out of control prematurely and was missing out on the hunt. It paced back and forth in the back of her mind, waiting for even a millisecond of weakness, for a tiny break to step in and take back the steering wheel.

A low growl began to build in Clara's throat. She would not be intimidated. The Crone's potion no longer buzzed within her. The hunger was appeased. The wolf was the weakest it would be all month. It would take a major break in concentration to lose her hold on her body now.

The scent of the group she was following was stronger now, and there were more than she'd originally believed. She slowed down, apprehensive. Donald's warnings resurfaced in her mind. What if these wolves weren't even from her pack? They didn't smell like normal wolves, which didn't inhabit this part of the forest anyway. They had to be werewolves, but who were they?

The breeze shifted, and the potency of the group's scent made it seem as if they were on top of her, surrounding her. She halted, afraid. She didn't recognize any of the wolves' scents. She raised her hackles, trying to prepare herself. The wolf inside grew excited and clamored harder for control. She had to get out of here, these couldn't be from her pack. She stepped back, preparing to turn.

The underbrush before her rustled. Something was coming.

Clara's muscles bunched as she prepared to leap into a run, but a massive gray wolf emerged from behind a large thicket, cutting her off. Flecks of white dotted its fur, making it shimmer in the half-light like a patch of the moon itself.

The wolf's yellow eyes pierced through Clara like an arrow. She stumbled back, growling. She shifted her weight, gaining her balance, and wrinkled her muzzle into a gritty snarl, her ears flat against her skull.

The gray wolf stepped closer, one ear flicking. Behind it, more wolves slipped out from the brush and from behind trees.

The new pack closed in on her, their calmness uncanny. Clara had so much adrenaline pumping through her system that her inner wolf already had its teeth in her. One wrong step and she would lose control.

Not willing to give it such a chance, Clara turned on her heels and ran. Even by werewolf standards, Clara was quick, but the thundering of a pack of running wolves mean they were pursuing her and keeping up. A few of the fastest were gaining on her. Fear spurred her to run faster.

She couldn't let them catch her. She couldn't. Their behavior was unnatural. They were in too much control. Why didn't it bother them that they had run into another werewolf? She hadn't been able to detect a trace of surprise from any of them and now, as they ran after her, she could feel nothing from them.

Her vision started to haze over again. She was losing control. The ragged breathing of one of the wolves was getting closer, and it matched her own haggard breathing in a frightening duet. All she could see was red.

A howl tore through the air and Clara's heart leapt. Donald! A misshapen mass hurtled through trees and crashed into the closest wolf behind her. Clara spun around, her paws sliding in the dirt and fallen leaves. Through the fog of red, she barely made out Donald's hybrid form fling the wolf away. It hit a tree and slid down, whimpering piteously.

The red haze darkened, the wolf's anger fighting to take control through her fear. Snarling and snapping exploded around her, followed by *thunks* from wolves smashing into trees. The wolf inside howled with need and approval, wanting to be let loose again. The fight fueled it, giving it strength it only had during an approaching full moon. She couldn't hold it anymore.

With a vicious snarl, the wolf took control and Clara slipped away into nothingness.

****

Clara's gasped as she opened her eyes to the blinding sun. Hazy spots dotted her vision, and she rubbed her eyes. The hard ground pricked into her human back and skin, and a root dug into her shoulder. Her muscles were sore, and there was mild pain in her right leg.

Slowly the green leaves and occasional splatters of blue sky above her came into focus. She sat upright, her heart pounding as half formed memories from the night before flooded her mind. Where was Donald and the foreign pack of wolves?

Climbing shakily to her feet, Clara studied the forest around her. She didn't know where she was, but the trees weren't too thick here. Donald wasn't close . . . Maybe he'd returned to the Lodge already?

When she stepped forward, her right leg throbbed from the sudden pressure and she fell to her knees, hissing in pain. Panicking, Clara scanned her leg for the damage. Stretching from her hip to her knee was a line of claw marks. The cut wasn't too deep, but it stung ferociously. The dried blood caked around her wound flaked off her skin every time she moved.

Upon closer inspection, she found she was covered in many other wounds, though none of them were as bad as the one on her leg. She drew in a few deep breaths then pushed herself to her feet again. She needed to figure out where she was.

Wincing, Clara took a few steps. Each time her foot fell, she grew more accustomed to the pain until she could walk almost normally. She could see more light coming from her right, so she headed toward it. With luck, she was near a road.

Clara stepped out of the thick of the forest and blinked in the sudden light. When her eyes had adjusted, she blinked again to ensure the massive log building before actually existed.

She was back at the Lodge.

The wolf hadn't made it all the way back this time, but thankfully it had been close enough.

Flooded with relief, Clara increased her pace to a lumbering shuffle. Climbing the stairs was difficult. Every time she lifted her leg, the cuts seared with pain. She made it with less effort than she'd anticipated, but she still nearly collapsed as she threw the door open.

The entire pack was gathered in a chaotic frenzy; everyone talking at once. In the center, Donald was trying to dish out orders, but he was not authoritative enough. Benjamin was pacing the room, looking ill.

As Clara entered, the entire room froze.

Without warning, the noise erupted again, and Clara was swarmed by the crowd.

"Clara! You're ok!"

"Where've you been?"

"We were worried! Benjamin about murdered us all for losing you."

"You made it, lass," Donald said as he forced his way through the crowd to grab Clara by the shoulders and inspect her. "I woke outside the door to the Lodge and you were nowhere to be seen. I thought . . . I thought we'd lost you."

"I'm fine." She was acutely aware of her nudity as the pack crowded around her. She hadn't been the only one naked before. "I just need to wash up."

Benjamin appeared at her side, glaring ferociously at anyone that tried to slow her as they made their way to the basement. Chelsea found her way to the Warren siblings, stepping in line behind Clara as a rear guard.

"Come on, Clare. Let's look at those cuts."

Cleaning her wounds took the better part of half an hour as Chelsea looked her over a hundred times over to make sure she was all right.

"Donald told us what happened," Chelsea said as she finished wrapping a bandage around Clara's thigh. "I can't believe that pack attacked you."

"If they're looking for a fight, we'll be more than happy to oblige," Benjamin growled.

"I don't think they were," Clara said through gritted teeth. Having Chelsea tugging at her cuts wasn't helping with the pain. "There was no blood lust. It was more like curiosity."

"Yeah, their claw marks say otherwise," Chelsea said.

"They only started to attack after Donald did."

"Doesn't matter when they attacked, Clara," Benjamin said, his expression dark. "If they think they can hurt us and get away with it, they've got another thing coming. I'll hunt every one of them if I have to."

"You'll do no such thing," Clara said, cringing as she hoisted herself to her feet. She limped over to her suitcase for some clothes. "The last thing we need right now is a fight between our packs. Just leave it alone."

"But look what they did to you!"

"I'm sure I landed more than a few good hits myself. Besides, it's really not as bad as it looks. The cuts aren't deep. I'll be fine by tomorrow."

Benjamin and Chelsea exchanged skeptical looks. Finally, after clicking his tongue in frustration, Benjamin left the room to vent somewhere else. Chelsea closed the door quietly behind him.

"He'll cool down eventually," Clara said.

Chelsea nodded. "You should probably get some rest. I'll make sure you get called for lunch."

"Thanks, Chels."

Clara lowered herself into her bed and closed her eyes gratefully. Chelsea waited in the room a moment longer before leaving. As soon as she was alone, Clara's eyes opened again.

The image of the gray wolf wouldn't leave her alone. He'd seemed so calm, so in control. It wasn't a demeanor often associated with werewolves. What was his secret?

Clara rolled onto her side.

It was doubtful that the pack in the woods would cause any trouble. They had seemed peaceful until Donald attacked. She wouldn't have to worry about them—she couldn't worry about them. Not when she needed to get back to Sean.

The plan was for Benjamin to drive her home tomorrow. This experience just solidified her ever-growing conviction that she needed to tell Sean about the supernatural world. There were forces moving in Colesbrooke, and the best way to keep her loved ones safe was to prepare them.

Clara closed her eyes, dreading tomorrow. When she revealed all, she'd find out just how understanding Sean was. Hopefully she could save him without losing him.

4 A Terrible Truth

When Clara returned to her apartment, Sean was no longer there. She searched the whole complex twice through just to make sure. But his normal scent mixed with the awful vampire stench was stale.

Frowning, she called his cell. The ring tone sang in her ears as she waited for him to pick up. Usually, even at work, Sean responded quickly. Now he was taking too long. Upon reaching his voicemail, she hung up and tried again. Still no answer.

Clara sank onto her futon, trying to decide what to do next. Her best bet would be to check with his work, normally he was there this time of day. She just hoped he wasn't with the vampires right now. If he was, things would get tricky.

Clara pulled out her phone to try one more time when a flash of white caught her eye. A small paper towel hung on her empty fridge. It had Sean's handwriting sprawled all over it.

I'M GOING BACK TO THOMAS'. HE'S INVOLVED IN SOMETHING DANGEROUS AND I CAN'T ABANDON HIM. YOU PROBABLY WON'T HEAR FROM ME FOR A FEW DAYS.

A lump rose in her throat. Leaping to her feet, Clara snatched her purse and hurried out the door.

The Café Compendium was a little over a mile away from her apartment. Every fiber of her wanted to run, but her leg was still sore. The pain would be gone by tomorrow, but for now she just had to be patient and walk. She ground her teeth the entire way, anger at her leg and a dull dread pulsing through her with each step.

He would be there. He had to be there. If not, then what?

The Café Compendium was a quaint shop on the ground floor of a towering white office complex. Modest window displays sported books and the checkout stand, but Sean wasn't behind the register.

Clara's stomach sank as she reached for the shop's glass door.

The rich aroma of the late-morning's coffee being brewed blasted Clara as she tugged open the heavy door. When she stepped inside, her curse helped her identify the underlying scents despite the overwhelming power of Columbian dark roast. There was the lovely scent of old paper wafting from the used book section, the sharper tang of fresh print in the new releases shelf, and the faded lemony hint of the wood polish the employees use to make their oak bookshelves glisten each morning.

This whirlwind of scents was normal for the café, but she froze not two steps from the door. A slow frown tugged at her lips, and she took in a much deeper breath through her nose, her mind processing the olfactory information.

Sean's scent was stale here, too.

As her heart sank into her boots, she scampered through the bookstore, processing every scent and looking for Sean anyway. She had to consciously remind herself not to tip her head back and sniff the air like a hound. That was an embarrassing habit younger werewolves got into and few managed to break.

Her mounting anxiety must have been apparent on her face because the senior bookstore clerk behind the counter frowned as she approached after two full rounds of the store.

"Hey, Clara. Everything alright?" Desmond asked in a voice that rattled in his chest like loose change.

Desmond had been a clerk at the Café Compendium for his entire life, the original owner having hired him as a teenager. He was the quiet, grandfatherly type, who spent the majority of his work hours reading gritty noir mystery novels behind the counter, and he spent his breaks on the back patio smoking an old pipe and trying to solve the mystery before the book solved it for him.

As a regular to the Café Compendium, Clara had always enjoyed a friendly banter with Desmond, as they were both avid book readers and she'd gone through a heavy mystery phase a few years ago. Though Desmond occasionally commented on Clara being an old soul, the kindly old book clerk had no idea he was younger than his favorite customer.

However, not everything about Clara was a complete mystery to Desmond. On the day Clara and Sean had officially become an item, Desmond had informed the new couple that they had earned him twenty dollars from Jackie the barista—she thought Sean wouldn't be able to work up the courage to ask Clara out for coffee.

"Hey, Desmond, I'm doing fine. Is Sean around?" Clara asked, doing her best to sound nonchalant.

The frown that wrinkled his face all but confirmed Clara's suspicions.

"I'm sorry, Clara, but Sean hasn't come in today. In fact, he hasn't shown up for several shifts," Desmond said, each word he rattled out coated in concern. "I've been covering for the kid so it's no big issue but . . . Well, I thought you'd know more about what's going on with him than me."

With a valiant effort, Clara managed to keep herself from cursing aloud. Sean's clove-scented aftershave was faint enough that she'd guess he'd been gone for over a week. She couldn't deny it any longer.

Sean wasn't there. That meant she needed to start snooping, possibly in vampire territory.

"Hey, I don't want to butt into a coworker's private life, but if he is sick or something could you have him call me? I've called him about a hundred times. I like the kid well enough and don't mind helping out, but the boss is getting frustrated."

Clara nodded and gave a weak smile. "Sure thing, Desmond. Thanks for helping him out and covering those shifts. I know he'll really appreciate it."

"Sure, sure. Like I said, he's a good kid. Happy to help."

Panic consumed her thoughts as she headed home. When she bumped into a man, she nearly lost control. A low, surprised growl rumbled from her throat, and the man stopped complaining. She hadn't walked into someone since she'd turned half a century ago, and she stared at the man as he shuffled around her, grumbling. Was her mind so vulnerable that even bumping into someone on the streets gave her wolf a chance to escape?

Almost like a physical sensation, the gentlest of tickles, Clara's nose twitched as another scent cut through her focus.

A young man leaned against the side of a building, sipping from a white paper travel cup with a black lid. The cup was emanating the earthy scent of tea. Lemon balm tea.

The last time Clara had smelled lemon balm was when Sean had introduced her to his friends at his sister's apartment. Well, everyone except Thomas. She still hadn't met him, and she didn't really want to. Being a good hostess, Sean's younger sister Artemis had fixed everyone lemon balm tea.

Though she'd only been there once, Clara was certain she could find the little basement apartment again. But it would do her little good—all of Sean's friends were living with Thomas now. Anyone who might be able to tell her where Sean was was in vampire territory, probably in their base, the Red Lightning Pub.

Clara gritted her teeth. Time to find out how brave she was.

****

The Café Compendium was a well-kept bookstore that had aged like fine wine over the years, becoming more distinct and graceful as it stoically marched on through time. The Red Lightning Pub, while sharing a similar age, was more like yogurt left outside in the hot sun all day.

The shoddy brick building had always looked like it was one condemned sign away from a wrecking ball. She'd only been near this part of town a couple of times, but it was enough to recognize the pub and its crumbling apartment complex at first sight. It was dirty and dingy with an awful plastic awning out front. On the pub's there was an insignia: a circle with a red lightning bolt bearing three drops of blood, the logo they put on all their signature drinks.

However, since the last time she'd passed the bar, the Red Lightning Pub seemed to have nearly collapsed on itself. The windows had been boarded up, a new door that didn't fit the 1920's motif had been hastily slapped over the entrance, and the area reeked of cordite and gun powder.

The vampires' cold war had gone hot, and this looked to be ground zero.

For an hour, Clara waited in the doorway to the office building directly across the street from the Red Lightning Pub. No one was going inside at this hour, but a few had come out. One was a massive brute of a man, just a towering statue of gray moving at a ponderously slow pace.

Clara recognized this vampire. One of her oldest pack mates claimed to have fought him a hundred years ago in Arizona. Her pack mate had been under the employ of the infamous Pinkerton and was getting paid to break up a factory worker's strike.

Jericho had been hired by the strike bosses to keep people like her pack mate away.

The two of them fought hard, but it had ended in a draw as soon as they realized they weren't dealing with an average human opponent. Her pack mate had waited for the next full moon to hunt the giant vampire at full strength.

Somehow both had managed to walk away from the scrape, or at least limp away.

Just more bad blood and ancient history between the vamps and wolves.

Another hour passed, and despite her concerns over Sean's safety, Clara knew she couldn't stride into a vampire pub during a vampire war. That could just create more tension and bloodshed.

She would have to wait for the perfect moment.

There!

Instinct took over and Clara pressed herself against the side of the lobby door.

Across the street, a woman with sapphire eyes and wild brown curls stepped out of the door and began an exhausted pace down the street. While she lacked any signs of the abundant energy she had when they had first met, Clara knew the woman was Artemis Butler, Sean's sister.

Before Artemis turned the corner at the closest cross street, she paused, turned around, and began her tired march back toward the pub. She passed the Red Lightning's doors and began ascending the steps up to the shared apartment complex's lobby.

Artemis froze on the last stair. She must have known she wasn't alone in the alley. Spinning around, she drew her hand back.

Clara was faster. Her hand shot out, taking Artemis by the wrist and squeezing tight.

A small glass vial reeking of holy water, hawthorn seeds, and garlic oil fell from Artemis's numbed fingers and shattered against the ground at her feet. The offending smell burned her nose, throat, and lungs, and Clara growled in a tone that would make even a bear flee in terror. The wolf inside was in agony.

"Don't scream."

"Clara?" Artemis asked, confusion apparent in her strained eyes, and she pulled her hand free. "What . . . what are you doing here?"

"I could ask you the same question, but I have a bigger problem to fix first," Clara said, too upset to care about anything other than her next question. "Where's Sean? Is he okay? Was he hurt in the war?"

Artemis blinked several times, processing everything slow like a human. She frowned and started to speak several times but stopped, selecting her words carefully.

"How did you know about the war? Did Sean tell you?" Artemis asked, her eyes narrowing. "I don't think he would have, so you're already involved. Are you a vampire?"

Clara had meant to keep her cool. She really had. But at the accusation that she might be associated with the vile her curse compelled her so strongly to hate, Clara could not help but spit on the ground in disgust.

"A werewolf, then," Artemis whispered.

The sudden change in Artemis' tone gave Clara pause, but only for a moment.

This wasn't about Clara. This was about Sean. Under normal circumstances, Clara would have shrugged Artemis' accusation off with ease. It didn't matter what the human thought. Besides, seeing how involved the Butler siblings were with the supernatural community now, there wouldn't have been much of a point. They would have found out eventually anyway.

"Yes, I am, but it doesn't matter. Did you know Sean hasn't been to work? Everyone is looking for him. I'm surprised Desmond hasn't filed a missing person's report yet, what with all those mystery novels he reads."

What little light left in Artemis' eyes faded. Something had happened. Clara growled, the wolf inside still not properly caged after the olfactory attack. She lunged forward, grabbing Artemis by the shoulders and shaking her.

"Where is your brother? Where is Sean?"

Before Artemis could reply, there was a soft hiss of a voice that made Clara's skin crawl.

She'd been so focused on Artemis that Clara's keen sense of smell hadn't detected the chemical reek of the expensive sunscreen vampires wore so they could function during the day without risking radiation burns.

"Put her down," a man growled from the mouth of an alleyway.

The man was a head shorter than Clara and whip thin. His heavy trench coat and gloves were the only things weighing him down enough to keep him from being blown around by stray gusts of winds.

Yet the hairs on the back of Clara's neck rose and she bared her teeth, the bestial part of her mind trying to break free and turn her into a mindless monster ready to flay the threat.

"It's okay, James," Artemis said hastily, pulling herself free from Clara once more. "She's a friend. . . . She's just worried about Sean is all."

A lump formed in Clara's throat.

James? As in *the* Jugular James?

This tiny man was one third of the dreaded Boston Boys. He was rumored to be more demon than vampire, though he refused to drink blood straight from the vein like other associates of the Red Lightning Pub. That didn't mean he wasn't interested in the jugular veins of his enemies.

A slight itch tingled her skin, and Clara glanced down at the thin vampire's hands and saw a bright gleam on each ring finger. Piano wires dipped in pure silver.

Like Jericho, many werewolves had crossed paths with Jugular James, but unlike the vampire giant, most didn't live to tell the tale. Jugular James was simply too quick and deadly with his silver-dipped garrotes. He could slit a throat or strangle someone so quickly he could be a block away before his victim's body hit the ground.

"You said this is a werewolf? I'm concerned there might be a bit of a misunderstanding," Jugular James answered in a deadpan. "We are hurt, ma'am. The kind of hurt that some might foolishly misinterpret as a weakness or the inability to defend ourselves."

Casually, Jugular James reached for the right index finger with his left hand and gave a tug. A glimmer of silver wire manifested itself between his hands, humming ever so slightly.

Clara tensed up, the wolf howling to be released and show this fool what it meant to threaten a werewolf. He was the prey here, not her.

"James, please! That won't be necessary," Artemis pleaded, holding up a placating hand. "Clara and Sean are dating. She just wants to see him."

The small man's expression didn't change much, but he did seem taken back. He glanced between them, as if there was some angle he wasn't getting about their story. Yet, after another tense moment, he slid the garrote wire back in place.

"Don't go inside," Jugular James said, not in a manner of warning but as if he was stating common sense. "But you can see him from the window."

48

He glanced at Clara and added, "I'm watching you, werewolf. Sara Foxe is keeping the peace around here, but Lawrence Foxe is keeping the muscle around as well. Remember that next time you and your pack start getting hungry."

Artemis threw her hands on her hips and started reprimanding him, but Jugular James was already gone, disappearing back into the alleyway.

Clara spun around and sprinted to the pub's windows.

"Wait, Clara, you don't understand," Artemis cried as she hurried after her.

By the time Artemis had caught up with her, Clara was staring through the slits of the boards hammered over the pub windows.

Inside she could make out a few figures.

There was Lawrence Foxe, dressed in a three piece suit and looking like a dandy as always, though his jovial face seemed to sag from his high cheek bones and his eyes were as red as the liquid he was drinking. The owner of the Red Lightning Pub looked as if he were a man determined to drink himself to death in the next hour. The several empty jars of the blood and moonshine concoction known as Red Lightning hinted it might be a possibility.

The young man seated next to Laurence wore an equally crestfallen expression. He was tall and gangly and would have been the type who tripped over their own two feet if he weren't a vampire. His colorless skin was pockmarked with violent bruises, and his eyes were puffy and red from crying. This must be Thomas. He was watching the doorway with desperate intensity. Clara followed his line of sight.

Sean.

He was being wheeled over to the others, pushed by a tired medic. Clara had met Nelson once before. During their brief meeting, he'd impressed Clara with his wit and level of playful energy. Now he looked like an entirely different man. There was a haunted look in his eyes as he pushed his friend over to the counter and stopped. He muttered something Clara couldn't hear, but it was clear from the expression on his and the others' faces that it wasn't good.

Shaking, Sean summoned up his strength and placed a hand on the bar. He was so pale his face and arms were roadmaps of blue blood vessels. To the untrained eye he looked terminally ill and, perhaps, in a sense he was.

"No. . . ." Clara watched in horror.

"It happened a few days ago," Artemis said, her voice breaking as she watched her brother. "We were attacked. We lost a lot of good friends, including . . . we lost a lot of friends. We nearly lost Sean, too."

Clara couldn't tear her eyes away from the inhuman act Sean was about to indulge in. With a shaking, weak hand, the love of her life grasped a bottle of red liquid and brought it to his lips.

Sean grimaced as he tipped his head back and gulped the blood and alcohol mixture, and in doing so, exposed two puncture wounds on his throat.

"But he's alive now because he's been . . ." Artemis trailed off, biting back a sob.

"Alive?" Clara spat. Fury, disgust, pain, betrayal, loss. There were so many conflicting emotions swirling inside she wasn't sure if she was going to scream, cry, or vomit. "He . . . he . . . he . . ."

"Is a vampire," Artemis said. "But listen, Clara, I—"

With tears flooding her vision, Clara turned and sprinted down the street. If only she could get far enough away, maybe she could fix this. If she could leave behind this crazy, horrible situation, maybe she wouldn't have to face it. Because Sean couldn't be a vampire. He just couldn't.

5 THE LONE WOLF

It was harder to control her instincts when in emotional distress. Confusion, guilt, anxiety, uncertainty—these were the feelings of a human mind, of a mind that found complexity a gift and not a burden. The wolf would have happily channeled all its feelings into either ferocity or hunger. Those two base instincts were all the lycanthropic curse cared to address, and when the werewolf's human psyche was stressed, the wolf was more than willing to take over.

The wolf inside was something that couldn't be tamed. Not ever. Clara knew some members of the pack who had forgotten and let their guard down or, even more foolishly, thought they had finally managed to leash their curse. They usually ran into tragedy for their lax behavior, a sudden flare of anger or fear causing them to shift into their wolf form despite the lack of a full moon. Only Rudy couldn't free himself from the guilt afterward and ran off.

Such an experience was terrifying but not nearly as damning as being forced to change by the light of a full moon. When the full moon forced the transformation, the wolf was allowed full control, as the original caster of the curse had no doubt intended. So potent was this transformation that many newer werewolves didn't even remember their nights as a werewolf. All they could recall was an overwhelming darkness as their human consciousness was suppressed by pure bestial fury. This was not the case on other nights, when a werewolf phased without the full weight of the curse on their back. Through a mental struggle, the human psyche was usually able to force the wolf back into its mental cage, allowing them to willingly change back into a human.

In nearly five decades, Clara had only accidentally phased twice. It'd been decades since then, and she wasn't about to start now.

Not even if Sean had been . . . Clara swallowed, as if the action could get rid of the foul taste in her mouth. Not even if Sean had been turned into a vampire.

Her hands clenched into fists that trembled with the thought. A strangled noise caught in her throat as she locked her jaw down, refusing to give into her reflexive need to scream her rage and frustration to the sky. She needed to curse. She needed to yell until her voice was hoarse and broken from the weight of her heartbreak.

Her silent struggle lasted eons before she could calm herself enough to move again. Her breathing remained ragged, and her emotions still hurt. She couldn't do this here. What she needed was a place to stay while she figured things out.

Clara set off down the street, huddling over and hoping no one noticed her. It wasn't a good idea to take public transportation. The subways were crowded with commuters and she didn't think she could take all the jostling. When a woman guffawed a few feet away, anger swelled in her chest and she broke into a painful jog, hoping it would take the edge off.

The first time she'd lost control had happened during her second decade. She'd gotten into a heated argument with a school admissions officer because her scholarship was significantly lower than her brother's. She'd lashed out with wickedly sharp claws.

Luckily, no one got hurt, but the shame of losing control was not easily forgotten. Benjamin, however, still thought the situation was hilarious and that the officer got what he deserved. He'd had always been a bit of a lone wolf, even by werewolf standards, but the bond they shared ran deep. Clara trusted him more than anyone.

Benjamin would understand. She could talk to him.

The thought of Sean's pale hand reaching for the glass of blood flashed through Clara's mind.

Shivering with revulsion and guilt, Clara sped up. Benjamin would know what to do.

****

When Clara opened the door to her brother's apartment, she found him in his usual spot. Sprawled across a couch with several books and old videocassette tapes heaped randomly on the floor nearby. She would never understand how someone could possibly spend more time agonizing over which book to read or movie to watch than reading or watching them.

His dark eyes glanced over at the door as it opened, and he scratched at the black stubble on his face. "No comments on the disarray?"

She couldn't stand how easily he could live in a cluttered pile of books, movies, and music. He'd respond to her suggestions with a comment about how she's his only visitor anyway. But she didn't care, not now.

"Benji, I think I'm in trouble," she said, almost to herself as she shut the door behind her.

Benjamin leapt to his feet. "Did you phase? Did you bite somebody?"

Benjamin's reaction was not surprising. Because of the nature of their curse, if a problem befell a werewolf, the first and immediate assumption of other werewolves was that you had lost control and let the wolf slip free. It could be annoying, but with it being such a justifiable concern it was hard to protest.

"No, no. Not that. You know me better than that. But this may take a while."

Distrust flashed through her brother's eyes as he sat up, pushing away some cassettes so Clara could sit down. Thanks to a series of unfortunate relationships, bad luck, and the constant maintenance of his curse, Benjamin was quick to suspicion. Distrust was not widespread among the Colesbrooke pack. Their curse and the help of the potion made the pack more social than others. Everyone was family, everyone wanted the same thing: to not have to hunt and kill vampires anymore. It forged a bond that made Benjamin's acidic personality stick out.

There was a duality in all werewolves. Most who suffered from the lycanthropic curse reflected some aspect of their bestial nature, even in human form. Some were fiercely territorial, some wildly rowdy, and others delighted in their superhuman senses.

Clara was guilty of overindulging her keen sense of smell with aromatherapy, enjoying it on a level humans couldn't even possibly dream of.

But Benjamin was different. Whatever manifestation of the wolf he had in his human life was kept private, hinting that he was either in constant war or there was a cold understanding between the two personas inhabiting his mind. Whether this attributed to or even amplified his jaded behavior was unknown, even to his sister. But Clara certainly knew it could be worse.

Some werewolves liked abusing their wolf advantages. Those were the werewolves who made appearances in the legends and myths that usually ended with a silver bullet. Werewolves who lived long lives embraced their curse and were smart enough to avoid causing problems in cities. They were more content to fight amongst their own pack mates, constantly battling to be Alpha.

"I don't like where this is going," Benjamin said, his tone blunter than a river stone, but he sat down on the couch anyway. "If you need help burying a body, ask someone else. I've told the pack a million times; I don't like you digging up the parks."

"Could you stop being snarky for two seconds? I need your help," Clara snapped. Despite how quickly her mind jumped between words to say, she slowly paced around the living room, walking in a serpentine fashion between the piles of books, movies, and unwashed shirts littering the floor.

Benjamin's bored expression meant he wanted to say something else that was probably equally sarcastic, but he held it in. His tendency to be snide was a sort of defense mechanism he'd developed through the years. It wasn't an easy habit to shake, especially when his doubting nature made him so averse to serious topics.

"Okay, so what happened?"

"Well . . . you've heard me talk about Sean. . . ."

Benjamin's eyes narrowed. "If this is about a breakup I'm going to be very upset with how bad you scared me."

Clara gave Benjamin a glare that on two separate occasions had made pit bulls roll on their backs and show her their bellies in submission. Benjamin matched his older sister's glare with ease. He'd suffered through too many of her dirty looks to be impressed by them anymore.

"Would you just listen? It's a very delicate situation." Clara shook her head and released a frustrated growl. "I was planning to tell Sean about myself tonight."

Benjamin shot up to his feet so quickly that he crushed a cassette tape underneath his foot.

"Clara!"

It wasn't that such things were completely unheard of. Unlike vampires, who had a predator–prey relationship with them, werewolves had a close relationship with humans. Some werewolves ended up sharing their true identities with a human they were in a relationship with. In some cases, they even intentionally passed the curse itself along.

Two married members of the local pack, Vic and Izzy, were known to have been a werewolf and human couple before they joined the pack, though they never did share who had been the original werewolf and who had been their human paramour.

Benjamin had shared this dark secret with at least two women over the past fifty years, but both of those stories ended sadly. One had believed Benjamin was mentally ill and the other could not bear the thought of her potential husband being something less than human.

"You don't understand. There are extraneous circumstances. I don't have a choice." Clara found herself at a loss of words. "But uh, something came up."

A look of confusion replaced Benjamin's initial expression of shock and outrage.

"What happened?" he asked again, his voice taking a much gentler tone.

Having had negative experiences with this sort of thing himself, he could only imagine what might be coming.

Clara opened her mouth to explain but found herself speechless. How could she possibly say what she needed to say? She fumbled for the right words—everything just sounded so wrong.

"So, maybe I should've told you this earlier, but I didn't want you to worry. And if the pack had heard . . . it might not have ended well. A while back, Sean's best friend got turned," Clara explained, giving more information than necessary to stall what she was sure would be a violent conversation.

"Into a werewolf?"

Clara shook her head and Benjamin's eyes grew wide.

Benjamin wouldn't be pleased that his sister was associating with someone who had ties to the vampires. He, like all members of the local pack, respected the truce that Sara Foxe had worked out with the supernatural community. It kept things simple and safe, not just for the supernatural factions but for the humans of the city as well. It was one thing to enjoy the benefits of a peace, but it was quite another to willingly associate with the enemy.

"The bloodsuckers are at war. I'm betting the strange attacks in the news are part of it," his voice had a sharp edge. He wasn't happy with the suspected casualties like many of the others in the pack. "Was Sean killed while we were gone?"

Clara shook her head and turned away before her brother could see how her eyes were starting to fill with tears. She took a couple of deep breaths and blinked until she could see clearly again.

"Sean got caught up in it. I didn't hear exactly what happened, but in the end the result is the same. Sean is . . . a vampire now."

As someone who had turned skepticism into an art form, there were few things that caught Benjamin so off guard. This was one of them. He fell back down onto the couch, his face blank as he tried to comprehend the magnitude of what she'd just said.

"So . . . your ex-boyfriend . . . is a vampire?"

"No, Benji," Clara said firmly. "My *current* boyfriend is a vampire."

Had Clara sprouted three different heads at that moment, her brother would not have been more surprised.

"What?" he shouted so loud that Clara winced, her sharp hearing ringing.

"I trusted him enough to accept me as a werewolf. It would be a pretty scummy move to not do the same for him."

Benjamin leapt to his feet again, crunching another cassette tape. "No! That's entirely different!"

"How?" Clara demanded, channeling her confusion into aggression toward her little brother, who was an easy target for her temper.

Benjamin stared at her as if what she was saying was so painfully stupid that he wasn't sure how to even address the issue.

"Because Sean is no longer human, Clara," he said slowly as he looked his sister in the eye. "I mean, he's a vampire. . . . We hunt them, Clara. We have for centuries."

"No, other werewolves hunt them. We haven't hunted vampires since we found the Crone. I want to be a person, not an animal," Clara said sharply. "That's why we stayed here and pay for the damn potion every month."

"What are you going to do? Because I honestly don't know what to tell you."

It was a question she didn't have an answer to. Where to go from here? Her entire world had been turned upside down. No, it was even worse than that. She'd left her world to appease her curse during the full moon, and on her way back she managed to stumble into a crazy new world.

If only she'd had more time to talk to Sean before she'd left for the Lodge. Maybe she could have kept him away from all of this.

"I need answers," Clara said at last. "We leave for a couple of days and suddenly everything's gone to hell. I need information."

Benjamin groaned. "No. Not happening. That is a bad idea."

"You have a better one?" When Benjamin only shrugged, she folded her arms and continued. "That's what I thought. I've got to talk to the Crone."

Benjamin snarled, a mindless animal noise that showed his distaste for the suggestion. After baring his teeth, he walked over and grabbed his coat, slipping it over his shoulders.

"Fine," he said as he headed toward the door. "I mean, hey. She couldn't possibly ruin our evening, right?"

Clara frowned, trying to figure out how to respond without killing Benjamin's willingness to tag along.

Benjamin rolled his eyes. "I'm kidding. Let's just get this over with."

****

Uncertainty, nervousness, and guilt always set the wolf on edge, and Clara found herself keeping an internal dialogue to keep the wolf caged as they neared the Crone's shop.

Sean must have been afraid with his perception of the world being destroyed and then dying and being reborn as a savage. Her own experience had been brutal, and she should have been there for Sean.

The night Benjamin and Clara had been turned into werewolves was an event she tried not to think about. It had certainly started out innocently enough. Her parents—happy, proud, and perhaps a little sad to see Clara and Benjamin grow up and move out—had decided to go on a family camping trip during the first week of summer. It was to celebrate their children's high school graduation, as well as get back in touch with one another and strengthen their family bond.

Unfortunately, it had turned into a nightmare when the full moon peeked out from the silvery clouds the second night.

She still wasn't entirely sure what had happened. The night was a tapestry made of bits and pieces threaded together by overwhelming terror. Clara heard screaming from her tent and scrambled out to see blood.

Her father crouched over the limp, bloody form of her mother. Benjamin was beside the tent, frozen by fear and shock.

A massive weight hit Clara from behind, sending her into blackness.

When she woke in a hospital a day later, the first person she saw when she opened her eyes was Benjamin. He was bandaged like a mummy in the bed across from her.

A police officer hovered near the door and questioned them about the wild animal attack. It was difficult to answer through the lack of memories and the fog from being heavily medicated.

The police officer said, several times, that it was a miracle she and her brother had survived, though, unfortunately, her parents had not.

The world miracle was used a lot over the next week, as the doctors were astounded at how quickly Clara and Benjamin recovered from their injuries. When they left the hospital a few days later, they didn't have any scar tissue or scabs. Clara didn't feel miraculous. She felt cold and hollow.

The next three weeks were filled with a constant state of heightened aggression. Clara and Benjamin were always at each other's throats when they used to hardly fight at all. She thought it was just part of the grieving process as they tried to get over the violent loss of their parents.

Everything changed the night of the full moon.

The first transformation was the hardest. Sudden pain wracked their bodies, and Clara thought she was being attacked again. Every bone broke and shifted in an agonizingly slow process, and her muscles ripped and reformed in strange ways. When she woke up naked among a group of strangers, she learned a pack had found her and Benjamin, guiding them to their first kills and helping them return to their human form. Five years later, the Warren siblings made their way to Colesbrooke after hearing rumors of wolves who didn't hunt vampires.

"We're here."

Benjamin's voice startled Clara, breaking her free of her bitter reverie. Her mood went from sour to purely vitriolic.

"Let's get this over with."

******

A squat brick building sagged heavily to one side, almost as if the entire structure was hunched by the sheer enormity of its own age. The windows were intentionally painted black, but the rest of the building was a mottled gray color, with years of grime making the thick, uneven coat of filth blotchy, interrupted only by the large, greasy brass knob of the door handle and a rotting store sign above the door.

If Clara hadn't known better, the building looked to be another condemned store unable to be touched by historical building regulations, waiting for the day when the outskirt city council might consider repurposing it into a much more useful space.

No crude slogans, gang signs, or obscene pictures had been scrawled, painted, or sprayed onto this particular building despite the neighboring buildings being covered in graffiti. Someone scuttled away in the dark, probably another emerging artist running away from the odd, unsettled feeling. Clara could smell the hint of spray paint following the figure.

As Clara and Benjamin approached, the store sign grew more legible, announcing the name of the place like a splintered whisper.

THE TROUBLE AND TOIL.

"I hate this place," Benjamin said, as per tradition for every werewolf who found themselves on the Crone's turf.

Even from the street there were offensive smells, sour stenches, and stomach-churning reeks that only a werewolf's delicate nose could detect. Clara, for all of her love of aromatherapy, could hardly identify half of the scents oozing from the cracks within the building's walls.

Despite all of her reservations about The Trouble and Toil and the mysterious woman who ran it, Clara needed to ask her questions. She moved forward with as much purpose as she could muster, her hand slipping once on the brass doorknob as she pulled the door open.

Gloom greeted her.

The interior of the shop was as poorly maintained as the outside, and it was much darker and certainly more crowded. If the contents of a Halloween-themed party, a furniture store, twelve different churches, and a curio shop were crammed inside the same room and then shaken around for a few minutes before cementing the wreckage in dust and cobwebs, Clara could have replicated the shop's insides.

An unknown light source dimly revealed molding plants in pewter bowls crowding several tables, a bookshelf displaying an odd collection of bottles with murky substances, chairs groaning under the weight of bizarre stones and crystals, and all sorts of strange symbols hanging from wires running along the ceiling.

"By the pricking of my thumbs, something wicked this way comes," hissed a voice from the gloom, though the direction was impossible to determine, even with Clara's sharp ears.

"That has never been funny," Benjamin growled, trying his best to look aloof as he followed Clara deeper into the shop.

"Oh, a young playwright I knew long ago would have disagreed with you," the voice cackled.

After maneuvering through the darkness and the chaotic clutter, the werewolf siblings found themselves facing the only place in the entire building that resembled organization. A glass counter full of all sorts of bizarre, hand-carved charms, and curious odds and ends on full display had been placed in front of a series of shelves with all manner of ancient papers and tomes piled neatly upon it.

Between the counter and the shelf was an emaciated figure, wrapped in layer after layer of twisting robes. The landscape of wrinkles made the figure's face resemble a prune and rendered it genderless, though there was something matronly in the wicked rasp of its voice.

What Clara hated most about the Crone and her shop—more than its unsettling aura, more than its ungodly reek, more than even the occultist herself—was the mystery. No one knew anything about the witch, and many went through great lengths to avoid her, but no one knew why. In a city with accursed kin like vampires and werewolves, Clara had no doubt about the existence of otherworldly forces like magic. But encounters with the occult were so rare, Clara couldn't tell for certain whether or not the few things she'd witnessed were true acts of magical mastery or simple tricks.

Clara found herself doubting the Crone's authenticity as a true weaver of spell, despite all of her mystery and the success of her supposed occultism. Her potions worked, but Clara hadn't witnessed the Crone perform actual magic.

"What brings you pups into my humble shop? The full moon has nigh a week gone, so you can't be struggling with your beasties," the Crone speculated as she casually turned the page to an old, yellowed booklet titled *Malleus Maleficarum*. "Don't tell me you want another brew? Or . . ."

Even in the gloom, the Crone's crooked yellow teeth gleamed wetly as her wrinkled face stretched out wide.

". . . have you developed a taste and want a chewier treat?"

Instinctively, Clara placed a hand on her brother's shoulder to keep him from making some toxic retort.

Whether the Crone was a true magic user or not wasn't important to the local pack of werewolves in this city. Her potion results were real enough to make her an absolutely priceless resource to their kind. Every month, the mysterious occultist would provide them with some foul-tasting brew to keep the wolf at bay.

"Or perhaps you want to secure your brew now, hmm?" the Crone chittered, setting down her booklet and reaching down underneath the counter to withdraw something.

Lifting her skeletal hand with fingernails that matched her yellow teeth, the Crone placed a small glass tube on the counter, stoppered with a wax-covered cork. The murky sludge within the vial was impossible to identify, though every member of the local pack choked it down twelve times a year.

Clara and many others of her pack theorized that these potions contained vampire blood or possibly bits of a vampire's heart. If this were true, she had no idea how a weak old woman like the occultist would acquire such ingredients. Honestly, it wouldn't surprise Clara to learn some desperate vampire was willing to sell his blood to the Crone in exchange for some other tincture that aided their kind.

After all, many vampires used a strange sunscreen to function during the daylight, and who was to say they didn't get such a thing from this very shop?

"Unless that potion is free of charge, I'd put it away," Benjamin said, folding his arms and failing to keep the anger from his words.

If there was one thing that brought fear to the Crone's heart, it was the thought of giving her merchandise away for free. The occultist actually turned her head and spat a glob of phlegm on the floor at Benjamin's mention of the word *free* before hastily putting the precious potion back out of sight.

"What he means is that I need information, not a potion," Clara said, shooting a sharp glance at her brother.

Benjamin snorted.

"Despite what people say, talk isn't cheap, pup. If it is information you seek, then even that has a price." the Crone coughed, once again reaching underneath the counter to withdraw a faded old tarot deck with hand-painted symbols that made Clara nauseated if she looked at them too long. "Shall I read your future?"

"No! Nothing like that," Clara said, her own words getting heated as her frustration grew. "What I need to know is what happened to the city while we were gone? What happened to the vampires? Are their elders going to get involved? Is this city still safe?"

It was impossible to tell when the Crone was frowning—she had a perpetual scowl—but the occultist's smile had noticeably vanished at the mention of the vampires.

Whether this was upsetting to her because it meant a lower price than a tarot reading or because it reminded her that some potential customers had died was impossible to tell.

"Ah, yes. The pups of the first werewolf fled the city for the full moon while the fledglings of the first vampire flooded the city with blood. Interesting times indeed. I can tell you what you wish to know. But first, payment," the Crone said, holding out a decrepit claw of a hand to Clara's face. "A lock of your hair, if you so please."

"My hair?" Clara glared in suspicion.

Benjamin was also taken aback. It wasn't like the Crone to ask for something so seemingly trivial. He'd told Clara he had dug into his reserves and brought along an emerald ring, the green gem a particular favorite of the Crone to demand when she was brewing their potions.

"Yes, pup. Your hair. You never know when the hair of a werewolf might prove useful." The Crone's sagging face spread out into another horrific grin. "Snips and snails and all that."

Clara paused. It wasn't a good idea to hand a bit of herself over to a morally ambiguous person like the Crone.

However, Benjamin knew her well, and had already pulled out his pocket knife and handed it to her. With a nod of thanks, Clara twisted a lock of her black hair from her ponytail and, with a quick slash, cut it free.

The Crone grinned as Clara handed the hair over to her.

As Clara folded the blade back into its handle, she started. Had her hair just wiggled in the Crone's grasp? No, it must have been a trick of the dimly lit room, or maybe the stench in this place was making her see things. Benjamin was staring, too.

"Good, good. A price paid in full and so shall service be rendered." The Crone cackled in her strange way, placing the lock of hair in a dusty box underneath the glass counter. "The war among the accursed blood suckers was heavy indeed. Yet a high price was paid to make certain none of the eldest of their kin took note."

Both Clara and Benjamin found themselves leaning closer to the Crone, scared to miss a single word.

"Not even your Pack Fathers are aware that the war has shaken this city so. The predator known as Ernest lost the war, he and his mad, blood-addicted clan all but wiped out. Even now the victorious vampires hunt his disciples nightly, looking to end his legacy once and for all. The keeper of the accord, Sara Foxe, had to bury her only daughter. A terrible price for victory indeed." There was not a hint of sympathy in her voice. Her callous attitude made Clara wonder if the hag had ever had anyone she could say she loved. "The vampires are disorganized and tensions run high. They now fear discovery by the humans and their otherworldly enemies more than ever before. They must reform, rebuild, or they will find themselves further divided and weakened."

She pictured Sean in a wheelchair. Not only was he weakened as his body slowly transformed, but those who could protect him were equally weak. He was caught up in the blood sucker's web now. Now and forever, if Clara didn't intervene. What would happen if the vampires began to squabble amongst themselves again? What would happen if the supernatural community decided it was safest to drive all the vampires out of the city before they stirred up the humans even more?

Clara knew from firsthand experience how savage both vampires and werewolves could be, but that was nothing compared to the savagery of a scared and angry mob of humans.

"Is the city safe?" Clara pressed, her voice tight as a piano wire.

The smile didn't fall from the Crone's lips as she replied. "Why, pup, the city is never safe."

6 The First Meeting

Benjamin glared at the road in front of them, frustration guiding his foot on the gas as he drove increasingly faster. Thin headlights were lost in the blazing glory of windows and frequent streetlamps, and Maggie turned away from her brother to watch the multi-colored skyscrapers pass by. They were nearly to her place.

The intensity of their argument worried her. It had become so extreme she was surprised the two of them hadn't transformed and gone for each other's throats.

"You heard the Crone! This city isn't safe! I have to get Sean out of here. If I'd done that in the first place, he wouldn't have been turned," Clara said for what felt like the hundredth time. "I am going to do this."

"That's exactly why I'm begging you not to do this. There's no way the vampires can keep their war a secret for much longer, even if the war is over. Have you seen the news? It screams vampire war even if the humans don't know it yet. What do you think will happen as soon as one of those ancient ticks decides to move into the city to see what the fuss is about? What do you think will happen if a Pack Father discovers this? Or even the chief of police? Something is about to fall hard on the vampires, Clara. That's what the Crone was telling us. Just leave them alone."

"No," Clara said, her breath fogging the window as she turned back to Benjamin. "And please don't get anyone else involved in this, okay? I trusted you with this secret."

Benjamin's knuckles turned white from his grip on the steering wheel. He opened his mouth to speak but only a guttural growl came out. His lips peeled back, revealing pearly fangs.

He blinked in surprise and shook his head several times, letting out animal-like snorts with each change of direction.

His temper was getting the best of him, and his inner wolf sensed it. Clara felt the same, the wolf pawing her mind to be released.

Benjamin calmed himself as he took the last turn before her complex and began slowing to pull over. His own struggle took the fight out of Clara, leaving behind bone-chilling exhaustion.

"I don't want to argue anymore, Benji."

He stayed quiet and parked the car in front of the lobby.

She reached out and grasped the handle to the car door. The plastic felt oddly weak beneath her fingers. "I might not be directly at fault for what's happened to Sean, but I've got to do what's right by him, okay? I'm going to see him. Tonight."

Benjamin breathed methodically, again trying to calm himself enough to control his curse. After several moments, he even managed to let go of the steering wheel.

Despite this, his eyes had a yellowish tinge when he looked at his sister.

"If I don't hear from you in the morning, I swear I'm going to call up the pack and demand the Pack Fathers call down an Omega Hunt. You got that? I promise you that's what's going to happen. If these blood suckers decide to take out their anger on you, I'm going to hunt them into extinction."

"They were at war with themselves, Benji. Not us," Clara said as she opened the door and climbed out of the car.

Benjamin started his car, shaking his head.

"Sometimes I don't know how someone so smart can be so dumb," he said bluntly as he turned on the car's left signal to reenter traffic. "We were never at war with the vampires because we were never at peace with them, Clara. For all this talk of peace accords and keeping the supernatural community hidden and safe, the fact of the matter is that our relationship with vampires is like their relationship with humans. At the end of the day, they are food. Even if we're not currently hunting them."

Not wanting to hear any more, Clara slammed the door to her brother's car shut and stomped into her complex lobby. She didn't need Benjamin's approval, and she was going to see Sean tonight, even if it meant she was going to walk there herself.

She needed the walk anyway. How was she going to say anything to Sean with her eyes turning yellow or her mouth growing fangs if her temper flared up?

Now more than ever she was going to need control.

****

The doorway of the Red Lightning Pub reeked. Badly. Considering the olfactory assault she'd just experienced at the Trouble and Toil, Clara figured the smell of cheap cigars, booze, fresh paint, and thick sunscreen wasn't that bad.

But those really weren't the smells that were making her so tense.

As she swung open the entrance door, the stench of decay nearly sent her to her knees. Her eyes watered and the wolf inside howled for release. She forced herself to walk inside, wiping her eyes, and breathing through her mouth. It didn't help. She could taste the foul mixture of rotting eggs and cabbage with a dash of moist mothballs, and it took all her will not to throw up in the main room.

For once, Clara was grateful for the awful chemical reek of sunscreen because it was more tolerable than the unending stink of a vampire hole. She tried to focus on the sunscreen as she glanced around the room, immediately identifying a dozen or so of the individuals inside as vampires. Their scent was undeniable, and their breaths were heavy with the blood drink that made the club famous red lightning moonshine.

Disgust clenched her insides and she had to fight to not gag again. The vampires were casually raising their tinted glasses to their lips, drinking deeply of the mixture of blood and moonshine whisky. The wolf despised everything it smelled and saw, and it was ready to attack and destroy the corruption before her. She had to focus on something else, anything else.

The interior of the Red Lightning Pub was not what she'd expected. Long-time members of the Colesbrooke pack knew the vampire hideout was an old speakeasy from a century prior, but now it looked like a strange bunker–bar mix with some random new improvements. Someone had been trying to hide the war zone, but the clean stage curtains and mic made the militaristic layout more apparent.

As she stepped toward the bar, a small itch in her sinuses made Clara wrinkle her nose. Scratching her nose didn't help, and a sneeze welled within her. She felt as if she were pawing at her snout like a dog.

Failing, she huffed like a wolf and nearly died inside. A few vampires glanced at her, but no one said anything.

The itch didn't go away, and another sneeze threatened. She had a sneaking suspicion at the cause but was hesitant. Vampires didn't like silver, either, so she wasn't sure why the pub would stash it.

Due to their incredibly keen sense of smell and heightened senses, werewolves were extremely sensitive to silver. Being in the same room with a moderate amount of silver could cause mild irritation, and silver embedded in their body was fatal. Such as a silver bullet. However, she didn't know the exact effect silver had on vampires, but it couldn't be too bad if Lawrence was using it liberally in his bar.

Breaking out in hives would give her away. Hopefully Lawrence didn't have too much silver hidden away or she needed to move fast.

Stepping across the floor, Clara sensed more than saw a few curious gazes thrown her way. However, her sharp hearing didn't detect anything alarming in the low murmurs of the vampires drinking away their eternity. She thanked the moon that vampires couldn't smell werewolves as well as werewolves could smell vampires.

Taking a seat on the stool at the bar, Clara drummed her fingers across the countertop as she tried to think of her next move. She was here, but now what? Should she just ask for Sean? How did she know he was even here? Maybe she was being too hasty. Maybe Benjamin had been right, and she was letting her emotions get the better of her.

As her resolve wavered and Clara started to leave, a voice nearly made her jump.

"Sorry about the wait." A figure stood up from behind the counter—he'd been out of sight while retrieving a bottle. "Can I get you anything?"

Clara looked at the barkeep and shook her head.

"Of course," she muttered to herself as she mentally cursed the universe for its horrible sense of humor.

Behind the bar, Thomas Spencer's tired expression fell behind a mask of confusion. They'd never met in person, so he wouldn't recognize her. But maybe Sean had described her to him at some point?

"I'm sorry, have we met?" he asked apologetically. "I've met so many people in the last few days I kind of stopped keeping track of peoples' names."

"No, we haven't met before." At least they hadn't spoken. She'd seen him through the window earlier that day.

He shifted his weight behind the bar, still holding the bottle in one hand, then started to pour her a glass.

"I'm not here for a drink. I'm looking for someone."

Understanding flickered in his eyes. "You're Clara, aren't you? Um, Artemis told me about you. . . ."

Clara tensed as the full implications of Thomas's words hit her. How could she have forgotten about Artemis? The last time they had spoken, Clara had revealed herself to Artemis, who had apparently gone straight to Thomas. Did that mean that Sean already knew, too?

She felt like throwing up again.

"Hey, are you alright?" Thomas asked, sounding concerned. "Here, let me get you some water."

As he filled a glass with ice cubes and a bottle of water, Clara was telling herself to calm down. Panic was strengthening the wolf inside, who was already ready to be released. Artemis couldn't have told everyone she was a werewolf. If Sean's sister had blabbed about that, there was no way Clara would have been able to enter the bar. Artemis must have kept the fact that her brother was dating a werewolf to herself. Hopefully.

Artemis was clever. She could have foreseen the stress and chaos such an accusation could have caused. That meant as far as everyone here knew, Clara was just some random human girl who had wandered into a shoddy bar.

There was also the issue of Jugular James, the other person in these parts who knew her secret. But again, Clara assumed the fact that she was seated in the Red Lightning Pub was a sign that none of them knew she was a werewolf. Jugular James must have kept quiet.

Besides, hadn't the Crone said that the vampires were still hunting down any who were loyal to Ernest and his cause? That meant the Boston Boys were probably out in the slums, looking for any blood junkies still hiding from retribution.

"Here you go." Thomas set down the glass before Clara.

Nodding gratefully, she sipped the ice water to help clear her throat, and the sudden freeze pushed back the wolf. "So . . . what did Artemis say about me?"

Thomas's smile fell from his lips. Her heart nearly stopped—had she miscalculated Artemis's discretion? The surge of fear thawed the wolf, and it wound tight like a coil, ready to spring.

"Just that she ran into you this morning and you were worried about Sean," Thomas said, lowering his voice as he leaned in close.

Clara swallowed nervously, wondering how fast she could flee the bar if need be.

"She said you knew about this place, about people like me." His eyes filled with a look of sheer guilt as he mumbled, "And . . . you know what I did."

Clara recognized the look in Thomas' eyes more intimately than he could have possibly known. It was the same look she'd seen in her own eyes, staring back at her every time she looked in the mirror during her first few years as a werewolf. It was a blend of survivor's guilt, of self-loathing, and of struggling to come to terms with the fact that you were no longer human—all the emotions that Sean himself would be going through right now.

"Listen, I've lived in this city for quite some time and I know that this city is unique. There are certain unbelievable populations who live here," Clara replied, doing her best to be diplomatic and vague for both her safety and the safety of her relationship with Sean. "Don't think you need to hide anything for my sake. I understand what you're going through and I understand what's happened to Sean. None of that scares me. What does scare me is that I haven't seen Sean in days. I need to see him."

Thomas looked reluctant and for a moment didn't seem sure of how to continue the conversation.

Clara could now understand some of the comments that Sean had made about his friend—he was "the smartest dense person you'll ever have the pleasure and frustration of meeting."

Perhaps Thomas had expected Clara to be furious with him for turning her boyfriend into a vampire. In truth, Clara was surprised over how little anger she felt toward Thomas.

Maybe it was all that wisdom she'd gathered over the decades reminding her that if it weren't for Thomas, Sean would be dead right now. Or maybe Clara knew more about transforming into something you didn't want to become better than anyone, even a vampire, could understand.

Or maybe, just maybe, Clara was angrier with herself over letting Sean fall into such trouble than she was with Thomas.

"I . . . it's not that he wants to avoid you." Thomas fumbled. "It's these changes, you see . . . it's really hard . . . and he was really injured. He was . . ."

Clara's hand balled briefly into a fist. Every second she wasted trying to navigate a conversation with Thomas—in which she was much better informed—was a second she could have spent with Sean.

"I really don't have time for this," Clara told him. "I need to see Sean. Now. There are things I should say before it's too late. You should at least understand that, right?"

Thomas stood rigid for a moment and hostility flashed in his eyes, but then he nodded slowly.

"See those stairs over there?" Thomas asked, nodding toward the far end of the bar. "There's a makeshift hospital at the bottom. Sean's down there getting some of his strength back. The first few days are hard, so don't do anything unnecessary."

"Thanks," Clara murmured, standing up. She was about to rush across the room toward the stairs, but then something compelled her to stop and say something that surprised even her.

"Listen, I'm sorry for your loss. Truly. And thanks for helping me avoid the same thing."

Thomas's expression hardened. After a pregnant pause, he nodded and pretended to organize the liquor cabinet behind him.

Maybe Thomas wasn't that bad a guy after all—for a vampire anyway.

Heading toward the staircase, Clara swallowed nervously and mentally forced the wolf back to a corner of her mind. Vocalizing her knowledge of how close she'd come to losing Sean forever had rekindled her need to set everything straight.

Clara reached the bottom of the stairs and stretched for the door handle. This was it. This was the moment she'd been psyching herself up for all day.

The door's hinges creaked under its weight as it swung slowly open.

"Clara?"

The cry was followed by heavy thuds as Sean not only dropped the weights he was using but also leapt to his feet from a single hospital bed propped in a sitting position. He was still on the mend, though, and his legs nearly gave out, making him pinwheel his arms about wildly before falling backwards into a sitting position.

Clara wasn't sure whether to laugh or cry. Seeing him before her was almost like waking from a nightmare.

"This isn't how I pictured our reunion," Sean said, his grayish skin managing to conjure up a bit of a blush to his cheeks. "I was hoping to at least be able to stand up to greet you."

Clara was suddenly breathless and she shot out a hand to steady herself against the door. He was still Sean.

The two of them stared quietly, on opposite ends of the room, neither knowing what to say.

What could they possibly say? What kind of conversation could possibly cover all that they needed to express to one another? How was she going to be able to ignore the rotting flesh smell that was now part of him?

"I'm just happy you planned on us having a reunion," Clara finally said, her voice thick with emotions she couldn't keep down. The wolf howled in frustration, wanting to be free and take over, to channel the overflowing emotions into a vicious attack.

Sean wore a haunted look for a fraction of a second. The expression faded so quickly that Clara wasn't even sure she'd actually seen it. But before she could think about it for long, Sean rolled his eyes.

"Of course I was planning on a reunion! Believe me, I wanted nothing more than to see you but . . . Look, Artemis said you were someone in the know."

Clara nodded in a neutral fashion. "You could say that. Anyone that stays in Colesbrooke long enough starts to figure out a few things."

Sean smiled, revealing two elongated canines. He hadn't mastered the art of controlling his fangs quite yet. Given the fact that he was struggling to even stand, she understood.

"Yeah, well. I've certainly learned a lot of them over the last few days," Sean joked and then fell silent. His fingers traced the armrest of the hospital bed and he groaned softly to himself. "Clara, I love you."

Hot tingles shot along her arms and down her spine. He hadn't spoken those words out of passion or desire. He'd stated it like a fact. An undeniable, inarguable fact.

He loved her.

She was doing the right thing.

"But . . ."

Her blood turn to ice, and her voice caught in her throat as Sean fumbled for the right words. He ran his fingers through his hair and his brow was furrowed in frustration. This wasn't something he could joke about.

"But then I walked in on a vampire war. I almost died. A lot of the vampires did. It just makes you think, you know? It made me think, anyway." He forced the words out so quickly it was a wonder he didn't overexert himself, and he leaned so far forward she thought he was going to topple out of his bed. "I was out for an entire day after that and when I woke up, they told me I was a vampire. And you know what? The only thought I had was how badly I wanted to see you again, to tell you how I felt."

Sean stopped talking, but the hard look in his eyes made Clara sure he wasn't finished yet. She kept silent. Words were hard. Maybe if she showed she was willing to listen, he would keep going.

She needed him to keep going.

"But then life happened. I wasn't even awake for two minutes before Nelson and Thomas began force-feeding me blood to keep me stable and keep my vampire—vampireyness?—from coming out. It was horrible."

He gave her a pained grin and leaned back against the bed. "I'm not human anymore, you know, and it really sucks. I love you, but how can I . . ."

"No, don't say it!" She glared fiercely at him, a hint of the wolf's fury mixing in with her own. "Don't say anything else."

Sean swallowed nervously and shook his head, "But what if I—you know—what if—"

In two brisk strides, Clara crossed the room, reaching out for Sean.

He pulled away instinctively. He didn't know she was a werewolf, but maybe his instincts did.

She stopped, her hands almost to his shoulders. "Sean, I swear to you that you won't hurt me or drink my blood. I've never been able to guarantee anything as certain as that."

"You don't know that," Sean said, his voice almost a whisper.

The need to confess to her own inhuman nature had never been more powerful in her life. Clara felt the truth beginning to rise up out of her, the enormity of it making it hard to catch her breath.

"Because Sean, I'm—"

The door slammed open, nearly blowing off its hinges.

Sean and Clara both made startled sounds. She spun around, doing everything in her willpower to bury the wolf that nearly escaped from the excitement.

Thomas was a blur of motion. He ripped a cabinet handle clean off of its hinges with one hand, swore, and then yanked open the cabinet without the handle. Grabbing several bags of blood, he tucked them under one arm and reached for a first aid kit.

"Thomas? What's going on?" Sean asked. His eyes followed the blood bags as Thomas jostled them around. Sean, with his newly-formed bloodlust, surely couldn't help but smell the overwhelming copper and iron mix from upstairs.

Blood.

"Jericho's been torn to shreds," Thomas said, not even looking up at his best friend as he grabbed what appeared to be massively thick sutures. "We think it was a werewolf."

7 UPROAR

Juggernaut Jericho. Jericho the Giant. The World's Biggest Vampire.

These were all titles the giant before Clara had earned throughout his time among the cursed. Most of them had been coined by the man's best friend, a vampire named Charles.

Many of the stories revolved around Jericho's brutish strength, but one was legend among the supernatural community.

If sources were accurate, Jericho was in the thick of the Battle of New Orleans during the War of 1812, trying to push the entrenched British soldiers out of the city. His hunger had gotten worked up and he foolishly advanced on his own through enemy lines with nothing but his bare hands, inhuman strength, and terrifying thirst for blood.

Saber blades, rifle shots, and even a cannon ball had all found Jericho during that scrap, but he somehow survived. He'd ripped thirty pounds of bayonets from his back that were keeping him pinned to the ground, and then the sun rose and torched him. Somehow the giant had managed to find refuge from the consuming light, despite taking an ungodly amount of abuse.

There was a reason the commander of that battle, the soon-to-be-president Jackson, had managed to defeat the enemy while being vastly outnumbered; not that there were many references in the history books to what a certain giant vampire's presence had done for enemy morale.

That was why, of all Jericho's nicknames, the one that circulated the most was "Eternal Jericho."

The moniker was being put to the test.

The injuries the giant vampire had sustained were nothing short of horrific, pushing his constitution to the absolute limit. His left arm, from the elbow down, had been torn clean off. Massive gashes ran along both thighs, across his chest, torso, and right down his spine. These cuts were not clean. Shredded skin hung from his wounds that looked like they had been made by claws rather than blades.

A chunk was missing from Jericho's right trapezius muscle. The injury looked as if some wicked bear trap had snapped down on the muscle where shoulder met neck and was then cruelly ripped free, taking with it a good portion of flesh. Had the injury been an inch closer to the neck, a piece of the giant vampire's spine might have been claimed as well.

"Out of the way!" Thomas shouted at the clump of vampires who had carried their injured companion down the stairs.

Clara stared in horror as Thomas rushed to Jericho's side. Whatever had the strength to rip apart the giant vampire was something to be feared.

"Bob, help me with these blood bags. Nelson, get me the cauterizer. And for hell's sake, give me some room," Thomas shouted at the crowd gathered around their collapsed friend.

Maybe in a regular operating room the small number of people gathered around Jericho wouldn't have been a problem, but the makeshift hospital was tiny, and Sean's bed already took up a good portion of it.

Clara begrudgingly admitted Thomas had talent. Though he was the youngest vampire in the bar, excluding Sean, he'd been forced to adapt to his curse quickly, because of the a brewing war. Thomas seemed to have already mastered the incredible dexterity and inhuman speed that came with his curse. His hands were a blur, suturing the worst of Jericho's wounds shut with an almost mechanical efficiency, bringing to mind some sort of twisted sewing machine as he bound the ragged flesh together.

"I swear upon all that's good and decent if you ain't gonna tell me where my wife is I'll reach into your chest and rip out your heart!" Lawrence Foxe shrieked as he struggled past Thomas, his eyes burning on Jericho, though his face was a mask of dread.

His carefully cultivated appearance of a spry and harmless dandy in his early fifties meant nothing when it took four vampires to hold Lawrence back. It spoke volumes of the hidden strength within the vampire leader.

"Sara," Jericho rumbled, fighting to stay conscious.

"Don't speak. Save your strength," Thomas instructed Jericho, inspecting the ugly stump that was the remainder of the giant vampire's left arm before he spared a glance over his shoulder. "Lawrence, you aren't helping. Back off."

"You shut your mouth and make him tell me where my wife is."

There was a terrifying moment when Clara thought that Lawrence was actually going to break free of his minders and charge Thomas. Before he could, another vampire approached the leader of the Red Lightning Pub vampires without the reverence or respect of the others.

Clara found herself instinctively wrinkling her nose. This new vampire reeked so heavily of cordite and gun smoke it cut through the overwhelming reek of blood and vampire.

While his scent was certainly foul, it was nothing compared to the new vampire's look. Ugly wasn't even close to a proper description. His squat form was wrapped in filthy clothes, his gray skin appeared clammy to the touch, and his face looked like it had been smashed in several times. Even vampiric regeneration had failed to properly align his broken nose.

"Lawrence, if you don't shut your yap and let the kid work, I'm gonna break your jaw," he said with a chilling certainty.

No local vampire would ever speak to Lawrence in such a manner. It all but confirmed Clara's suspicions on the newcomer's identity: This was Boston Bob, leader of the infamous Boston Boys.

The wolf howled again, sensing her fear.

Boston Bob, along with his fellow gang member Jugular James, were the solution many in the supernatural community turned to in times of trouble. Their expertise as death dealers was so trusted that the elders in the supernatural community, be they century old vampire elders, matrons of witch covens, or even werewolf Pack Fathers, sought their services.

"You'd better watch where you're putting those mitts," Lawrence thundered. "Look at Jericho. He was mauled by one of those mongrels, and he was with my wife."

There was a collective gasp as Boston Bob delivered a right hook to Lawrence's jaw that sent him staggering backward. Sudden chaos broke out as some of the vampires pulled the stunned Lawrence further out of harm's way and others circled around Boston Bob, shouting at his sudden attack.

The room was on the brink of a riot, but the ugly vampire had succeeded in his probable goal of taking the pressure off Thomas. He had plenty of space to work, now that everyone was concentrated on Boston Bob and Lawrence.

"We should go," Clara found herself saying, turning her gaze to Sean.

"What?" Sean asked, clearly more confused than surprised.

83

Glancing around, Clara double-checked to make sure Jugular James hadn't arrived along with the other Boston Boy. Or Artemis. They were the only two who could identify her as a werewolf, and right now, that could mean her death. She needed to get out of here. More importantly, she needed to get the man she loved out of here, before he was dragged any further into the bloody affairs of these vampires.

"Go. Leave. Get out of the city," she said, trying her best not to sound like she was pleading to avoid suspicion. "This is just going to get worse."

For a moment, Sean looked tempted. He glanced back and forth between Clara and Thomas.

"Last time I tried to bail on my friends, it didn't work out so well," Sean said at last, rubbing the back of his neck uncomfortably.

"You don't really know these people, Sean. You've already been the victim of one war they've fought; isn't that enough?"

Sean watched Thomas in silence for a few moments. How could she tell him about her curse without the others finding out?

"Look, Clara, I might not know these guys, but Thomas is my best friend. He saved my life. And he might be dense, but he's never going to leave these people. So, neither can I."

Clara wanted to be angry. She wanted to scream at him, but she should have expected this. There were some loyalties that took priority over everything else. She understood. It was the loyalty she felt to her brother and to her pack. For Sean, it was to his friends.

"Please, Sean. I can help you. Let me help you." Clara reached out and took his hand. "Thomas will be fine. He has Lawrence now."

For a moment, Sean's face was impossible to read, a pale, blank slate. But then regret slowly ebbed into his features as he looked away from Clara.

"I'm sorry, Clara. I can't. Even if Thomas would be fine on his own, Artemis would never leave him."

"And you'll never leave Artemis."

He refused to meet her eye. "She's my baby sister."

Clara knew exactly what Sean meant. No matter what was thrown their way, Clara knew she would never abandon her brother.

Before she could say another word, Lawrence started shouting again. "My daughter's in the ground, Bob! If I've lost my wife too, I swear I'll . . . I'll . . ." There was a tremor in Lawrence's voice that was borne from equal parts pain and anger. His distinguished features were twisted into a look of agony at the thought of his wife not coming home. The burden of guilt and sorrow caused his once proud shoulders to slump under their weight.

A moment of compassion from Lawrence had cost him the life of his daughter and several close friends during the vampire turf war. At least, that was the tale the Crone had told Clara, and as she watched the leader of the Red Lightning Pub vampires nearly crumble under the weight of his grief, she found herself believing every word.

Ernest had started the turf war among the Colesbrooke vampires just a few months prior, and he'd recently slain Julia Foxe, Lawrence's adoptive daughter. According to the Crone, Ernest was the leader of the blood junkies and had once been Lawrence's best friend and partner.

"I understand, Lawrence. I really do. But I didn't fight a war on your behalf just to leave you twisting in the wind the second more trouble scratches at your door," Boston Bob said. His scowl hadn't softened in the least, but the tone of his voice had. "If the mongrels of this city think we vampires are easy pickings 'cuz of the war, they're gonna find out real quick there's little difference between putting down a werewolf or a rabid dog."

Clara's wolf was shredding her mind. What it heard was a declaration of war, and it was ready to fight. She grimaced, trying to keep from rubbing her temples as the wolf's attack turned into a sharp headache. She was going to lose control.

Not every werewolf was like the Colesbrooke pack. Some loved hunting bloodsuckers, and the out-of-towner vampires may not be aware of the thin pact Sara Foxe maintained. If she was really gone, that meant the Colesbrooke supernatural community no longer had a moderator, and this city was about to face a lot of problems as old alliances were broken.

She had to get out of there—to get Sean out of there.

"Sean, this city isn't going to stay safe for much longer. At least think about getting out. For me," she said, squeezing Sean's hand. She may have squeezed too hard with the wolf demanding to fight.

Sean glanced at her hand and made a noncommittal grunt. She pursed her lips in dissatisfaction. He needed to be more serious about this, but he didn't know which side yet she was on.

"I wouldn't be too worried," Thomas reassured Clara as he washed his hands in a small sink. "We have some friends who are good at resolving conflicts. They'll take care of it."

His face was flushed and beads of sweat dotted his brow. He'd worked hard and done all that he could for Jericho, and it looked like it was going to be enough. The giant vampire, with his wounds now sutured shut and tended to, was sitting at a table inspecting his arm stump and draining his fourth blood bag to assist his regeneration. The legend of Eternal Jericho was going to continue on.

It took a lot of willpower for Clara not to growl at Thomas's intrusion into their conversation, especially now that Sean was nodding along in agreement with his friend and dashing any hopes she had of leaving this chaotic city with him.

"And by 'take care of the problem' do you mean murdering a werewolf?" she asked, more sharply than she'd intended.

Her wolf was adding an edge to everything she said. Her control felt feeble against its mental attack, and the wolf's strength was fueled by her fear, its perceived threat, the reek of vampires, the silver hidden within the Red Lightning Pub's foundation.

Thomas didn't seem to notice the aggression in her voice; he was too busy checking Sean's vitals. Clara felt a twinge of guilt. She'd been getting distracted by the vampire's debate when she should have been focusing on Sean's health, too. He looked greener from when she first walked in, and he wasn't trying to lean forward anymore. She claimed to want to save him, yet she couldn't even tell when he was feeling ill.

"If that's what it comes to, yes," Thomas said, his voice cold. "Vampires and werewolves have a long and violent history. This kind of thing was bound to happen eventually. We've already suffered enough loss. We won't take a frontal assault lying down."

Did he know her true nature? The wolf growled inside her, and it took everything Clara could muster to not growl, too. His words sounded like a warning, maybe even a threat. If he knew, why wouldn't he have said anything? Colesbrooke's supernatural community was larger than in other cities because of the Crone's potion. More supernatural creatures meant more humans who knew about the interactions of their more private neighbors. Thomas had to believe she was one of those humans or he would have attacked.

Still, it was best to be cautious.

"I may not know much about vampire history," she lied, putting her hands on her hips. She had to convince them attacking random werewolves for revenge wasn't the answer. "But I know a bit about what can happen when vigilante justice gets out of hand. If you act hastily and retaliate without knowing for sure what's going on, it will only lead to more trouble."

Thomas and Sean glanced at one another. They didn't look convinced. The wolf reared its head again. They were being unreasonable, and their refusal to listen only made the wolf want to attack more. She was right, she knew she was. How could they not see that? After having just gone through a war of their own, they should be reluctant to start the bloodshed again. Or had they been numbed to death and simply didn't care about the possible consequences of their actions? Or did they feel invincible somehow?

"You may not understand, but these people are our family," Thomas said. "If Sara really is . . . if something really did happen to her, then we will punish anyone who hurt her. What kind of justice do you think people like us can depend on?"

Shaking her head, Clara fought against the wolf that so desperately wanted to silence the vampires before her. Deep down, she knew if the situations were reversed and one of her pack had been attacked, maybe even murdered, that her fellow werewolves would already be on the hunt. But she buried those thoughts under layers of fear and anger.

There was no way she could let the vampires act on their desire for revenge. She would not let harm come upon her pack or Sean.

"I don't think you understand what you're saying—"

A cold voice cut her off. "My sentiments exactly, my dear."

Lawrence stood behind her, his face an unreadable mask.

Her wolf reared in anger and frustration at the perceived sneak attack.

There was an unholy mixture of sorrow and rage burning in Lawrence's eyes, but his face was a placid mask of forced neutrality. "Now I'm just an old man, but to my ears it sounds like you need of some sense." He pointed at Jericho. "See that man over there? He's three hundred years old and has survived everything that life's been able to throw at him, includin' two world wars and several revolutions and civil wars. He can tell you what mustard gas feels like when it fills your lungs and describe the sound of a Panzer tank exploding. That man was out there tonight, accompanyin' my wife while she tried to get this city back in order after a murderous lunatic attacked our home and killed our friends and our daughter. If there's anyone there who coulda protected my wife, it was that man. And now he's dragged himself into my home, barely alive and tellin' me about a werewolf attack and my wife's death."

The weight of Lawrence's words and the chill of his gaze, made her shift uncomfortably. Even the wolf recoiled slightly.

"My wife worked hard to keep the peace with all manner of people in this city." Lawrence paused for a moment, a brief flare of emotion causing him to stumble before continuing. "If she's dead, then all the order she maintained died with her. So I'm gonna re-establish order immediately, beginning by makin' it clear that anyone who tries to harm a vampire loyal to me will catch a silver bullet right between the eyes."

The wolf howled, and Clara shouted with it. "That's not order. That's an invitation for war."

"So be it," Lawrence spat. "I already crushed one army, what's another? I'll put as many bodies into the ground as I need to keep this city together. An outsider ain't gonna understand."

"A war with the werewolves will turn this city into a graveyard," Clara said bitterly, but Lawrence wasn't paying her any more heed.

Boston Bob spoke to Lawrence casually as if he were commenting on the weather instead of organizing a werewolf hunt. "If these mutts could do such a number on Jericho, I want to hedge our bets and have a decent sized team hitting the bricks to find out what happened. We'll start as soon as James is back from his hunt in the slums. He should be back any minute, but in the meantime, let's get some hardware passed around. Time to crack open that case of silver buckshot you have."

Lawrence grunted and headed upstairs.

Clara started to growl and bit her lip hard to stop herself. There was nothing she could do. She would never be able to derail the vampire's plans, and the narrow window she had until someone realized what she was threatened to snap shut any second. The wolf inside was in a full frenzy now, and she couldn't stay any longer. Ignoring Sean's hand reaching to stop her, Clara stomped up the stairs and stalked across the pub.

She'd almost made it out when her sharp ears caught something that made her sick to her stomach.

"Maybe we don't have to fight the whole gang of mutts," one of the vampires was muttering to another. "Maybe it'll be enough to pick off one of them as a message. A lone wolf."

Clara glared back at the vampires in the bar, not sure which had said it. Sean was shouting her name, unable to follow after her. But it was too late. She spun on her heels and pushed past the door into the street. She had to warn the pack.

8 ACCUSATIONS AND ULTIMATUMS

The Den was a hard place to describe. It wasn't a bar, though it did serve beer. A few rickety pool tables were set up in the middle of the floor, and the bitterest coffee known to man brewed at the counter, but neither of those defined it. Cramped and usually dirty, the dive joint was located in a remodeled cellar of a canning factory near the edge of the city.

It was fitting that only a place that was dirty, smelly, and isolated could have possibly appealed to Donald. Though he did burn heavy incense to keep nasty smells at bay, adding a layer of smoke to the gloom of the room. The incense did help, though.

"Hey, hey! If it isn't my favorite pup," he called, raising a mug in greeting to Clara. "Finally looking to enjoy the finer things in life?"

"The finer things in life?" Clara wrinkled her nose, glancing around the Den. It was, as usual, an abandoned dump where only Donald and a handful of the braver pack members cared to meet and waste away their nights. "In what universe does this cheap swill count as fine?"

"I was actually talking about my company." He grinned at her and leaned heavily on the crooked counter of the bar. "And the Den ain't so bad. Why, it would have been a downright paradise back home."

Originally from Scotland, Donald had been in the United States long enough to lose the coarser parts of his native tongue. He talked about his homeland constantly, and few people who met him had much tolerance for it—he was rarely taken seriously when he rambled on about the golden days back home.

Oddly enough, the only thing that Donald never mentioned about his homeland was how he'd come to leave it and ended up in the United States. Any approach to the subject was met with a sour look and mumbling in Gaelic.

"Yes, yes. Good old home. Where the haggis runs free and it rains golden beer," Clara said as she itched her nose. She must still have silver in her system from her brief visit to the Red Lightning Pub because the itch wouldn't go away and the wolf was pacing inside. "Listen, Donald, I'm looking for Benji. He hasn't answered any of my texts and he wasn't home. Have you seen him tonight?"

The bushy eyebrows on Donald's crinkled brow shot up in surprise. Setting down his beer, Donald's face became the very picture of seriousness as he waved her over.

"No, I haven't seen your brother, and you've just about got my hackles raised with that voice of yours, lass. And the full moon was not that long off. You should have more control over the wolfie inside you by now," he said over the crack of the pool cues across the room. "What's wrong?"

Clara took the seat Donald had motioned to, trying to compose her thoughts. Benjamin was nowhere to be found, and he'd make the perfect lone wolf target. That and she needed to confirm he wasn't the wolf who had killed Sara Foxe. She needed to find him quickly and needed to warn the pack. But she also needed to keep guarding secrets because she wasn't ready to tell her pack Sean's fate.

The number of things she was keeping to herself were steadily growing, first with Sean and his friends, now with Donald and the pack. Her web of lies was getting more and more complicated. It wasn't that she was bad at keeping secrets, but these were people with whom she'd rather be honest.

But there was just no way she could explain the situation in its entirety. If her own brother had a difficult time accepting she was in love with a man who had become a vampire, how could she possibly expect anyone else to understand? Besides, she wanted to keep Sean as uninvolved as possible. If the pack knew about her relationship with him, they might feel the need to investigate. That could only lead to more trouble.

"I just need to find my brother. He won't answer his phone and . . ." she trailed off as Donald held up a finger.

His eyes closed and he took in a deep, deep breath through his nose.

"Blood and silver. That's what you smell like right now. Not your blood either. The metallic reek is in your hair. The wolf in you must be furious," Donald said, opening one eye and squinting at her.

Clara frowned, reaching up and running a finger through her dark hair. She should have gone to wash off the lingering scents from the vampire hideout, but she had to find Benji and warn the pack of what may be coming.

"Listen, you remember that pack we ran into the other day? You said they might be trouble and I think you were right," she said, skirting around the issue. She had to give Donald something he could believe even if it wasn't the truth. "It seems that the vampires are finishing up their war."

Donald nodded, "That's good. Didn't want to have to play moderator and trash both sides. But the ticks are always fighting amongst themselves. They don't value bonds, not like us werewolves."

That wasn't what she saw in the pub. Maybe werewolves had gotten the bloodsucker's culture wrong. Or they'd changed since she started taking the Crone's potion.

"Yes, well, there is a rumor I heard," Clara began, stumbling for a lie. "That Sara Foxe has also been killed. That means the peace is gone."

Once more his shaggy eyebrows shot up in surprise and Donald began cursing in a low, coarse whisper. He looked down at his mug, picked it up and tossed it back in a single, wet gulp.

"Who told you that?" he asked, healthy skepticism in his voice.

Clara paused for a moment. She was possessed by a sudden urge to tell Donald where she'd been that night, of all the horrible things that she'd seen at the Red Lightning Pub. The other werewolves were still playing pool and drinking too much. No one was listening to their conversation, and if there was anyone who could have had the wisdom and experience to help her, it was Donald. After all, he'd been the one who had found her and Benji after their first transformation. He was part mentor, part friend, and part surrogate father. But that didn't mean she could tell him everything.

"The Crone," Clara said. "I got a bonus from work, so I thought I'd buy the next potion early. She tried to talk me into buying more, since there is more trouble brewing."

He cursed again as he drummed his heavy fingers across the countertop.

"That old hag, eh? Well, I wouldn't put it past the old witch to make up an entire war story just to make a little extra coin on another one of her foul potions." He gave a heavy, tired-sounding sigh. "But even she wouldn't lie about Sara Foxe's death. The Crone has profited from the peace between us inhuman types more than anyone else. Hard to run a business in a war zone, and it looks like we just might have that without the Lady Foxe around."

"Exactly! This city is going to have some trouble," Clara said, seeing an opportunity to springboard off of this lie and actually do some good with it. "I think you should suggest to everyone to get out of town for a few days. Leave the city. Who knows what's going to happen? Maybe we could all meet up at the Lodge for a while? Until things cool off?"

"I'll suggest it, but I don't know who's going to be inclined to listen. The full moon has passed, and many of the pack just want to go about their lives as normal. Skipping town might not be something they want to do, especially if they have to work." He shrugged his meaty shoulders.

He'd made his decision, but it wasn't good enough.

"Even if it means getting killed?"

"Lass, I was in Scotland when the Seven Ill Years was sprung upon us. Families starving to death on their farms due to famine, vagrants packed elbow to elbow in the cities, and abuse after abuse thrown our way by the wealthy who owned our tenets." Donald's voice grew grim as he remembered the story he refused to tell.

Clara almost gaped at him for sharing, and her wolf paused its frustrating whines and huffs to take control of her emotional mess.

"Still we stayed. We had no cattle, no food, no trade, and no hope. We certainly didn't have any reason to stay. At least that's what I told my family."

She'd known Donald for over forty years, and this was the most he'd ever told her about what might have driven him out of Scotland. More than anything, his sudden candor was a true sign of just how dire things might be in the coming days.

"But they stayed behind. Stayed in Scotland where neither God nor king looked kindly upon us. Why? Because it was 'home.'

That was it." Donald said with a bitter laugh. "So, let me tell you that come hell or high water, people will not leave home. And us stubborn old beasts? Well, we would probably be more worried about high water than any vampires trying to force us out of a city we call home."

How was she to argue against his own experience? He'd lived much longer than her; he understood the nature of wolves better than her. But this time he was wrong. If he just tried he could convince everyone to leave and get to safety while this whole mess was figured out. She could save her pack *and* Sean.

Donald wasn't trying to save Sean. He wasn't trying to save the pack. He was trying to save the pack's home. And on the nature of werewolves, he was right.

The pack would rather fight than flee.

That was just the werewolf way.

"It's a real shame though. About the Lady Foxe. She was a good one," Donald grumbled, sitting up in his stool and reaching over the bar to grab a bottle of beer. "For a vampire that is. I might have never been able to call her a friend, but I could respect her as a kind soul."

Sitting back down, he popped the cap off the beer with his thumb and began to pour it into his mug.

"You said something about that pack we ran into though?" Donald asked.

"Yes," Clara said, remembering suddenly what she wanted to say. "Remember how weirdly calm they were? How in control? It has to be because they had killed vampires recently, right? And then a few days after they get in town, Sara Foxe shows up killed by werewolves. Don't you think that's a little suspicious?"

"Maybe," Donald said, scratching his chin. "Don't much want to go stirring up trouble though, not if we have a vampire war on the horizon."

"Trouble is already here! If the vampires think we're to blame, they'll come for our blood. Wouldn't it be better to have a suspect to give them and let them fight the right pack?"

Donald nodded slowly. "Maybe, maybe. I'll keep it in mind, pup. Maybe call in some long-distance favors. But you keep your nose out of it. Wouldn't want you getting hurt again, would we?"

The wolf inside wanted to be a part of the fight, the hunt. Her human half wanted the same if that's what it took to keep Sean safe. Donald's request wasn't a promise she could keep.

"Fine. I'll keep out of it for now, but I still need to find Benji. If you see him, tell him to call me immediately, okay?" she said, standing up and moving to race off, hoping she could find her brother before any vampires did.

"Oh, you certainly are adorable at times, pup." Donald chuckled, pausing to take a noisy slurp of beer. "It's nearly four in the mornin'. Did you ever think Benjamin might not be answering his phone or opening the door because he's asleep? At home?"

Clara's eyes went wide and, for a moment, she was at a loss for words.

One of the perks of being a werewolf was she didn't need a full seven to eight hours of sleep to function normally like humans. Prowling through most of the night didn't fatigue her, and it would be difficult to sleep anyway with the wolf riled up because of her mental state. Benjamin had probably fallen asleep out of boredom a few hours ago. Maybe he'd slept through her knocking—or ignored her. But she'd almost broken down his door with her banging.

"Uh . . . thanks, Donald. I'll try his place again." Her face felt hot as she turned to go.

Calling after her, Donald gave her one last piece of advice. "Whatever you've got to do, pup, be sure you do it quick so you can get that silver off of you! It'll be driving your wolfie outta its skull, and the more the wolf gnashes its teeth the more your mind is gonna be bogged down! You hear?"

******

Benjamin's wooden door was solid oak. Clara could break it down if she needed to, but it was going to hurt and wake the neighbors.

She smashed her fist into the wood several times, no longer willing to knock like a normal human. Benjamin had to be in there, and she refused to let him ignore her.

Besides, if she summoned the strength to knock down the door, she may release the wolf, too. Her control still wavered, and her frustration with her brother made it worse.

She knocked again, hoping the door would splinter. No, an urge for destruction was not what she needed to be feeling. She stopped knocking and took several deep breaths. The wolf had been allowed too much free reign as she took her frustration out on the door. If she didn't get the wolf under control soon, she might be struggling with it until the next full moon.

Dammit. Benjamin still wasn't answering. What if he wasn't home?

Fear clutched at Clara's pounding heart. How long had he been gone? What if he was the one who had killed Sara Foxe? His fury over her love for a vampire had been alarming. If it mixed with his anxiety and his wolf got out, he could have slaughtered more than one vampire during the night.

The sight of Benji's eyes turning their wolfish yellow and his mouth twisting to accommodate lupine fangs wouldn't leave her alone.

This was wrong. All Clara had wanted to do was confide in her only living family, to turn to her brother for help because he was the only one she could trust with everything. And now, there was a possibility that in turning to Benjamin for help, she'd released the wolf inside him.

If Benji did it, she was to blame.

This time, when her knuckles connected with the wood, there was a loud *crack* noise, and a jagged line appeared, running along the front of the door.

Exhilaration and guilt over damaging the door flooded her, and the wolf began breaking free.

The door flung open, an annoyed and tired Benjamin shouting in the doorway. "What the hell?"

Clara's knees buckled and she pulled him into a desperate hug.

He awkwardly hugged her back, patting her shoulder as he mumbled, "Are you trying to kick open my door? Why didn't you just use the key under the mat?"

The key. She released him and stumbled backward. Her agitated state was becoming embarrassing. First forgetting the time of night and then the key?

"Because . . . it's not important." She slipped past Benjamin and into his apartment. Finding him had calmed her enough to bury the wolf again. "The important thing is I need to know where you were last night."

Furrowing his brow, Benji shut the door behind him. He turned over and walked sleepily to the couch and flung himself down on it, not even trying to sweep some of the DVD cases off it first.

"What do you mean where was I last night?" he asked with a yawn, closing his eyes. "I spent most of it listening to my sister as she made a stupid plan to go into a vampire club because she's acting like a love-sick puppy. As you may remember, I spent a good deal of time trying to convince her not to do so."

"After that, Benji! After!"

One eye cracked open at her harsh tone and Benji looked more irritated now than ever before.

"Would you relax?" Benjamin asked. "Obviously whatever's happened isn't bad enough for you to be in wolf form, so I think we would all benefit from you calming the hell down."

Clara stopped in her tracks. He knew something had happened. Had he really been involved?

"What do you mean?"

He tossed a DVD aside and closed his eyes again. "Well, obviously you and lover boy are broken up now. Once you saw he was a blood sucker, either your common sense kicked in and you broke it off, or the tick dumped you. I know it hurts now but it's for the better. Trust me."

It took several seconds for what Benjamin had said to sink in, and when it did the flames of Clara's fury turned mind numbingly cold. Her eyes narrowed as she stepped across the room, over to the couch.

"You think I'm this upset over a breakup?" she snarled. "You really think I'd be hunting you down for that?"

"Well, aren't you? You're acting rabid!"

"That's not what this is about."

Benji shook his head. "You didn't tell him, did you? C'mon, Clara. This is ridiculous. You had me worried sick last night and at the end you didn't even have the guts to tell him?"

"I didn't have the chance," Clara said, more defensively than she should have. "A vampire was killed, Benji."

Sighing, Benjamin sat up on his couch. "Yeah, I know."

No. Shaky breathes rattled her lungs as she turned away. He really was involved.

"They had a war. I was there with you at the Crone's place, remember?"

Clara could have screamed at him for being so infuriating. She turned back and locked eyes with him. "No, Benji. Last night a vampire was killed. A survivor from the attack managed to get back to the bar. Sara Foxe is dead."

Benji frowned but didn't look too concerned, simply kicking his feet up onto the couch.

"So? As far as I see it, the fewer vampires around the better." He'd summed up the werewolf mentality toward their accursed kin as succinctly as possible. "I know you're doing the whole Romeo and Juliet thing right now, but you have to remember they *feed* on people, Clara."

Perhaps it was because Benji was a loner that he didn't recognize the name, but there was no doubt that he would recognize the importance that Sara Foxe represented.

"Ugh! Next semester I'm going to throw your butt into some sort of critical-thinking class to make sure that brain of yours doesn't rot any further," Clara growled as she began pacing again. "Sara Foxe was the peacekeeper between our kind and theirs. She was killed last night by a werewolf. That's as good as a declaration of war."

Benji sat up. Good; he was taking this seriously now. "That can't be right. The full moon was a few nights ago. Everyone in the pack changed back."

"Then it was someone else. There was a survivor. He's already told the whole Red Lighting Pub he and Sara Foxe were attacked by a werewolf."

"That doesn't mean—"

"I saw his injuries, Benj. It was a werewolf. The bite marks were some of the biggest I'd ever seen," Clara said, trying to get out all of the highlights of the horrible night. "And if they didn't phase back into humans after the attack, that must mean the attackers shifted intentionally. There's no other way to have such control. She was killed deliberately. So, please, tell me where you were last night."

Benjamin was still trying to digest all the new information when his sister's last question finally struck a chord with him.

"Wait, you're serious?" he growled, his own eyes flashing as he leapt up from his seat. "You think I murdered someone in cold blood? That's why you came all the way out here right before dawn?"

Clara held her ground. Benjamin's anger was justified, but so were her doubts. She couldn't afford to let this one go. She didn't think it could've been Benjamin, at least she hoped not, but she had to be sure. She had to be absolutely sure.

"You weren't in full control of yourself last I saw you. You nearly ripped the steering wheel right off of the car," she said, her voice calming down, as she did her best not to provoke Benjamin further. "And all that talk about calling down a blood hunt, what was I supposed to think?"

Benjamin threw his hands out wide in an almost helpless gesture of frustration.

"You're not supposed to think your brother is a murderer, that's what."

"That isn't something we can assume. We always have to be on guard. Always! What did you ask me yesterday when you saw me like that? You asked if I had lost control. It's the same damn thing, Benjamin."

Benjamin scowled at her, his lips curling back and showing a sliver of white teeth.. "I'm not an idiot."

"No. You're a werewolf."

She sank onto the couch, ready to give way to the exhaustion tugging at the corners of her mind, steadily creeping further and further into her thoughts.

"I'm sorry, Benji," she said, leaning her head onto his shoulder. "I didn't really think . . . I just had to be sure, you know?"

"Me, too." Benji sighed. "I mean, Colesbrooke is our home, y'know? And the pack has been a pretty good family."

Clara patted his arm. It was a little surprising he was expressing this at all. Usually his jaded nature made him tight-lipped when it came to any emotion that wasn't related to boredom or anger.

"I know, I feel the same way. That's why I'm trying so hard to make sure we all make it out okay. Listen, I'm really sorry. A lot has happened today and I was terrified the vampires would start hunting my little brother." She wouldn't bring up had been worried about him being the murder, either.

"I'd like to see them try."

Clara lifted her head from his shoulder to stare him down.

"I'm serious, Benji. There are some really bad vampires in town right now, the kind of vampires we were warned to avoid when we first transformed. Professional killers." The cold evil of Jugular James' eyes still haunted her, and her skin crawled with how casual murder sounded from Boston Bob's lips. "We have to figure this out and quick. If we don't, we'll be in over our heads. People will die, Benj."

Drawing in a deep breath, Benji grumbled.

"Clara, you need to step away from this mess, not get further into it. If what you saw is true, and a werewolf murdered a vampire, then the dice have already been cast. Especially if that vampire was the peacekeeper," he said, sounding rational rather than pessimistic. "What's done is done. There's going to be blood spilled no matter what, and all we can do is make sure that blood doesn't belong to anyone we care about."

There was a cold, detached kind of logic to what her brother was saying, and on some level, Clara found herself even agreeing to what he had to say. At its core, Benjamin's approach to the coming storm was the same as her wish to get everyone out of the city. It was all about protecting the ones they loved. She was just trying to protect someone extra, too.

The werewolves weren't leaving and neither were the vampires. She could neither persuade her loved ones to flee nor to hide. But if she somehow discovered the truth of what had happened, then maybe she could avert any further bloodshed. If she could find the werewolf who had slain Sara Foxe and get the truth from them, then perhaps a new peace could be forged?

Hunting down one of her own would be difficult, especially if they really had just lost control. But she could worry about that when she found the culprit.

Right now it was a race against time to ensure the vampires and werewolves didn't start a whole new war. A new tension filled her, a sickening sensation in her stomach as she realized how much every second mattered, that at any moment a potential war between her pack and the Red Lightning Pub vampires could erupt.

Hopefully Donald had already spread the word to the rest of the pack, and the werewolves were going to lay low for a while. At the very least, it could help buy them some time. Vampires couldn't sniff out other species like werewolves could. They would be forced to use more methodical means of discovery.

If the accursed kin could continue avoiding one another, Clara may have just enough time to figure out who had slain Sara Foxe. What she would do with that information was a question for another day.

"Who do you think it could have been?" Benjamin asked.

"I don't know. I asked Donald to look into that pack we ran into, but I'm not sure that will pay off."

"Better than nothing, I guess."

"I'm going to get to the bottom of this, Benji." She raised a finger to cut off his protests before they could be voiced. "I'm not doing it just for Sean. I'm doing it because I love our pack and I love that this city has become our home. I'm going to fight for peace because some things are worth fighting for."

Benji issued a low groan and rolled his eyes., "Oh, give me a break. You sound like Donald."

Clara offered a weak smile.

"Now that's a scary thought," she said, getting to her feet and heading for the door.

"Clara!" Benji called out, all mirth gone from his voice. "You can fight all you want, but you're going to have to accept the fact that when the worst happens, you'll have to choose a side. If you don't choose, you won't be able to save anyone, not even yourself."

She swallowed, trying to remove the dryness in her mouth, and pretended she didn't hear her brother. The door clicked shut behind her, sounding like the sealing of a tomb.

9 INTERNAL DILEMMA

Human running was depressing.

The wolf yearned to leap into a forest and sprint away the frustration and confusion welling within Clara's chest, and human legs were so awkward the way they pounded and balanced. The speed was terrible, and the short breaths forced by burning lungs were almost unbearable.

Yet Clara ran, desperate for a release of endorphins.

Most of her packmates ran as humans. The exercise helped ease the desire to run and hunt throughout the month, even if it did feel incredibly lackluster compared to loping through nature as a wolf. Clara found running more enjoyable when she went with her packmates, and they'd joke about the wolf's frustration and their own discomforts in human form.

She missed their company as she ran, but her mates couldn't relieve the indecision in her thoughts. She didn't want to sacrifice her pack to save Sean. But she wasn't going to let Sean die in another supernatural war, either.

Unable to bare the soreness in her legs any longer, Clara stopped at the corner. The soreness had turned into sharp pain from pushing it too hard, and she winced as she massaged and stretched the painful muscles.

There was something familiar in the air here, and she inhaled deeply, trying to remember. The stale stink of lard hung in the breezeless morning, mixing in with the general scents of gasoline and exhaust.

She knew this corner.

A small diner was tucked into the corner of a massive skyscraper. Mack's Eats used to be its own building half a century ago and had long been absorbed by Colesbrooke's expanding skyscraper districts. Clara hadn't been to the diner since its once owner, Joe Jack, had been murdered decades ago near where she was now standing.

That night was the second time she'd phased from loss of control. Joe Jack had become a good friend despite his coarse outward nature. He'd suffered the loss of much younger brothers to the beaches of Normandy during the Second World War and then later on his own son to the Chosin Reservoir during the Forgotten War. His ability to survive had inspired Clara during some of her darker moments when she missed her dead family and mourned her own trial of death she'd left behind in her early years as a werewolf. Joe Jack's diner was her solace, and she frequented it after every full moon when her memories ached the worst.

After an evening of listening to Joe's stories of his son's bravery, she'd hung around as he locked up to ask if he'd hire her to work as a waitress. As Joe stepped out of the diner and turned the key in the door, a group of eight men reeking of liquor rounded the corner.

She still wasn't sure what had sparked the fight. It might have been the color of her skin, or it might have been because Joe Jack looked an easy target. But once the spark was caught, it flared in an instant.

It started with yelling. Then one of the drunks said something to make Joe Jack throw a punch.

Then there was a flash of steel.

She couldn't be sure, but Clara remembered screaming as Joe Jack was stabbed in the chest. The screams that followed weren't hers, though, as her fear and horror had allowed her wolf to break free, and she'd phased into a werewolf.

The police had never been able to figure out what happened that night at Mack's Eats. It was easy to see the poor old cook had been killed by a switchblade that had pierced his heart. But his was the only body that was easy to identify—the eight other corpses had been torn to pieces.

To this day, nearly thirty years after the event that had born countless urban legends, the case of what had happened at Mack's Eats remained open and unsolved. The diner had been taken over by one of Joe Jack's daughters and remained a popular eating spot since. Clara hadn't returned, unable to face the grief of causing such destruction.

Even now sorrow overwhelmed her and she stopped stretching. More lives were going to die if she didn't do something.

If petty differences like race, religion, or gender were enough to cause hatred and murder, what chance did Clara and Sean have to be happy? Their differences weren't petty. They were beings that were created to hate one another on the most fundamental level.

The hatred between those suffering from vampirism and lycanthropy was just as much a part of the curse as their unnatural hunger. It was inescapable.

Sean would want to work through it. She knew he would. But he wouldn't understand what it was like for her. Vampires didn't hunger for werewolves. All he would know was that the hunger he felt with humans, even with his own sister, would not exist toward Clara. He would probably start making jokes the second he found out. She could see him now, petting her head, offering her treats and pretending to teach her tricks, telling her she was a good girl.

She snorted. He would think he was being charming.

But her humor was short lived. How infuriating it was that her little brother of all people was right.

She was going to have to choose what was more important: her relationship with her pack or her relationship with Sean.

Giving one last glance up at the spot where Mack's Eats had once stood, Clara issued a heavy sigh and began jogging. The pain in her leg had resumed its tolerable soreness level.

How could she have gotten herself into a situation like this? Being forced to make such an impossible choice? Her mind worked itself into a furious circle, going around and around and trying desperately to figure out a new choice, a new angle, a new option that she could take and change the equation.

But how?

Tensions were high. The Red Lightning Pub vampires were armed to the teeth and preparing to take retribution in the form of werewolf pelts. Sean, having been adopted by them in a sense, might be expected to join. And what reason did he have to object?

All it would take is one werewolf death before Clara's pack would strike back. Donald, now informed of Sara Foxe's death, was probably already preparing for a blood hunt, or perhaps even an Omega Hunt. A blood hunt was terrifying enough, where an entire pack of werewolves would gather and willingly transform and let their inner wolves go wild until their enemies had been hunted down and devoured.

An Omega Hunt was even worse. It was sanctioned murder by a Pack Father, who would declare to all packs that a particular danger must be put down immediately. It could mean the potential gathering of several packs, dozens of werewolves turning a massive hunt into a competitive slaughter.

Clara shivered. She'd never been involved in an Omega hunt. She'd never even taken part in a blood hunt. But the thought of it was enough to get her wolf growling.

"Hopeless." Clara sighed as she turned a street corner, heading back in the direction of her own apartment. "Completely and utterly hopeless."

There was only one thing to do, and it was what she'd been planning to do in the first place. Sean loved her. He'd told her only hours before. If that was true, they could figure out a plan together. That was logical. That was fair.

She just had to tell him she was a werewolf first.

****

Going straight to the Red Lightning Pub was too dangerous. With vampires thirsting for revenge, she needed to meet with Sean somewhere were she wasn't outnumbered by enemies. She hoped if she talked with Artemis, she'd help her meet with Sean away from the vampire den. So at noon, after Clara had grabbed a few hours of sleep, she got dressed, fixed her ponytail, and ran out the door.

The sting of manure clogged Clara's nose as she approached the small brick home where Artemis rented a tiny basement apartment. Freshly turned dirt lined the narrow cement path leading to the apartment in the back, with some clots of dirt spilling over onto the cement. They crunched beneath Clara's shoes, and the manure scent amplified. She could barely breathe.

Was Artemis setting up a nasal attack to ward off werewolves? Clara's heart dropped—maybe Artemis wasn't as accepting as she'd hoped.

Dirt was sprinkled across the metal stairs leading to the basement, and Clara cursed with each clanging step. She had to be careful not to slip, and there was no way Artemis hadn't heard her approach.

As she raised her fist to the wooden door, the door swung open, revealing a dirt smeared Artemis wearing a flowery apron and ragged gardener's gloves.

"Clara."

The wolf whined at the surprise, and Clara had to inhale deeply to calm herself. Artemis' intense glare didn't help, keeping the wolf on edge because of a perceived challenge.

"May I come in?" Clara found herself asking after a moment, growing a bit impatient.

Artemis glanced behind her. With the door open, the mix of sunscreen and rotting flesh escaped from the apartment. It was strong, overpowering the manure in the air. Sean was home.

"Look, I've kept quiet about your little hairy secret because I think you truly care about my brother." Artemis raised a gloved finger and shook it. "But if I think for one second that you are going to hurt him in body or in spirit, I will not hesitate to take action."

Sean. A small smile tugged at her cheeks as Clara watched Artemis' wagging finger. Here was this little waif of a girl in gardening attire, knowing full well that she was chiding a werewolf of all things, and she made it seem like it was the most natural thing in the world.

Just one sibling looking out for another.

That was a bond that not even the supernatural could break. Clara knew that from experience, thinking of her own brother and how she wanted only the best for him.

"That makes two of us, Artemis." How could she get Artemis to understand? "Thank you. Please, I want to talk to Sean. Just talk."

Artemis hesitated, her intensity slipping as she glanced behind her again and chewed her lip. She took a small step to the side of the doorway and just in time. Thomas popped out from the darkened apartment, reeking of that horrid sunscreen.

"Hey Clara. Sorry it's so dark. We taped up all the windows until Sean gets used to the change. It's really rough the first bit," he said, his tone shockingly casual for someone discussing the elements of the supernatural.

"I'll manage, thank you," Clara replied in a neutral tone, doing her best to try and keep her face politely composed. She hadn't expected Thomas, but she was certain the clove scent from inside the apartment was fresh. Sean was here.

"Yeah, no problem. Oh, and . . ." Thomas said, glaring at her as he pulled something out of his pocket. "I don't mean to worry you or anything, but a lot of the blood donors we get at the pub feel safer wearing one of these. Just a peace of mind kind of thing."

Sharp chills spread down her back and along her shoulders and arms. Every muscle tensed as the wolf's fight or flight was triggered. Silver.

He opened his hand, a small necklace with an ornamental cross on the front slipping from his palm until it dangled from his fingers.

Crosses and other holy items didn't affect Clara the way they did vampires, but this one was made of silver. Even at this distance, her skin crawled with revulsion.

Artemis's eyes grew wide, and she snatched the necklace with her thick gloves. "She doesn't need it, Tom. Sean's been really good about this."

It was only then that Clara realized Artemis herself wasn't wearing any visible religious symbols that were a protection against vampires, nor did she smell of silver or garlic. Although the small, glossy hair stick she was using to keep her locks tied up in a bun did have the look of hawthorn, a type of wood that was infamous in the supernatural community for disrupting a vampire's regenerative power.

"I know she doesn't." Thomas took back the necklace and tucked it into his pocket. "I was offering it in case she wanted it."

"Thank you for your concern, Thomas, but I'll be all right," Clara said with the same forced politeness. She wasn't sure whether the presence of silver or Thomas's blasé attitude was getting to her more. From the way Sean had talked about him, she'd thought Thomas was more caring. But maybe getting turned into a vampire just did that. Maybe the curse made vampires cold just like it spurred her temper.

"She's fine," Artemis grabbed Thomas and tugged him out of the way. "We're sorry to hold you up, Clara. Sean's excited to see you in there."

Sean. Clara pushed past Thomas. He wouldn't meet her eyes, but she didn't care. As she stepped into the apartment, Artemis began furiously whispering a lecture, Clara catching the phrases "social train wreck" and "insensitive idiot" as she focused on searching for Sean.

The apartment looked just like it had when Clara had last visited. It was a mess of tightly organized chaos that included items from just about every type of arts and craft profession that didn't involve an arc welder. Only a few things had changed.

All the windows were sealed shut with liberal applications of duct tape, and the room was full of new smells that included cologne, foodstuffs, and recently burned incense.

But the biggest difference was the fact that Sean was now seated at small table, looking at her with a guarded smile on his lips. His clove after-shave was stronger than ever.

"I thought they'd never leave," Sean said after a few heartbeats. "Thomas is one of the smartest guys you'll ever meet, but I swear he can be so dumb sometimes. I guess I just let him get under my skin too much. It's bad for the blood, you know."

Clara couldn't bring herself to laugh at Sean's terrible humor like she normally would. Not when there was such a pressing issue they needed to discuss.

"It's good to see you, Sean," Clara said softly, meaning every word.

Sean groaned and plopped on sunglasses. "Oh! Sorry about that! You can turn on the light if you want. The switch is just on the wall to your left. I'm still kind of getting used to all of these new senses and things. . . . It's really distracting. But at least I can wear these sunglasses! Makes me look like Mission Impossible, don't you think?"

"No, the light's fine." Clara took another step toward him. He didn't know she could see well in the dark, how much he was like her now. Waiting wouldn't make this easier. There was no point in delaying any further. "I've got something to talk to you about, and it's going to be a doozy, so just stick with me, okay?"

He cleared his throat and adjusted the sunglasses. "Okay."

Clara closed her eyes, hoping she could say the right words.

"Sean, remember what we were talking about last night? Before Thomas came in?" she began. The resolve she'd felt the night before was slowly being sapped from her. Clara took a deep breath and reminded herself that she couldn't afford to lower her head here. She wouldn't admit defeat.

Of course, that didn't stop her from feeling cold all over.

"Yeah, I remember. Just because I'm nearing thirty doesn't mean I have Alzheimer's. You know, Thomas is a doctor. He could probably check you out," Sean said, laughing weakly. When Clara didn't smile, he coughed to clear his throat before continuing. "I told you . . . I told you I love you."

Last night those words had burned through her like fire. They had made the world make sense, had ensured her she was doing the right thing.

Now they just stung.

"And we talked about how I was scared you wouldn't want to be with me anymore." Sean coughed again.

Taking a deep breath, Clara clenched her trembling hands into fists.

"Hold on to that feeling for a minute," Clara said in a rush, the anxiety beginning to ebb and turn into adrenaline. "But before I say anything else, you should know I love you, too."

In the gloom, Sean's expression seemed to dispel some of the darkness. His eyes went wide and a smile spread across his lips as if he hadn't been expecting those words.

"And I'm a werewolf," Clara finished.

Now that the words were out, her fear had disappeared. Good. She squared her shoulders and glared at Sean, daring him to reject her.

Sean opened and closed his mouth a few times, unable to form words. Clara resisted the urge to fidget. She'd made her move. It was up to Sean now.

"What?" Sean asked after what surely must have been an hour.

"I love you."

"No, after. After that."

"I'm a werewolf."

Sean's face was a blank slate.

"Well shit."

He shook his head, trying to process her words, and cradled his face in his hands.

Clara licked her lips, itching to fill the silence.

"I was bitten about fifty years ago," Clara found herself saying as she paced back and forth. "I wanted to tell you when you got involved with the vampires, but I was scared. I thought it would be too much or it was too soon. I told myself a lot of things."

Still no reply from Sean, though he did raise his head to stare at her.

"You're actually the first person outside my pack that I've ever told that I was a werewolf," Clara said. "I've never found someone I loved enough I wanted to tell."

His silence grew more stifling by the second.

"When I got back to Colesbrooke after the last full moon, I was determined to tell you, but all hell had already broken loose and you were a vampire, and I didn't know how I was supposed to feel about that and then there was the whole mess with Sara Foxe. I mean, it just seemed like really bad timing," Clara continued, desperate to make him understand through her clumsy attempts to justify her behavior. "I guess if I had just sucked it up and told you before I left for the full moon, I could have told you before things got so messed up, but when I saw you in that wheelchair, when I realized what had happened—"

"Wait, what?" Sean broke through Clara's babbling, looking horrified. "You saw me like that? But that morning, I was—" Sean's face was drained of the little color he still had. "I was feeding."

"Yes, but that isn't why I waited, I swear," Clara tried to explain in a hurry. "See, I tried to ask Artemis about it first, but she had me figured out in about two seconds and how was I supposed to know she wouldn't go running off and telling you what I was? And then that psychopath James showed up and I thought I'd be killed for being so deep in vampire territory and . . . You're a vampire, Sean! It was a lot to take in!"

Sean dropped his face into his palms again.

"I'm going to kill Artemis." His voice was muffled by his hands.

Clara was quickly losing control of the conversation. In her hurry to get the whole story out, she was focusing on the wrong details. She was trying to tell Sean she loved him.

"She was trying to do what was best," Clara said. "She didn't want you to get hurt. But that isn't the point. Sean, I want to be with you—"

"Great!"

"—but we're in a tight spot. We're on opposite sides of a blood feud that goes back for centuries. Centuries, Sean! It would have been easier if you were still human, but we're so different now. And there's no way our packs will let this slide."

"Our packs?" Sean snorted with laughter. "We vampires are called flocks. Figures a mongrel like you wouldn't know. But I know you have an undying love for learning, so I'm more than willing to help out."

"Sean . . ."

"Wait, wait, one more. Fangs to me, you won't have to look foolish when I introduce you to my flock."

"Sean," Clara snapped.

"Sorry," Sean said, trying hard not to smile. "But you have to admit this is kind of funny. I mean, what cosmic power did we piss off for this to happen?"

"I'm trying to tell you we're in danger." She crossed her arms and glared at him.

"What's the big deal? Are you seriously telling me this has never happened before?" Sean asked. "I mean, come on! In all the history of vampires and werewolves, there was no one else that fell in love?"

"We're cursed to hate each other," Clara said. How did he not get this?

"Yeah, but we got over it," Sean shrugged. "So how hard can it be?"

"Don't be naïve!" Clara shouted in frustration and as she did, her features contorted into a ferocious snarl.

Sean's jaw dropped.

"Our very lives are in danger just by associating with one another. At best, we'll be pariahs in the eyes of our friends and family," Clara said as she remembered Benji's reaction. "At worst, we'll be considered traitors to our own kind and hunted like animals. And that was what would have happened before the peace was broken!"

A look of cold dread filled Sean's eyes as the last of Clara's words sank in.

"You mean, before Sara was murdered by a werewolf. . . ." Sean said, looking as if he might faint. "Oh lord. Lawrence! He's on the warpath and . . . and he saw you!"

"Doesn't matter," Clara said stubbornly. "The point is, we're in a whole lot of trouble, and Sara Foxe's murder is only going to make it worse. If we want there to be the slightest chance that our clans will accept us, we have to restore the peace."

"Oh no," Sean said, trying to climb to his feet. "No, no, no. I see where this is going, and no. No. This is not a good idea."

"I know there's no way you'd ever leave, so the only chance we have is to stop this fight before it happens," Clara pressed on before Sean could say another word.

He was standing directly in front of her now, still a little unsteady, and he placed his hands on her shoulders, adopting a careful tone as he tried to talk her down.

"Clara, listen," he said. "If you stick your nose into this, it'll just get worse. Lawrence will go nuts if you're involved. Just lay low and let this blow over. We can try talking to them once things calm down again."

Clara shook her head. "We can do this, Sean. I can do this."

"Clara, they're out for blood. All of them. You just lectured me on how dangerous this was. Are you seriously going to just jump into the middle of it?"

"Do you want to be with me?" she demanded.

"What?"

"Do you want to be with me?"

Sean mouthed wordlessly before saying, "Of course."

"I'm going to make a place for us." She slipped out from under Sean's grasp. "Just wait for me."

Clara ignored Sean's protests and made a beeline for the door. She threw it open and marched right past Artemis and Thomas, who had been lurking on the other side.

Artemis stuttered a half-formed question, but Clara ignored her. She briefly made eye contact with Thomas but didn't wait around to see what his steely expression meant.

She'd done what she needed to do. She'd told Sean what she was and he wanted to be with her.

The fire was lit. Now it was time to get to work.

10 THE PACK

The Den wasn't a place Clara enjoyed hanging out. It was cramped, dirty, and had a real boy's club vibe to it. She liked the roof of the building much more. Originally it was a smoking area for the employees at the canning factory, but some of the more industrious workers had slowly turned it into a sort of lounge. There were several potted plants, a small flower garden, and plenty of folding chairs. When the factory went under and the pack bought the building for their own personal hang out, they had kept the rooftop lounge intact. Now the pack members went up there whenever they needed fresh air from the dark, smoky lounge.

There weren't many places in the city limits that could be considered tranquil, but for Clara, this was as close as it got. There was always a gentle cross breeze that wiped away the stench of the city, leaving nothing but the fragrance of flowers in its place. More importantly, there weren't any pool tables or card games that brought out the competitive nature of werewolves. Up here they could relax and think or hold small pack meetings, though rambunctiousness still continued.

So while she was hoping for a peaceful meeting with Donald, her hopes were dashed as she heard thunderous smashes on the rooftop as she ascended the stairs. A brawl was already underway.

"You almost got him, baby," Izzy called, clapping encouragingly at her husband. "C'mon. Go, Vic!"

Clara reached the roof just in time to watch Izzy knock her glasses askew from a lounge chair. Clara still didn't know why Izzy wore them when she didn't need to, but she was never seen without them except on the night of the full moon.

In the center of the rooftop, Vic was wrestling with Donald, doing his best to break Donald's balance so he could knock him over. Unfortunately, Vic's strategy was destined for failure. There were some oak trees that would have considered his opponent sturdy. While Vic was tall and had a superior reach, he was a bit on the gangly side. Donald outweighed him by a good thirty pounds. More importantly, Donald had years of rough and tumble experience to call upon and upper body strength that would have shamed a silverback gorilla.

There was no way Clara was going to have a private conversation with Donald until the brawl was over and he'd calmed down. She settled into a lounger next to Izzy and sighed. She was just going to have to wait.

Vic lunged, looking to shove Donald back a step instead of trying to pull him off balance. Donald gave a hearty laugh and twisted his body as his own hands shot forward. Donald gripped Vic's wrists as he continued moving at the hip, his broad shoulders bulging as he drew upon their impressive strength.

Vic hollered in surprise as he was lifted off his feet and thrown flat onto his back.

"Ho, ho, ho, pup. First to fall buys the drinks," Donald shouted, throwing his hands high. "I've been drinkin' for free for years, thanks to you young'uns! All bum and parsley, the lot of ya!"

Vic jumped back to his feet and began to argue about the rules of this wrestling match. The argument grew louder with the additional commentary from Alban and Albert, collectively known as the Von Grimmel Brothers. The twins seemed more like one soul sharing two bodies than two separate entities.

"Pah! These wolf-men and their yapping," came a low, syrupy voice from behind Clara and Izzy. "Sometimes I think we should get them all neutered so they can finally end this obsession to become a non-alpha leader."

This was not the first time such a statement had come from Deva, a come-and-go member of the local pack, but she didn't mean it. With dark and rich skin that contrasted the bright and vividly colored clothes she favored, Deva was the second oldest werewolf in the city but refused to take any leadership role despite how invaluable her experience and advice was. Maybe Clara should talk with her first before talking to Donald again. No, Deva would never support a relationship with a vampire.

Deva tutted as she adjusted her vibrant emerald traveling peacoat. She had a bad habit of vanishing without a trace and then reappearing months or even years later with no explanation. Deva had claimed that the urge to roam and wander was in her blood and that being a werewolf had made it worse.

"Oh, boys will be boys," Izzy said, reaching down to the cooler, pulling out a beer, and offering it to Deva before giving her a coy smile. "Besides, I don't think I'm too keen on having Vic neutered. I like him just the way he is, thank you."

Deva's following remark was lost in the commotion caused by the Von Grimmel brothers joining in the brawl.

Using a long violet fingernail to pop the tab of a beer can, Deva settled into another chair next to Clara and Izzy, taking a mighty gulp as she continued to stare in a disapproving fashion at the ruckus.

"It must be the wolf within that turns all the males of our pack into such a lively and lowbrow lot," Deva said in a huff. "They concentrate all of their focus on the fang instead of the fluff, if you get my meaning."

Clara and Izzy shared a look when Deva continued to tut in disapproval. From the little they knew about Deva, she hailed from the Romanichals, her family having fled from the British Isles during the reign of Oliver Cromwell. She'd ended up in a nomadic circle that encompassed most of North Africa and the Middle East, which was where she was bitten. With her newfound strength, she'd quickly become a heroine to her people. She easily fended off bandits who targeted the poor foreigners for the only thing they had worth stealing: their women.

While such a harrowing history could give root to negativity, the local pack knew Deva's bark was worse than her bite. After all, every time she came back to the Colesbrooke metroplex after one of her mysterious disappearances, she always seemed to end up staying at Donald's place until she re-oriented with city life.

Donald simply said he was doing right by a fellow member of the pack; though many pointed out that he was less flirtatious and more well-behaved when Deva was around.

"Oh, a lot of men are just competitive, that's all. It's probably a cultural thing," Izzy told Deva and then glanced over to Clara. "I mean your boyfriend isn't one of us, and he's the competitive sort, right?"

Despite her best effort, Clara couldn't keep from wincing at the mention of Sean, something Izzy unfortunately noticed.

"What?" Izzy asked, perking up immediately at the prospect of gossip.

Clara took a long drink to stall for time. She hadn't shared her revelation about Sean's new status as a vampire with anyone but Benjamin. There was no way the pack was ready for that kind of news. She'd planned to talk to Donald with a different angle, one that conveniently left out Sean's supernatural status.

But maybe she could trust her pack members with a partial truth? "We're going through a bit of a rough patch.

"You think you'll break up?" Izzy asked.

"No, but I think I've pissed him off."

That part was true. Sean had called her almost ten times since their confrontation yesterday. He was stubborn and was still against Clara's determination to investigate Sara Foxe's death herself, but she planned to show him her own stubborn streak and the strength of her resolve. After the second call, she started to ignore her phone entirely.

"So let it go," Deva shrugged. "It's more trouble trying to keep men in line anyway. You'd be better off without him."

Despite the jumbled mess the other werewolves made, there was no doubt that Deva's eye singled out Donald, who was currently holding each of the Von Grimmel brothers in headlocks as Vic tried his best to escape being trapped underneath his three pack mates.

"Deva," Izzy said sharply, chiding the older werewolf. "Have some tact, will you?"

Deva just gave a shrug and placed a hand on her hip. "What? Since when was it bad manners to be honest?"

Before the two could begin a more heated argument, Clara surprised them both by giggling. It was so like Izzy to lecture Deva for doing exactly what Izzy herself was guilty of.

After the last few days of enormous tension, it felt good to laugh, and Clara had a hard time stopping. When she did, she wiped away a few tears crinkled in her eyes and shook her head.

"I think I'll stick with him for now," Clara said, her breathing heavy. "But who knows if he feels the same. I just told him what I was."

Deva's drink clattered against the ground, golden liquid spraying their shoes.

"You did what?" She tried to say something else, but all that came out was sputtering.

"Oh relax, Deva. Telling a man about the curse isn't the end of the world," Izzy said, rolling her eyes. "He probably didn't even believe her."

Izzy might have been more at ease with Clara's decision than most werewolves because of her relationship with Vic. They had come to the city as a couple secretly, having secluded themselves from the supernatural community just long enough to confirm that the rumors about the Crone's potion were true, and that the worst of the lycanthropic curse's effects could be contained by her bizarre concoction.

Once that had been confirmed, one of the lovers intentionally, and consensually, turned the other into a werewolf so they could be together for as long as their unnatural lives would carry them. It was only after this change occurred that Vic and Izzy had revealed themselves to the other werewolves of the city, eventually joining the pack.

Izzy and Vic's story sounded like a cringy teen romance novel. In a world of curses and full moon massacres, most werewolves were unwilling victims of their curse, and many resented anyone who would willingly accept it. For this reason Vic and Izzy never revealed who was the original werewolf in their relationship.

"Spoken like someone who has never caught the wrath of a blunderbuss across their face," Deva said icily to Izzy before turning to Clara. "And what would ever possess you to actually tell a human about you being a werewolf? What do you think will happen when he begins to gray and you are as you will always be? Hmm? Or were you thinking of adding him to our pack like our two lovebirds here?"

"Hey now," Izzy growled.

"Oh, knock it off," Clara said, feeling particularly tired after her rich laughter just moments ago. "I don't know what I was thinking, but I told him. And things got tense after that."

Izzy and Deva fell quiet and quit their posturing.

"Well, it takes time to wrap their heads around it," Izzy said after a moment, taking a step over and sinking down in the chair next to Clara. "For me and Vic, it was the same way. We needed a lot of time to be certain that the curse was worth passing on."

While she hadn't dropped her frosty scowl of disappointment, Deva did add in a much softer tone, "And how does this man of yours feel about your confession? Does he believe your claim? Or does he think you are sick in the head?"

She needed a reason for his connection to the supernatural that didn't include vampires. "He believes me. That's what's making things even more difficult. Sean has had previous contact with the supernatural."

Deva and Izzy looked at her with raised eyebrows.

"He works at the Café Compendium," Clara explained, hoping that would be enough to cover for Sean's belief in her curse.

There was a pause, then Deva nodded and huffed, "Witchery was once very prominent in that building. I'm surprised anyone still frequents that place without being turned into a toad. There's bound to be all sorts of books no one's bothered to clean off the shelves."

Izzy gave Clara a sisterly pat on the knee. "Then you're already in a better position than most. If he has experienced the supernatural for himself, that's a giant barrier already broken down between you two."

"Yeah," Clara said, but him being a vampire added several new fortress walls to overcome.

Much to Clara's surprise, it was the usually abrasive Deva who offered words of wisdom to help calm some of Clara's fears.

"What will be, will be, girl. That's how life always has been, and it won't be changing any time soon," Deva declared as she reached into the cooler and pulled out another beer.

A smirk spread across Izzy's face as she fixed her glasses. "Why, Deva, I didn't take you for a romantic."

Deva huffed and replied indignantly, "I'm not, and you best not be getting any silly ideas in that head of yours to the contrary! I still think you two are both daft for thinking that any man is worth such trouble. Headaches, a bit of physical labor, and changing wagon wheels are the only things they've been good for in my experience."

Clara grinned, the tension leaving her shoulders as Deva lost control. "Is that all men are good for? Then why did you decide to stay at Donald's place again?"

Not even an icy glare from Deva could stop Izzy from giggling.

"This is what I get for sharing all of my hard-earned wisdom?" Deva lamented with an exaggerated shake of her head. "I don't know why I even bother. Maybe that's why those old coots who call themselves Pack Fathers are always secluding themselves in forests or mountain caves. It's less of a bother than looking after insolent whelps."

Izzy started to mock gasp but was interrupted by a loud clatter near the fire escape.

"Blimey! Is that how you plonkers have a bit o' sport?"

Bert, a mustachioed gentleman in a heavy coat stood on the fire escape. An old pipe hung from his mouth, but he tucked it away as he swung his legs over the side of the building. In one practiced motion, he took off his coat, removed a golden wristwatch, dumped them both near the fire escape, and charged right toward the fight.

Clara, Izzy, and Deva winced as Bert's full two hundred pounds collided with the jumbled mess of wrestling werewolves, which brought about a whole new bout of loud cursing and struggling.

Vic managed to separate himself only to be tackled by the Von Grimmel brothers with enough force to shatter human bones when they hit the ground. After they all rolled to a stop, the fight seemed to drain from the trio, and they stopped to watch the other two werewolves tussle.

Brawl might have been a better word for what was going on between Donald and the latest contender. Though it had started as a good-natured grapple, their aggression was slowly starting to mount, as neither one of them was able to gain an edge. The pair had their hands on each other's shoulders, each trying to out muscle the other, but both stubbornly refusing to give ground. Bert tried to deliver a cuff upside Donald's ear to break their little stalemate, and he was rewarded with a similar counterattack.

Huffing, they released one another, freeing up their hands as they began to circle around the other, each smiling smugly. While Donald was crouched low with his big, gnarled hands looking ready to shoot out and throttle his opponent, the Englishman held his fists up in a classical pugilist style that would have made modern boxers cringe.

From the sidelines, the odd bout in which these two were engaged looked ridiculous. Considering they could both turn into several hundred-pound wolves, their entire conflict felt flat.

Before the two of them could exchange anything more than glares, a hand fell behind each of their heads. They both grunted in surprise as they were forced toward each other.

A hollow thud rang when their skulls collided together, so loud the onlookers winced in sympathy.

The two combatants sank to the floor, each swearing loudly.

Deva brushed her hands off on her dress, a glint of satisfaction in her eye as she put an end to the competition that was slowly getting out of hand.

"If you two are finished trying to rekindle hundreds of years of idiocy between Scotland and England, I think we should get on to business," Deva hissed, her commanding posture saying she wouldn't tolerate any objections. "Or should I go grab some muzzles to make sure that some of our more uncivilized members keep their yipping to a minimum?"

Other than a few mumbles from Donald as he climbed to his feet, no one seemed opposed to Deva's suggestion.

"Well ain't that just a kick in the teeth, Deva. Had I known you were back 'round I would've been on my best behavior," Bert said in an overly sincere and apologetic way before quickly jerking a thumb to Donald. "All I was trying to do is show the pups over there how real wolves play. Honest! Was I informed you'd be joining us today, I'd have greeted you properly with a dozen roses as lovely and radiant as youself."

Donald muttered under his breath, folded his arms, and scowled at the man next to him, though he didn't rise to the verbal bait and defend himself. Deva seemed to have just as much experience dealing with Bert as she did with Donald and kept her expression level.

"You're certainly one to talk about giving notice, Bert," Izzy said as she and Clara joined the rest of the pack. "Last I heard you were on a ship heading straight for London. That was ages ago."

Laughing, the newcomer just gave his mustache a twirl and winked at Izzy, not bothering to provide a proper response.

Bert Ashworth was one of those rare individuals who seemed to be right at home no matter what city or town he found himself in. Charismatic in his own way, Bert had traveled the globe many times over in his long years as a werewolf—there was at least one pack on every continent that had welcomed Bert into their midst with open arms. Unlike Deva, Bert's travelling was not spurred by some sort of wanderlust. Instead, he was dragged from place to place by extraneous circumstances that never seemed to end.

No matter where he ended up, Bert was always lamenting about his need to return to London, his home city.

"Oh, I got back to England but never made it past the Port of Immingham before a spot of trouble got me on a flight to Quebec," Bert said, giving a grateful nod to one of the Von Grimmel brothers who had collected his bowler cap and handed it to him. "When you're as charming as I am, there's always someone wanting to get ahold of you."

Deva snorted but Bert ignored it as he placed his bowler hat back on his head and his pipe between his teeth.

"But you shouldn't have swung in unannounced. We could have grabbed a few bags of that horrible tea you're always going on about." Vic laughed as he stepped over to Izzy and wrapped an arm around her waist. "Come to think of it, all the veterans of the pack are here. We should give everyone a call and have a proper get together."

Pursing her lips, Clara realized Vic was right. Deva, Bert, and Donald were the oldest werewolves who frequented Colesbrooke. They were probably some of the oldest werewolves in the country. Not only that, every werewolf gathered here had been a member of the local pack for over three decades, giving them the distinction of being cornerstones of their little community.

Clara's stomach sank. A gathering like this could only mean there was serious business to discuss. She may have been too late to talk to Donald again on her own.

"He makes a good point," Clara said, trying to sound friendly instead of suspicious. "What brings you back to the city, Bert?"

"He's here because I asked him to come," Donald said in the business-like tone he usually only used close to the full moon. "Same with Deva. I figured since none of us put much stock into that alpha nonsense, we could do a counsel. If we all work together, we can get the entire pack on the same page."

Clara's stomach twisted into a knot.

"The city we left during the full moon isn't the city we came back to," Donald said, turning his eyes toward Clara. "In fact, if we aren't careful, we might not be able to call Colesbrooke our home for much longer."

11 STUMPED

As lazy, careless clouds drifted over a sky the color of a robin's egg, seven mismatched chairs were pulled into a rough circle around a cooler half full of ice and beer. Looking from the outside, it would never have been obvious that those assembled had done so to discuss the possibility of a genocidal war.

Clara wished with all of her heart that there had been an eighth chair, one for her brother. She could have used his support right about now. Before today, she'd never considered that she might be central enough to the pack to be considered one of its leaders. Now she was going to be asked for her input, and she was biased with a secret.

This was a bad decision. She had no place being involved right now.

Take Deva for example. While she'd never been one to call the city her home, she'd extended her guidance and affection to the local pack numerous times. Just as well traveled, and possibly more knowledgeable than Deva, was Bert, a respected member of the supernatural community worldwide despite his constant jokes and refusal to take any matter too seriously.

Neither the Von Grimmel brothers, nor Vic and Izzy, had been around as long as the others, but they had all been integral to the pack for several decades as well.

And then there was Donald.

Clara glanced over at Donald, the unofficial leader of the pack, despite not wanting to be an Alpha. The role of leader just kind of fell on his shoulders since he was the oldest. It was more of a burden than a blessing for him; yet he bore the responsibility as best he could, doing all in his power to ensure the safety of his pack. When push came to shove, there wasn't a single werewolf in the city that wouldn't follow Donald's orders; they all knew he had their best interest at heart.

The fact that he'd been able to get both Deva and Bert back to Colesbrooke upon request showed just how much sway Donald had—and how much trouble he thought the local pack might be facing.

"Now, I don't think anyone here would call me a liar if I said that I wasn't too big on politics," Donald said, raising his voice just enough to make all other conversations putter out. "But politics is why I thought we all needed to meet up today, and why I'm going to be asking for all your help in figuring out what our actions are going to be like from today forward. What we're going to decide here is going to affect every member of our pack."

The sudden tension those words brought made Clara squirm in her seat. Izzy reached over and interlocked her fingers with her husband.

"Okay, I'm lost," Vic said after a moment. "What are we talking about? What politics? Did someone in the pack bite somebody? Do we have a rogue werewolf to track?"

As a living example of what could happen when a rogue werewolf goes out to hunt, Clara knew the dangers of lycanthropy being passed on to someone completely ignorant of the curse. She and Benjamin had been lucky. They had been found. Just three years ago, a man had been infected during a hunting trip. Completely ignorant that the bite he received in the forest had been the work of a werewolf, he'd gotten into trouble in Chicago and was arrested only two days before the full moon.

He'd transformed and managed to escape his jail cell, which resulted in the deaths of four civilians and two police officers.

The attention gained by that tragedy was the kind no one in the supernatural community wanted, which was why most werewolf packs made it a top priority to find rogue werewolves as quickly as possible.

"No, Vic. I'm proud to say that our own little happy family can be held up as a great example to other packs, keeping our own affairs and business amongst ourselves." Donald grinned as he added, "It isn't our politics that has turned this city upside down."

"The blood sucker," the Von Grimmel brothers said at once, their voices flat.

All eyes turned toward the twins.

"The one gathering criminals and slum dwellers. Ernest." Alban said with a disgusted look on his face. "Not subtle at all. Set up his own little operation that turned into an all-out war."

"Blimey, and you didn't tell me?" Bert adjusted his hat.

Donald shrugged, "Vampire war. Ernest and his blood junkies wanted free range on the humans and to take over the Red Lightning Pub. Some of us kept an eye on it. It got bloody fast. Lot of human casualties and talk of vicious serial killers and attacks. They're still raving about it on the news, though humans don't know it was supernatural. The pub vampires ended it during the full moon."

Albert rubbed the back of his neck. "Did you see what happened to the Church of Saint Wilgefortis? It got trashed. All religious items were stolen. Crosses, rosary beads, even the door to the rectory. But not the tithe box. The neighborhood went door-to-door for collections to hire an artist to repair the crucifix of Saint Wilgefortis. The nails of the statue got torn right out. Made of silver."

"Collecting silver is a problem," Vic said. "Normally I don't care when vampires kill vampires, but involving silver . . ."

Clara resisted the urge to tell them off, but she'd never cared about how werewolves talked about vampires before. To have changed so suddenly would draw unwanted attention. The last thing she needed right now was the pack finding out that Sean was a vampire before she could prepare them for the news.

"So the vampires are squabbling in Colesbrooke this time," Deva said. "They are far too involved in the affairs of humans. Sure, we have our problems, but it's never as devasting or common. Wherever vampires go, you can bet trouble will follow."

As Deva finished speaking, Bert erupted into deep, bubbling laughter. Every eye turned to him as he tried to control his mirth.

"Blimey, trouble is just a fact of life. But we have to give the blood suckers some credit. Their war could've been much larger and closer to the surface. They've been covering their tracks, even with some of the human casualties on the bloody news. I keep my ears pretty low to the ground on principal, and Donald's call was the first I'd heard of this."

"I doubt the humans sweep it under the rug. There were some gruesome deaths flashing all over the internet," Izzy groaned.

"Don't worry about the humans," Bert said as he reached into his coat pocket and pulled out a small leather bag of tobacco. He packed his pipe while everyone stared at him then stuck it between his teeth and smiling lips.

The wait was tedious, and Deva started sniffing. "Worrying about humans is how our packs have stayed hidden, Bert."

He kept smiling as he lit his pipe. "Bloody humans always have something to worry about. Their sensational news will find something new to report and stir up the masses. They never fail. It's the vampires you have to worry about, honest."

Everyone but Clara rolled their eyes.

"The vampires may be as spineless as rats but even a cornered rat can bite. On the way here I put some questions out to some well-connected friends, and it seems this war was big enough that the vampires called in some heavy hitters. A bunch of Yankee gangsters turned vampires calling themselves the Boston Boys. You've heard of them. They whore out their bloody services to anyone, even human cartels," Bert said between puffs on his pipe. "I cannot stress this enough: no punches were pulled in this war. What happened among the vampires ain't a struggle to determine who the Alpha was. This was a one hundred percent ideological war, and the dust is still settling from that."

The Von Grimmel brothers both opened their mouths to speak, but they were silenced by one of the sternest looks anyone had seen from Bert.

"Don't waste your breath yapping with false bravado, pups. I know how tough our inner wolf makes us, but this ain't some street brawl." He exhaled a long stream of smoke. "Donald brought me in to do some digging and that's what I did. The blood junkies were well prepared to go to war. They used their drug connections to manufacture a whole lot of firepower that would work against their own kind, including an entire truckload of silver bullets."

Any protests that the Von Grimmel brothers might have voiced died as Bert spoke. While they weren't as intimidating as Bert or Donald, the twins were some of the greatest hunters in the Americas. Anything or anyone who had the misfortune of becoming their prey rarely lasted a few hours after the Von Grimmel brothers caught scent of them. But even they were not keen to engage an enemy heavily armed with the only weapon effective against them, especially if it was a vampire packing silver.

Vampires had better aim than humans, and no matter how quick and lethal a werewolf was, they weren't faster than a bullet.

"The blood junkies were beaten, and to the victors so go the bloody spoils. So not only do you have some of the most dangerous vampires in your city, it's safe to say they're sitting on a small fortune of silver weapons."

The muscles in Clara's legs felt tight as she rubbed her clammy hands on her pants, and she had to force herself to relax. That was why Donald was taking this so seriously, why he'd called a gathering. The vampires were angry and they were armed. They wouldn't hesitate to act. And Sean was in the middle of it.

The Von Grimmel brothers leaned toward each another and began speaking in hushed voices. Vic took Izzy's hand and held tightly, while Deva was harrumphing to no one in particular. Clara did nothing but watch. How could she dispel their fears and convince the vampires to dispose of the silver bullets?

"But the vampires went to war with themselves," Izzy said over the chatter. "Why should we even worry about them? We have the treaty."

She had a cautious amount of hope in her voice but given the scowls from Vic, Deva, and the Von Grimmel brothers, it was not a sentiment everyone shared.

"Normally that would be the case. Everyone minds their own business and cleans up their own messes. That's what all of us non-human folk have agreed on," Donald said, squaring his meaty shoulders as he came to the brunt of the issue. "But as of a few nights ago, the truce has ended."

The pack fell silent, no one moving. It was the first they were hearing of it, and their flat gazes unsettled Clara. She glanced at Donald, who was joining their solemn silence. Long lines weighed down his face, making him look older than Clara had ever remembered.

This was her time to talk, to explain before they could jump to their own dangerous conclusions. She just hoped she could say the right words.

"The truce hasn't ended," she cut in. "Not necessarily. It was violated by an act of war and the vampires are looking to retaliate. Sara Foxe was murdered by a werewolf."

The spell was broken.

"That's impossible," Alban said.

Dammit. She hadn't been able to finish.

"Couldn't have been killed by a werewolf," Albert agreed. "Stupid to think otherwise. All of us took the potion and hunted at the full moon, and none of our members are dumb enough to attack a vampire in the thick of a vampire war on our own."

"It couldn't have been us," Vic said. "We were all outside of the city. And even if the vampires were at war, they know not to enter the forests during the full moon."

"Yeah, what would possibly have made them think it was a werewolf anyway?" Izzy asked, pushing up her glasses as she glared at Clara. "We've kept the peace in accordance with the truce, like we promised. We don't hunt them and they don't hunt humans. That was the deal."

It was moments like these that Clara was almost positive that it was Izzy who had been turned into a werewolf by Vic. Life in Colesbrooke was different than it was for werewolves elsewhere. If Izzy had been turned after she and Vic had already come here, then she'd always had access to the Crone's potions during her time living with the curse. She would never have had to experience losing control of the wolf to a regular vampire hunt.

If that were true, Izzy might be the only werewolf in the history to have never murdered to sate her curse. She wouldn't really understand what it was like to be a werewolf. But there was a positive side to that as well. Her hatred of vampires wasn't as strong, which meant she could be a useful ally.

138

"A deal that was only made possible by Sara Foxe herself," Deva said. She had an odd amount of respect for the late vampiress, having shared a certain sisterhood with her because of their mirrored positions among their own kind. "If she was truly killed by a werewolf, then it was intentional. It could have been hunt for sport or perhaps even a declaration of war, as Clara claims."

Vic shot a glare at Deva and held his wife's hand even tighter. "But she wasn't killed by a werewolf. Other than you and Bert, every member of the pack ran with us on the night of the full moon, and I doubt the two of you are stupid enough to commit an act of war."

Bert chuckled as Vic spoke. Deva, on the other hand, pursed her lips and her cheeks flushed. When Vic was done, she opened her mouth to speak but was cut off by Donald.

"He raises a fair point," he said, staring right at Clara. "Are you sure that Sara Foxe was killed by a werewolf?"

All eyes turned to Clara and she felt her mouth go dry. She couldn't tell everyone here she'd been at the Red Lightning Pub the night of Sara Foxe's murder, that she'd seen Jericho's wounds with her own eyes. The massive bite marks, the precision of the claw marks, not to mention the strength it would take to rip off the giant vampire's arm.

Even if Jericho hadn't witnessed Sara Foxe's death as he claimed, his injuries were proof enough of werewolf involvement.

"Yes," Clara said with conviction.

"How?" The Von Grimmel brothers demanded at once.

Deciding it was best to stick to her original cover story that she'd told Donald, Clara put her hands on her hips and fixed the twins with a stare.

"I heard it straight from the Crone herself," Clara lied, making sure to add enough of a glare to remind the Von Grimmel brothers they weren't due the same respect that she was showing the older werewolves.

"And we're going to believe that manipulative hag?" Albert asked, not wanting to back down. "Why would we trust a witch that extorts us?"

Bert snorted. "Because war is bad for business? The only reason she's made a living here is because we aren't hunting vampires. Without the peace, she has no business."

The twins didn't look convinced, but they weren't about to argue with him. The only thing Bert loved more than Virginia aromatic fire-cured tobacco was loud, obnoxious debates. Since those debates often ended in a fist fight, and Bert had demonstrated his prowess in those several times, it was wiser to back down.

"There is no need to doubt the Crone or Clara. We are treating these as facts. The vampires are armed with silver. The peace is broken. Not only that, the peacekeeper was killed by a werewolf," Donald said in a commanding tone, putting an end to the reproachful looks the Von Grimmel brothers kept shooting in Bert's direction. "What I need from everyone here is ideas about what we are going to do about it."

This was where Clara needed to step in. The pack had believed her lies and was looking for her input. "We already know that none of us did it, all we need to do is convince the vampires. They don't want a war, they just want justice. Just as any one of us would."

"But how can we?" Izzy asked mournfully. "The only proof we have is trust. That won't hold with the vampires."

"We find the real culprit," Clara said.

"How?"

She didn't respond immediately. This was the part she was unsure about. How was she supposed to go about finding the other pack? They could be anywhere by now, and it would be difficult to

140

track them. The Von Grimmel brothers were probably her only chance.

"I mean, our pack is the only one in Colesbrooke, and we were all out of town during the full moon," Izzy rambled. "And none of us could possibly have lost control so soon. And no one would do it deliberately, at least I don't think they would."

"She's right," the Von Grimmel brothers said, starting to come to the conclusion Clara had hoped for. "It wasn't our pack."

Vic frowned, "There was the other pack we bumped into in the forest, but they weren't in the city either."

"Something else is going on. Maybe something big," Clara said. "We were out of the city for the full moon when the vampire war reached a boiling point, and the blood junkies were getting their hands on a lot of silver bullets without us noticing. Then, right after the full moon Sara Foxe gets mauled to death by a werewolf? The timing is all off, and we can't verify if the other pack had other members elsewhere. It's almost like . . ."

Izzy and Vic's eyes went wide as they realized what Clara was implying.

"It's almost like someone wants another war to break out in this city," Donald grumbled, though he didn't sound as alarmed as the younger members of the pack.

Given their equally unsurprised expressions, Deva and Bert had also seen the pattern in the timing. Or maybe the idea of war was just not that terrifying a prospect after living as long as they had.

"It does make a twisted bit of sense, doesn't it? If you look at the big picture," Bert mused. "Had the blood junkies won their spat, they would've known we wouldn't have brokered a truce with them because they actively hunt humans. Or perhaps they were planning on gunning us down next. Either way, that meant they would have to contend with werewolves, and so they armed themselves with silver bullets. They may also have had a contingency plan if they lost."

A great weight lifted off of Clara's heart. She'd thought it would be harder to convince the hot-blooded leaders of the pack that the Red Lightning Pub vampires weren't looking for conflict. Colesbrooke was everyone's home. Every single one of them would be ready to fight to keep it, be they werewolf or vampire.

Perhaps that meant Sean had been right to refuse her offer to flee the city.

Clara shook her head.

No time to think about that now.

"So someone else had to put things in motion and kill Sara Foxe," Vic said.

Izzy shook her head, a stubborn look on her face. "This is wrong. We're jumping to conclusions. Who would do something like that? It's insane! Why would anyone want to start another war? And why are they targeting us? We haven't done anything!"

Clara was unable to watch as desperation slipped into Izzy's features. She couldn't blame her friend for rejecting the pattern so violently. Clara didn't want to believe that the unfolding events were the result of a sinister plot either, but neither did she believe someone in her pack had gone rogue and killed Sara Foxe. They did not have the luxury to hope for the best—at a time like this, it was better to prepare for the worst.

"I don't think whoever is doing this needs a reason. Sometimes people do things that can't be rationalized by the likes of us," Deva said, a dark look in her eyes. "However, if you look hard enough, you might be able to see the pattern behind their actions even if you cannot understand them."

"What's that supposed to mean?" Izzy asked.

"We don't need to understand why someone would want a war between us and the vampires. The why is irrelevant," Alban explained in a distracted sort of way. "Just need to figure out how they are doing it."

"We're the how. It's like how wolves hunt," Albert said. "They pick off the weak."

"Oh no," Izzy said, her face growing pale in the dim light.

Clara felt a little sick herself. To be hunted by the very creatures she and the pack transformed into was unsettling.

"I'm afraid they're right," Donald said. "Without the peace, we go to war. As soon as that happens, every faction is going to be weakened. Werewolf or vampire, occultist or human, we're all going to be easy prey."

"All the more reason to stop this before it escalates," Clara said, jumping to her feet. "If we move quickly, we could—"

"We could make it worse," Bert cut her off. "Every vampire in the city has an itchy trigger finger. We best not give them a target."

"But—"

"That's enough, Clara," Donald growled.

She dropped back into her seat, heat rising in her face.

"Any pack-wide gathering on our part would be seen as hostile," Donald said, clasping his hands together. "I want everyone here to spread word to the pack that they are to steer clear of vampire territory and avoid them at all costs. They have no way of finding out what we are, but we can smell a vampire from a mile away. That'll buy us some time until we figure out what exactly is going on."

Clara gritted her teeth. A few nights ago, that was exactly the type of strategy she would have endorsed. But now, hiding looked like the worse option. The longer she and the pack sat still, the longer the vampires would have to stew in their anger. If they could just settle everything before it got out of hand, they would have a chance.

But Donald and the others were beyond listening. They had chosen their path, even if it was one Clara didn't agree with. And by wanting to protect Sean, Clara had chosen hers.

From now on, she would be on her own. If Donald found out that she intended to act, there would be hell to pay. For now, they just needed to think she was cooperating.

"So we just back off?" Clara asked. "Do nothing?"

"Well I didn't say that." Donald scratched at his ear. "Why do you think I called in Bert and Deva?"

Clara shook her head, nonplussed. Deva smirked and Bert chuckled.

"Lass, there's no one who knows the supernatural community better than these two here," Donald said.

"You mean . . . ?" Clara said, excited.

"Bert and Deva, at your service," Bert said, bowing low. "The pack's personal sleuthing agency."

12 LOYALTIES

Not wanting to rely only on Bert and Deva, Clara tried doing some investigative work on her own, but had come up dry. She'd never found the spot where Sara Foxe was killed, nor did she find any more information about the strange pack.

She'd also been busy warning the other pack members with Donald, the Von Grimmel brothers, Izzy, and Vic. It had only taken a day to spread the word to the rest of the pack that they needed to keep a lower profile than usual. That suited everyone just fine, as most of them had plenty of things keeping them busy as they made up for the work they had missed during the full moon.

Life could get pretty hectic juggling a professional and social life. Throwing a curse into the mix didn't make things easier.

The only member of the local pack who had been overly concerned with this new order to lay low was, of course, Benjamin. Her brother didn't think all the trouble would simply disappear if everyone kept their heads down for a while. Luckily, he'd been called out by the forest service to fill in at a ranger station because some unlucky recruit had managed to roll his utility vehicle into a ravine. But once he was back in town, he would fall back into his stubborn ways doing whatever caught his fancy, regardless of whether it was advisable or not.

Benjamin had at least promised Clara he wouldn't do anything stupid while he was gone. She'd seen him off the morning he left with a smile and a wave. As long as he didn't get too bored, he would probably stay put. When he was back, she wouldn't have that guarantee.

That was two days ago.

So for now, her most pressing concern was Sean. She hadn't seen him since she'd left Artemis' place, but they'd talked frequently on the phone. Every day it was getting clearer that Sean was deteriorating. His jokes were worse than she'd ever heard before. He couldn't even bring himself to laugh at them.

She couldn't put off seeing him any longer. It wouldn't be fair.

So Clara had agreed to meet with Sean tonight.

She sat at her tiny table, staring at her hands and the aromatherapy diffuser puffing lavender throughout the room. In a way, tonight would be easier than the last time she'd seen Sean. He would try to talk her out of digging deeper, but she could handle that. At least the uncertainty around their relationship had disappeared. She was sure of her path. All she had to do was hold her ground.

A loud knock at the door interrupted her thoughts, but she didn't even need to look up. The clove mixed with death scent announced Sean's presence. She didn't smell sunscreen though, but it was after dark.

Clara took a few deep breaths to steady herself as she stood up and began to move toward the door. Before she could open it, however, Sean knocked again. He was understandably impatient.

"Clara? Is that you? I think I hear breathing but I'm still not really used to how loud things are." Sean's muffled voice came through the door. "Like, maybe there's actually a hurricane raging inside. Who knows, right?"

Clara smiled. He could be so dumb sometimes. Her nerves melted away.

"Of course it's me, you dork. Just a sec, I'll open the door."

She twisted the doorknob, pushed the door open, and groaned at what she found standing in front of her. Despite her best efforts to control herself, she laughed.

"What's so funny?" Sean asked. "Don't you like my outfit? I thought I looked awesome."

Where Clara had spent half an hour to make sure that her outfit was both casual and cute, Sean had probably spent the same amount of getting dressed, but only because he wore so many layers he looked like something a bargain bin at a secondhand clothing store had spat up.

He wore a wide brimmed fisherman's hat, and sunglasses with massive lenses covering up what little of his face the mismatched scarf didn't wrap around. Faded workman's overalls poked out underneath the trench coat draped over his shoulders. Despite Sean's best effort to shove his hands back into his pockets once the door opened up, Clara still caught sight of the gardening gloves he wore.

"Wow . . . you look like . . . well, actually, I don't think I've seen anything that looks like you." Her laughter faded into giggles she couldn't suppress. "Just wow."

"You like it, don't you?" His scarf crinkled from his grin. "It's just too bad it's dark outside. I was looking forward to showing off my style."

"You're the pinnacle of fashion," Clara assured him. "But seriously, what gives? Are you doomed to dress like a stalker forever? Thomas didn't look this bad."

Sean shrugged helplessly. "I haven't picked up clothes from my place, and this was all I could find in my sister's closet in my size. I'm hoping to move back to my old place soon, anyway. Then I'll have all my old clothes back."

She smirked and stepped away toward her futon so Sean could come in.

"Clara? Sorry to be a pain but uh . . ."

Sean was still standing outside the doorway.

"You gotta invite me inside."

Clara's eyes went wide.

"What? That whole thing about the threshold is true?" she asked, unable to keep the surprise from her voice. "Are you serious?"

Sean's floppy hat bobbed up and down as he nodded.

"Yeah, it's super weird. I'm still learning the rules but check this out," he said, holding up his gloved hands and pressing against the empty space of the doorway.

Despite there being nothing but air between the doorway, Sean's hands pressed up against some unseen force, preventing him from entering the apartment no matter how hard he appeared to shove. He even took a step back and leaned forward, looking as if he were somehow suspended in midfall.

"That's . . ." she said, unable to form a complete sentence as she watched Sean's bizarre antics.

"Freaky, right? It's just residences, so things like stores and hotels are ok. I can get into other vampires' places okay, too. Like Thomas' apartment at the pub complex," Sean said, doing a one-handed push up against the magical threshold blocking him. "But Artemis needs to invite me in every time."

"You could have a promising career as a mime."

"Aww, thanks. That's the sweetest thing anyone has said to me all day."

"So how do I invite you in?" Clara asked and regretted it immediately.

Her words must have broken whatever magic was preventing Sean from entering her home because he let out a cry of alarm and caught himself in a malformed push up, half in and half out of her apartment.

"I'm not sure, but the words 'welcome' or 'invite' always seem to work." He groaned as he picked himself up off of the ground and then shut the door behind him. "Or 'come in.'"

"Sorry about that." She stifled a giggle.

"Yeah." He removed his sunglasses and his hat but kept the scarf on.

Clara had a sneaking suspicion the scarf was to hide his fangs, something that she'd heard took a while for a new vampire to control. But they were here to talk openly, weren't they? Not to hide from one another.

"Why are you dressed like that anyway? It's night."

Shrugging off his gloves and trench coat, Sean began hanging them on the coat hooks on the wall. "Well, I wasn't sure how long this was going to take. I wouldn't want to get stranded if we talked through the night."

He hung his hat on his coat, but it fell off. Shrugging, he adjusted his scarf and tried to hang the hat again.

Clara frowned. "So that sunscreen stuff that vampires wear doesn't work on new vampires or something?"

She may be a veteran werewolf, but that didn't mean she was all knowledgeable about vampires. Last time she'd hunted them, they were still nocturnal because they didn't have sunscreen protection yet.

"No, it does, but the stuff is pretty potent and smells chemically harsh, even to me, so I figured it would be better to cover up with lots of clothing. I didn't want to hurt your nose. Might affect your skills as a huntress. We wouldn't want that."

"True. Then how would I track you down and rip out your heart? Just leave that hat on the table. It's too big for the hook."

Sean chuckled and tucked his hat away next to the diffuser and then stood there. While she knew there wasn't much space in her studio apartment, he still could have sat on the futon by her like he used to. She'd pushed it into the couch position and added decorative pillows with galaxies on them.

"You're allowed to sit down, you know."

"You sure? I was prepared to stand."

He was so cute worrying about her nose. She waved him over and rolled her eyes. They weren't going to work if they couldn't sit by each other. She kept her back straight as Sean collapsed onto the futon next to her. She'd known that things would be different than they were before, but now that Sean was next to her, smelling fully like the vampire he was despite the heavy lavender in the air, she was beginning to understand what that might entail. An electrical tension hummed in the air that had nothing to do with the emotions of either party involved. It was beyond reason. Clara wondered if Sean could feel it, too? If she hadn't told him she was a werewolf, he would never have known. Now that he did, was his curse as averse to her presence as hers was to him?

A werewolf and a vampire. It was unheard of.

"So I guess there isn't going to be any easy way to say anything we need to say, huh?" Sean finally said after a moment.

Clara nodded. "I think you're right about that."

"Well, would it be okay if I said some things first?" he asked hesitantly. "Since, well, I asked to come over and whatnot."

Clara just nodded, not really trusting her voice.

"Okay. I tried to rehearse this all in my head, but when I actually saw you, I forgot it all," Sean said with what might have been a smile hidden underneath his scarf. "So, if it doesn't really make sense or if I ramble, I'm sorry."

"It's okay."

He took in a few deep breaths as he turned to better face Clara. She really wished she could see his entire face, even with his fangs, so she could read his expressions as he talked.

"Okay, so, before I say this," Sean said, swallowing nervously once more, "Promise you won't get mad?"

Immediately her gaze narrowed.

"Why? Is there something I should be mad about?" she asked, an edge to her voice.

Drawing in a big breath and exhaling to steady his nerves, Sean began to babble.

"So, Thomas figured out you're a werewolf." Clara felt a sense of satisfaction mixed with panic. She knew he was on to her if he hadn't eavesdropped on her revelation to Sean. "And we lost a lot of people in the vamp war, see? So he's gotten a bit intense since then. Like, seriously, the difference is amazing. Artemis thinks he just needs some time to mellow out again, but I'm not so sure. He's gotten a little cold. Like, he's willing to do whatever it takes to keep his friends safe, you see?" Sean began to stammer. "But . . . Thomas knows that it's impossible for vampires to track werewolves because of your senses and that's when he got this stupid plan, which I didn't agree to by the way, I can't stress that enough but . . . um . . ."

Clara forced a smile onto her lips and reached up, peeling Sean's hand from her shoulder in a grip that would have left bruises on a human.

"Sean, sweetie," Clara said through her forced smile, "What exactly are you trying to say?"

"I hate this. Thomas asked me to . . . ask you to help us spy on the rest of the werewolves."

"What?!" Clara was on her feet immediately. "Are you serious? What in the hell makes you think I would do that?"

"No, I know," Sean said, getting to his feet as well and holding his hands in front of him in a placating manner. "Trust me, I know. He wants to investigate all the local werewolves. He just doesn't want things to get bloody, I swear!"

"So I should just betray my pack?" Clara snapped. "They are my family, Sean."

"I know," Sean said again. "I told him it was a terrible plan and that you'd never agree to it, but—"

"But you decided to ask anyway? Do you have a death wish? No one in my pack is a murderer."

"I know. Clara, listen. I believe you, I really do. But Thomas is having a hard time trusting anyone right now. It would put him at ease, calm him down a bit. Just consider it, ok?" Sean pleaded.

"I'm not going to sell out my pack so Thomas can sleep at night," Clara said coldly. Sean was going to have to figure out that he needed to be on her side, too, if this was going to work. "What's it going to take to get him to back off?"

Sean scratched at his earlobe. "Um, a solid lead on a different suspect."

"Fine," Clara said. "You want proof, I'll get it."

Clara stalked away from Sean and picked up her wallet and jacket from off of the table.

"Wait, where are you going?"

"I'm going to the woods," Clara replied shortly. "I need some time alone."

"Wait, let me come with—"

Clara shut the door before Sean could finish and raced down the stairs. So the vampires wanted to play, did they? Not if Clara had anything to do with it.

******

Though it wasn't exactly the kind of fairytale forest Clara had imagined as a girl, the woods were well preserved and looked after.

It took the combined efforts of state, federal, and several private organizations to keep it that way, sectioning off certain areas that were approved for camping and strictly regulating hunting and fishing licenses.

Another big contributor to keeping the vast stretches of trees, streams, lakes, and wildlife as safe and pristine as possible was an endangered species of owl that dwelled within these lush borders. This allowed the area to be categorized as a local wildlife reserve, which greatly limited what kind of industry could crop up in the surrounding areas.

This meant that there were neither factories polluting the air nor any massive saws hewing away entire swathes of trees.

Though it was just a few hours' drive from the city, it was almost like traveling back in time to a much more peaceful era. No rumble of subway trains, no reek of thousands of people living in confined spaces, no swarm of neon lights that made it almost impossible to see the stars at night.

Certainly no stupid boyfriends trying to convince you that you should turn over the identities of everyone you cared about so a grief-ridden vampire with a vendetta could interrogate them or track them like dogs.

Clara let out a frustrated growl at that last thought, slamming the door to Izzy's borrowed car as she stepped out of it.

She was in the vicinity of the Lodge, but closer to town in a small clearing at the beginning of the woodlands. It was difficult to guess where the rogue pack might be, and in human form she wouldn't be able to smell them unless she cross walked through their path. However, she suspected they would be keeping close to the city limits if they really were trying to incite a war. She hoped if she transformed in the right location, her lupine form would pick up their scent on the breeze and she could track them down faster.

The wolf within was practically wagging its tail, sensing what was about to happen.

Hidden from the road, Clara felt no need to be modest as she stripped down, folding her clothes before tucking them in the trunk.

Rolling her shoulders a bit to loosen up her muscles, Clara closed her eyes and began to walk toward the forest.

Werewolves spent so much time with internal struggle that sometimes it was hard to remember that they were a single being. The wolf was always trying to break out and roam free and the human was always setting up more and more barriers to prevent the wolf's escape from ever happening.

Other than the full moon's light, the only escape the wolf had was through raw emotions that tore holes in the mental cage that contained it. Though, in rare moments like the one that Clara was trying to initiate now, the very cage that kept her lycanthropic curse locked up tight through constant mental discipline and vigilance, could be willingly opened.

It was harder for Clara to transform on purpose than for some of the others in her pack, though this was because she didn't do it often. It took a lot of effort and concentration to consciously lower her guard, almost as if were a communication of sorts.

In Clara's mind, both sides of what she was, the woman and the wolf, agreed on a temporary truce. The wolf would be allowed free to roam as the woman was allowed a respite from the woes of the world.

It was almost intoxicating, this agreement between the two personas of her mind. When they were in accord with one another, even the physical transformation was less painful. Her jaw did not ache as her teeth morphed her face into a muzzled visage. She didn't feel muscles spasm and spine contort as she shifted, her human form slowly molding itself into a lupine form.

Mentally, Clara felt herself become a creature of pure emotion, one that was not weighed down by complexities, woes, or future worries. It was all she could do to mentally process all of her heightened senses and the fierce, animalistic joy of charging off into the forest.

Despite her very existence being of an unnatural, accursed origin, Clara never felt more in tune with the natural world than when she'd willingly phased into her wolf aspect. An unbridled joy filled her, and it was easy to see how some werewolves became addicted to using their curse in such a manner.

The unmatched speed and power, the heightening of all sensation and the true depth of primal power—why would she ever think of changing back?

This was old territory for any werewolf, and Clara knew the dangers of such thoughts. Or perhaps they weren't thoughts at all? They were just the impressions that her suppressed human side was given by the wolf that was freed. Currently, the wolf was content just to roam and enjoy itself, which Clara also found pleasurable thanks to their mental link, but that was because the wolf was not hungry, not angry, and not dangerous.

Time was a complex concept that Clara, in her wolf form, had a hard time comprehending. However, the wolf could notice the movements of the moon poking through the treetops as its golden eyes adjusted to the new lighting. Each time the breeze shifted, she inhaled deeply, scanning the new scents.

Then, suddenly, there it was.

She could smell the rival pack.

The reaction from her bestial psyche was so violent, so fierce that even lacking a physical form in the realm of shared consciousness, the human side of Clara flinched.

She felt her lips peel back in a snarl, exposing her fangs, as a rattle of a growl escaped her throat.

The massive gray wolf emerged from the thicket, still wrapped in that unnatural calm. It was by far the largest wolf that Clara had ever laid eyes on, seeming even larger than the last time she'd seen it.

Every muscle in Clara's body tensed as her hackles were raised and she growled even louder.

Yet her growls were easily drowned out by the gray wolf as it threw back its head and issued a thunderous howl that echoed throughout the surrounding forest.

It was a howl that was answered by chorus distant howling.

13 Big, Bad Wolves

Clara struggled to maintain any kind of control of the lupine form. The initial shock of seeing another werewolf had destroyed most of her control, and the wolf was caught in the primal instincts it had: fight or flight.

Weakness was not something that could be tolerated in the eyes of a potential threat, and Clara, in any form, had never been one to roll over and show her belly when the going got tough. That went double for the wolf. Her primal, wolf-like mind was rearing to confront this new threat.

Claws digging into the earth to gain purchase for additional traction, the wolf caused Clara's lupine body to tense up, preparing to strike.

Her vision was clouding over with red again. Attacking head-on such a large opponent alone would be futile. Clara knew that and was desperate to find a new angle. The wolf was more ambitious. It could feel her protesting and was trying to shut her out.

As Clara struggled to retain control, a surge of adrenaline spiked through her: the wolf had noticed something she hadn't.

The gray wolf had begun to move forward. It was a casual, almost loping fashion as its powerful muscles began to twitch. The gray wolf shook its shaggy mane as it began to change shape, bending backwards. Sickening cracks shattered the night as a skeletal structure rearranged itself.

For a brief second, the wolf was some hybrid monster of man and beast, walking on its hind haunches as its forepaws became more humanlike.

Over the course of several heartbeats, the gray wolf faded away into nothingness. What was now approaching Clara was a tall and muscular man with stormy gray eyes that matched some of the coloring of his salt and pepper goatee.

Now that the threat of the other wolf was gone, Clara's wolf was momentarily confused as to what to do with all of the adrenaline and tension it had built up. She capitalized on that confusion, forcing the wolf back into its cage and becoming a shuddering mess for several heartbeats as she phased back into her human form.

Her heart pounded as she steadied herself on her human feet, far less graceful than the strange man had. He stood several feet in front her, and his height was so impressive that she had to tilt her head back to stare him in the eyes.

"For a second there, I thought you and I were going to have a moment," the stranger said. His voice dripped with low-key aggression. "Not many attempt to tussle with me, even those who wish to be an Alpha."

Alpha.

That single word put Clara more on edge than even the big man's haunting eyes.

"I didn't expect anyone to be in this section of the forest," she lied, doing her best to maintain eye contact and not let an ounce of discomfort show in her body language or voice. "This is usually a good spot for a run."

The stranger had stopped his approach at about an arm's length, but that didn't mean he'd stopped moving. In casual strides, he circled Clara, his eyes not bothering to remain on her own. That intense gaze swept over Clara's lithe form, as if trying to memorize every inch of her. She was painfully aware of her own nudity but fought back the urge to shy away. Werewolves had to show dominance, and she refused to lose to this stranger.

Something told her such actions would have made her seem even more vulnerable than just standing as she was. He was looking for some sign of weakness.

In that regard, all Alphas were the same.

"I've seen you before," he said, completing his circle of Clara and stopping in front of her. "I saw you during the full moon a week ago. You were in control back then, too. It's not often you find a like-minded hunter."

The stranger's body language relaxed and he smirked, the turning of his lips odd against his harsh face, though his stare was just as sharp and focused as it always was. He extended a large hand to Clara.

"The name is Leon Tipton, Alpha of this pack."

"Clara . . . Scott." She gave her mother's maiden name as she shook Leon's hand. "I haven't seen or smelled your pack around before the last full moon. You must be new."

As she and this Leon were no longer metaphorically baring their fangs, Clara took stock of her changing surroundings. The pack's smell seemed stronger, some of them almost on top of her. Underbrush rustled and a handful of werewolves in human form began emerging from the surrounding woods, at least six, both male and female. She could smell more around her, and she'd no way of knowing if there were other members elsewhere.

"Yes, my pack has just recently arrived," Leon said. "We've been roaming for a while as we were forced to relocate our hunting grounds. The tick population in our last region has been depleted. Isn't that right, Howlers?"

Despite being in human forms, the other members of the pack each opened up their mouths and released a wolf-like howl that made Clara's blood run cold.

"Depleted?" she asked, her heart racing. "What do you mean?"

"We hunted them to extinction," Leon said in a disturbingly calm voice. "We heard of a mass migration in these parts and came to investigate."

His conversational tone concerning localized genocide made Clara's stomach turn, but she made sure to appear calm. The statement all but confirmed her fears; these werewolves had given far too much to the wolf within and saw vampires as nothing more than prey.

Many times had Donald warned Clara and the others about this type of werewolf. Some allowed the wolf within to win, so to speak, giving in completely to the wild exhilaration. That meant that their human and rational persona, the section of their psyche capable of complex thought slowly faded away and became dormant. Certain events still allowed for the werewolf's human mind to surface and, if need be, take control.

"That's . . . impressive," Clara said slowly. "The need for vampires isn't that strong and you are a relatively small pack."

"We found the more we feed our curse, the more control we have. I want my family to have control. It grants greater power." Leon resumed his pacing. "But surely, you understand that. You have been in full control both times we've met. And your Alpha was in control as well."

Clara fought back the rising nausea in her stomach. These people killed vampires for sport.

"I don't have an Alpha. I'm more of a lone wolf." She then added in an off-handed manner, "The wolf you saw is an acquaintance of mine."

"I see," Leon said, leaning toward her with a murderous gleam in his eye. "I guess it can't be helped that there are those who reject being a part of a family. It's sad. Perhaps life would be better for you if you seized a little more control of the wolf. We've recently stumbled across a hive of the blood suckers. Won't you join us for a hunt?"

Clara swallowed nervously. Leon talked so casually of murder, and he had a strange perception of family. He professed to be looking out for his pack, but none of the pack members would meet his eyes. Something wasn't right.

This was exactly what Clara had been hoping for, wasn't it? Proof that would absolve her pack of ending the truce? It all fell neatly into place, after all. Every blood junkie, clan-less, and craven vampire within a five-state radius had been flocking to the city in the preparation for the Red Lightning Pub war. Such a migration would have attracted an aggressive pack of werewolves who would have seen it as nothing but a golden opportunity. The bravest packs may have even followed the migrating vampires to Colesbrooke in search of a new challenge.

Clara knew that none of her pack mates would have doubted her suspicions—they trusted her instincts. Donald, Deva, and Bert could have quickly confirmed her story with their century old contacts in the supernatural community.

The vampires were a different story.

Other than Sean's good word, the other vampires had no reason to believe her. She needed evidence more substantial than a gut feeling.

She needed proof.

"Perhaps," she replied tactfully. "I have not yet begun to feed more often than the curse demands, but I admit that you and your pack have an impressive hold on the wolf."

Arching an eyebrow, Leon drew himself to his full towering height and stared down at Clara with a small smile. "I would love to try and convince you. After all, you can never have a big enough family."

A few guttural laughs echoed from the other pack members surrounding Clara, but she didn't let it shake her. Nor did she allow herself to be intimidated now.

When confronted with a savage beast, there were few things worse than showing weakness.

Leon's smile fell from his lips as his body tensed.

Clara's right hand became a blur, sickening popping sounds filling the air as her joints distorted and her fingers elongated. Blackened fingernails, more akin to claws now, rested against Leon's throat, and Clara made sure her golden, wolfish eyes were locked onto his.

The pain was excruciating, but Clara was in possession of a laser focus. For the first time in her life, Clara found that both her consciousness and the beast within were working in perfect concert during a fight. She needed to show her skill or she would end up dead. The wolf knew it as well.

It took all of her willpower, but Clara was allowing only a section of her curse free, turning her hand into a dangerous claw. Losing partial control was much easier than controlling a partial phase. It resulted in both physical and mental strain, but she was no stranger to either.

"I'm no one's hound, Leon," she said in the lowest growl she could muster to mask the pain surging up her wrist. "If I hunt with you, that means you've given me a reason, not an order."

The surrounding wolves tensed, a few of them growling as they circled closer to Clara and Leon. She was certain they'd attack, but their attention turned from her when a sharp whistle rattled everyone's sensitive ears.

"Hey, Leon!"

Leon's eyes remained locked on Clara's for a heartbeat longer before he turned his head to glance over to the source of the disturbance. He didn't even see her as a threat.

"What is it, Boyd?" he called.

Her gamble had paid off. She dropped her hand and willed it back into its human form as she turned to the edge of the tree line to the newcomer, Boyd.

The new arrival was dressed in tattered jeans and a jacket, holding what appeared to be an old school radio.

"Dirk and Kale made it back to camp. Got big news," Boyd shouted, his voice ringing out through the forest.

"What about Schmitt?" asked one of the werewolves, the taller of the two women.

"That's the big news."

With the tension between Clara and their leader gone, the other werewolves left and joined Boyd.

Leon followed with a sweeping gesture for her to come.

"Care to join us, Clara? Maybe I could give you a reason to run with my pack?"

Clara glanced after the pack. This was the chance she'd been looking for. She was being invited into the wolf's den without being forced to stay there. If she could find something, anything, to prove her pack's innocence, it would be worth it.

"It would be my pleasure, Leon."

******

Much deeper in the forest than Clara had ever traveled, in either of her forms, was the Howler's camp. Although, camp might have been too generous a word to use. It looked like the beginnings of

163

a shanty town, basically a series of tents and random odds and ends set up in a cramped clearing.

On the way there, Clara had learned that, including Leon, this pack was about fifteen members strong. The longer she spent with them, the more Clara came to understand the type of people that inhabited the pack. They had all learned to give into the wolf by feeding it vampire hearts whenever the slightest inclination arose, and despite his cold treatment of them, the pack seemed to adore Leon. They hung on his every word, never meeting his eye, and were always eager for a chance to be praised. Yet, though they all loved their leader, none of that love was for each other.

They were like children. Children who had forgotten what it meant to be human.

"We got him loaded up into the back of the jeep and drove to the river. He got about a mile in and then quit on us, coughing up blood and all that," a chubby werewolf named Dirk said around the mouth of a whiskey bottle. "We thought about tossin' him in the river but figured you'd want to see him."

On full display in the center of camp was the werewolf that Clara had learned was called Schmitt. Or at least, the remains of the werewolf. Freed of life and his lycanthropic curse, Schmitt was in his human form, a scrawny man that had been heedlessly dumped near a fire pit. Even in death, his face was distorted in a painful expression, dried blood ringing his lips and his throat and chest covered in deep, ugly bruises.

The death and corpse of one of their own seemed to do little to disturb the pack, with the exception of the woman who had asked Boyd about Schmitt. Upon seeing the corpse, she let out a furious howl and shifted into her lupine form right there, charging off in a rage.

No one followed her. Leon barely spared her a glance.

"This is . . . disappointing," Leon said in a frosty voice, causing both Dirk and his twitchy counterpart named Kale to flinch. "To lose a member of my dear family is tragic."

Clara pulled back, glancing at the other werewolves. The tone of his voice didn't match his words. Neither did the ferocious scowl forming on his face.

In savage frustration, the Alpha kicked the dead body. When Schmitt still didn't respond, Leon kicked the corpse again and again and again.

Something about the sheer indifference and lack of respect to the dead made Clara want to scream, but she fought back the urge. When she checked on the other pack members, hoping to find someone acting as she felt, all she found were blank stares as they watched their leader take his anger out on a dead man. One or two of them looked amused. Most of them looked like they were empty inside.

Clara shivered.

Breathing heavily, Leon finally stopped kicking the corpse. He paced back and forth, spitting into the dirt. Then after a deep breath, his eerie calm returned.

"Did you at least find new marks for us?" Leon asked, his voice level.

"That's what we were doing," Kale said, a nervous tick making his right eye twitch wildly. "But then Schimtt goes off, smelling something, and when he comes back, he's hurting bad."

"Did he go to the slums?" Leon asked. "Was it Ernest and his crew?"

"Ernest?" His name slipped from her mouth before she could stop herself. Were they working with him?

Leon's sharp ears must have picked up her surprise, and he glanced over his shoulder.

"A mover and shaker for the vampires, especially the ticks who like to feed off of humans. His sloppy operation has been feeding us for months. We've been picking off his incoming recruits. But they got their hands on some silver bullets. I told my pack to steer clear of them for a while," Leon said, turning his eyes back to Kale and Dirk. "Apparently that was too much to ask."

Glaring at Dirk and Kale, Leon turned and walked past Clara, stopping at the entrance to the largest tent.

"See what happens when people don't obey their Alpha?" he asked. "When the Alpha is ignored, our family gets hurt."

"Schmitt wasn't shot," Boyd said.

While Leon's presence and volatile temper cowed every other member of the pack, Boyd seemed immune to the Alpha's intimidation. He was indifferent to Leon's anger.

He must be the Beta male, the second-in-command to this pack. The closest Leon had to a right-hand man.

"What?" Leon asked, reaching into the tent.

"He wasn't shot," Boyd repeated, not caring to elaborate.

"Yeah and we weren't near no slums or bars, like you said," Kale hastily added.

"When we were putting him in the jeep, Schmitt was moaning about troubles and boils," Dirk said. "Well, he was before he started to cough up blood and go all blue in the face."

The Crone.

Clara tasted blood as she bit her cheek to keep from demanding her own questions of the incompetent pair. If they had avoided the slums, then the oldest part of town was close to the Trouble and Toil.

Clara gave the bruised corpse a second look. Perhaps the ancient occultist might have more substance than flash to her after all. But would that be enough to protect her from a vengeful pack of werewolves?

Sharp pain shot through Clara's palms, and she forced her hands to relax from their tight fists. She needed to leave and warn the others, especially Donald. If the Crone was killed, that meant no more potions and at the next full moon, her entire pack would be forced to be murderers. She also needed to tell Sean that she'd found the proof they needed.

Behind Dirk and Kale was a line of boot prints and drag marks, probably from Schmitt's body. The drag marks lead north, and if what they said about a river was true, then all Clara needed to do was get to that river. If she could make it there in her wolf form, she could phase back into human as soon as she hit the waters, completely masking her scent as she rode the current to a safer distance.

According to the Von Grimmel brothers, such a maneuver wreaked havoc on the werewolf's sense of smell. Werewolves would be forced to phase back into human form or risk the scent of their own wet fur masking the smell of prey, which would slow them down considerably. Hopefully, by the time any pursuers picked up her scent again, Clara would already be halfway to the city in her lupine form.

She just needed a moment when the Howlers were distracted enough for her to get a small head start. Most of the wolves were still arguing with Dirk and Kale, and Leon was shrugging on a long leather jacket as he walked toward her. Shit.

The jacket sparkled in the sunlight. It was adorned with random items, worn like military badges across the chest, jingling with each step. Several of these badges were gruesome to behold: long, white vampire fangs and one was a withered, mummified finger wrapped in barbed wire. One in particular caught Clara's attention and made her forget the overwhelming need to escape.

Replacing the top button of the leather jacket was a golden pendant the size of a quarter; impressed upon its surface was a lightning bolt and what appeared to be three teardrops. They weren't teardrops though but droplets of blood.

The symbol of the Red Lightning Pub.

Clara's heart nearly leapt into her throat.

The pendant had to have belonged to Sara Foxe, which meant that it was the proof she was looking for.

It would not only prove her pack was innocent, but also provided the means to restore the peace of the city, as the local werewolves and vampires worked together to get rid of a common enemy.

"Like it? A trophy from every hunt I lead," Leon said with obvious pride. "As well as a trophy from every pup who tried to disrupt the peace in our family."

Steadying herself and taking a moment to make sure that her voice didn't tremble as she spoke, Clara did her best to casually raise a hand and indicate the pendant.

"What's the story behind the golden one?" she asked, hoping that her question hadn't given away the fact she'd actually recognized the symbol.

Stepping up to her, Leon's intense gaze found Clara's eyes again as his finger ran along the pendant with an almost loving touch.

"Good eye. That's from my latest hunt. Right in the city itself. I found a tick and struck. This was the only thing I was able to get before a giant appeared. Nearly finished him off as well," Leon added the last bit without much enthusiasm.

"Sounds dangerous," Clara said.

"Being at the top of the food chain just means that there are more fangs waiting if you fall down," Leon said, staring intently at her. "So why don't you run with my pack? If you're a part of our family, I can promise no one is going to try and take a bite out of you. How's that for an offer?"

Every part of Clara wanted to break away from Leon's gaze. But she didn't. Instead, she steeled her stomach for what she needed to do next.

"Hmm. It's good. I'll consider it."

She reached out and plucked the pendant off his jacket. Leon watched as she ran it through her fingers, making a show of looking longingly at is.

"I'll hold onto this," Clara said, stroking the pendant. "The next time you see me, I'll have something even better for you."

Every eye in the camp was weighing on her back, and for a moment Clara was afraid her ploy had backfired. But then Leon released her from his hypnotic stare. He reached up and grasped the front of his jacket to adjust it, making the other trophies he'd collected rattle.

"I've never failed to find quarry worth hunting and never failed in getting a trophy worth taking. Keep that in mind," Leon told her and then walked right past her. "I hope to hear from you before the next full moon. If I don't, I promise you'll hear from me on that night."

Grasping the golden pendant so hard she was afraid it might break her skin, Clara didn't reply. Instead, she walked out of the camp, keeping her back straight.

Once she was free from the clearing, she stuck the pendant under her tongue, shed her human form, and raced toward the city with as much speed as her paws could muster.

This time, the run carried no thrill for her. All she felt was anxiety for what was to come.

She'd discovered a den of monsters and they knew her name.

14 PREVENTATIVE MEASURES

Clara huffed as her paws pounded on a cement path toward Artemis' apartment stairs. Clove clung to the cement and grew stronger with each bound. Good—his scent had been stale at his place.

"Sean," Artemis' muffed voice shouted from inside. "Don't put half-full blood packs back in the fridge. And if you're going to, at least put them in a baggie first. That's so gross."

"My eyes were bigger than my stomach! I'm still a growing spawn of the night."

It was a relief to hear his voice as she leaped down the stairs, though she was disgusted at his words. But it didn't matter—she needed to show him the pendant immediately.

She started phasing as she crashed through the door, entering the apartment in a gruesome mess of a humanoid wolf. She started explaining about the pendant, but only emitted low growls as she shook, twitched, and shuddered as her bones popped and cracked. With every contraction of a muscle or jerk of a limb, more of her fur seemed to fade away into nothingness and she shrunk in size.

Penny, Artemis' best friend, was seated at the tiny table trying on several different pairs of earrings. As she started screaming, she dropped the mirror she was holding and fell out of her chair.

Oops. Maybe Clara should have transformed outside first.

Once she was fully human, Clara spat the pendant into her palm. "Sean, we need to talk."

For a moment, there was silence as Penny calmed herself and everyone stared. Then Sean let out an agonized yell.

"Stop it," Sean cried out, nearly tackling Nelson as he threw his hands over his friend's eyes.

Flailing about, Nelson tried to shove Sean off. "Gah, stop what?"

"Looking at her. You creep."

"Dude. Get off of me."

Shit. She needed clothes, but she'd left them in Izzy's car. She'd have to go back and pick that up sometime.

"Sean," she said, trying to gain back his attention. Did he not understand how important this was? Why else would she have rushed here before warning her clan, before returning to her human form at home where she could dress and fix her hair?

The men continued to grapple on the floor.

"This is sexist," Nelson howled. Sean had easily placed him in a headlock and was forcing his face onto the floor. "You're not covering Penny's eyes and she's just as into girls as I am."

"Don't even think about it," said Penny as Sean's head whipped in her direction. She was climbing back to her feet and fixing the chair and table. "First of all, I'm not a teenage boy. And secondly, my eyes didn't bug out of my head the minute she walked in. It's nothing I haven't seen before, and I was more concerned with the grotesque human shapeshifting thing."

Artemis draped a thick blanket over Clara's shoulders.

"Thanks, Artemis. Thanks for that," Clara stumbled through her words as she pulled the blanket tight around her. "Hi, Penny. How's work going?"

Penny gaped for several heartbeats while Sean kept Nelson pinned down. Clara hadn't blushed earlier, but she did now. She should have prepared a better entrance. Her jumble of thoughts while she ran as a wolf had been a mix of panic and a need to talk to Sean and her clan.

"Just fine, I guess," Penny managed to say. "So . . . you're a werewolf?"

"Yeah. Sorry 'bout that. I'm cursed." Clara tried to smile. "It's this whole . . . thing. Anyway, *Sean*."

Glancing over his shoulder, Sean's distraction was enough for Nelson to shove free and grumble at his friend.

"What?"

"I'm not here just to hang out. Why else would I have barged in here as a wolf? Oh, sorry, Artemis. I'll get you new hinges. And Sean, be more respectful of your sister's place. Her fridge is not your blood storage.

"What?"

"In other words, don't be a tactless moron," Nelson said, giving him another shove as he stepped past Sean and headed toward Penny. "Be more of a gentleman, like me."

"Nelson, if I rolled my eyes any harder, I'd lose a contact," Penny said, completely deadpan.

Nelson's and Penny's antics had provided a great bit of amusement for Clara back before Sean had been turned into a vampire; but right now, she couldn't allow herself to enjoy the lighthearted banter.

There was a war to avert and a pack of psychopaths to drive off.

"Sean, this is incredibly important, and it can't wait. It's about our . . . arrangement." She glanced at Penny and Nelson, unsure if she wanted them involved quite yet.

"Babe, I think it's safe to say that our little secret has been spilled to the people who just saw you transform from a rabid wolf to your hot bod," Sean said with a wry grin then shot a glare at Nelson. "Though some people saw a bit too much."

Clara ignored the muttering at the table, though it was hard to miss Nelson flipping Penny off.

"Hey," Artemis growled. "Clara, would you like us to step out while you and Sean talk?"

Clara opened her mouth to reply but found herself momentarily tongue tied.

It was the first time she'd actually been in the presence of several people who knew what she was and weren't already werewolves. It was a monumental event, yet no one was panicking. They were being respectful. Even after she'd scared them half to death by bursting into the place mid-transformation.

"No, it's fine. Sean makes a good point."

"Vampires and werewolves hate each other, and we're trying to figure out how to avoid a war between them by solving Sara Foxe's murder," Sean told everyone, standing in front of the table and glaring at Nelson. "Until that happens, we've gotta do the whole secret lover, forbidden fruit thing."

"Oh," Penny and Nelson said in unison.

"That's a gross simplification of a complex subject," Artemis said disapprovingly. "Should we maybe let Clara actually say what she has to say?"

Clara sighed, the urge to hug Artemis overwhelming her. "Thanks. I know who did it."

She shifted the blanket so she could show everyone the pendant in her hand without uncovering herself. Everyone froze,

173

watching the pendant swing in her hands and clatter on the tiny table.

Penny groaned. "Isn't that—"

"The insignia for the Red Lightning Pub," Artemis sat down on her bed, setting down a pot of tea next to her. "It has to be Sara's."

Although it saddened her that it had come to this, Clara did feel a huge sense of relief that the others connected this pendant to the late peacekeeper of the city.

Clara had risked her life to obtain it.

"I thought so, too. I went out into the forest to look for this pack that I ran into during the last full moon, and damn did I find them. They call themselves the Howlers." She let go of the pendant's chain. "They aren't from the local pack. In fact, they're unlike any werewolves I've met. They've eaten so many vampire hearts that the wolf doesn't even try to oppose them. They have complete control over their curse and relish in the power it gives them. Their Alpha is some guy named Leon."

The pendant and serious tone in Clara's voice had sucked the mirth from the room. Even Sean didn't have a quip for her.

"Well, Leon calls himself an Alpha, but he's really just a dictator. He collects trophies from his victims. This was one of them. He followed the recruited blood junkies to Colesbrooke, specifically to hunt vampires. I don't think he knows much about the city other than there is a lot of prey here. He barely even recognizes the local pack. If I had to guess, I think it was just terrible luck that Sara was attacked when she was. He was probably just scouting the area and saw the opportunity and took it."

Sean's eyebrows drew together and his thumb passed over his lower lip slowly. She braced herself for an argument, figuring he would not think that Eternal Jericho and Sara Foxe would have just been at the wrong place at the wrong time.

"Are you okay?" Sean asked.

Clara tightened the blanket around her. "I—what?"

"You got this all by yourself? From a lunatic who kills for sport? I'm asking, I mean, did he try to hurt you?" His eyes narrowed dangerously.

Clara had never felt more certain than this moment that Sean cared about her.

"I'm fine, Sean," she assured him, reaching over and gripping his shoulder. "He thought I was a lone wolf and tried to convince me to join his pack. I managed to get the pendant from him in exchange for a promise to meet with the pack before the next full moon."

Sean's expression relaxed some, and Clara gripped his shoulder harder.

"It's a promise I don't intend to keep. We're going to take down this pack of rabid dogs. Together, as the team we promised to be."

Sean snorted. "Team my ass. You ran out on me and wouldn't let me help."

"Because you were asking me to spy on my pack," Clara reminded him coldly.

"I said it was a bad idea!"

"But you still—"

"Oh yeah. You guys are a great team," Penny interjected. "Well done."

"So what's the plan then?" Sean asked, shooting Penny a glare. "You said the forest? Anywhere specific? That's a lot of ground to cover."

"Not for my pack. Take the pendant to Lawrence and tell him that the local werewolves are innocent and taking care of the problem." She grinned, holding back a laugh. "These Howlers may think they're tough, but they've never gone against a full pack of werewolves. I think Leon is the driving force behind the violence. If we bring him in, the rest of the pack will break and flee."

"What? No way!"

"Sean, what part of my plan are you so violently opposed to?" He was going to doubt her again?

"All of it! You can't just waltz off into the forest and try to apprehend this guy."

"Why not?"

A collection of sighs rumbled around the table, and Artemis resumed preparing tea.

"It's dangerous—"

"Any ideas you might have about me being a damsel in distress need to end here and now, lover boy," Clara growled. "I've been in this game way longer than you. I know how to take care of myself. You're the newborn, here. So, you get a newborn job. Leave everything else to us."

Shaking his head, Sean pressed on.

"I'm not saying that you can't take care of yourself. I'm saying that it's dangerous. If this guy is our killer, he can't be underestimated. Do you honestly think that you could go toe-to-toe with Jericho and Sara Foxe? I was there when Sara Foxe fought five blood junkies armed with hawthorn stakes and she won."

Nelson grunted. "Over the course of the week I personally dug out half a pound of silver buckshot from Jericho and shoved four feet of intestine back into him after he was caught up in a bomb's blast. Then I helped Thomas reattach his arm."

As a werewolf, Clara was quite used to being completely reassured that, unless it came to a silver bullet, there were few things she had to fear in life. Being nigh invincible was just something you grew accustomed to when you suffered from a curse that allowed you to turn into a vicious beast and regrow major organs in a day's time.

But could she have held her own against both a vampiric giant and the vampire matron of Colesbrooke in a fight? At the same time? She felt no shame in admitting to herself that was simply an impossible feat.

"Irrelevant. I'll have my pack with me. Besides, I don't even think a fight will break out. If my pack shows up in full force, the Howlers will probably turn on Leon or abandon him. We'll be able to drop him right on the Red Lightning Pub's doorstep if you wanted us to. I'm just asking you to tell Lawrence to back off and let us handle it so we don't have to get anyone else involved: vampire, human, or werewolf."

Doubt began to worm its way into Clara's chest when she saw how hard Sean's gaze was, how he rubbed his hands on his pant legs. She couldn't ignore how worried he was.

Reaching down, Sean picked up the pendant and held it close to his face. He was silent for several moments, just looking at the impression of the Red Lightning Pub's infamous sign.

When he spoke, his voice was like gravel. "It just isn't possible to convince Lawrence to let the werewolves handle this on their own. The only people he has left are soldiers like the Boston Boys. Everyone else he trusts has been killed in less than two weeks."

Nelson grumbled an agreement, and Artemis hushed him.

"But we'll hand him the killer," Clara protested. "I don't think it'll take much for Lawrence to get the truth out of him. And whatever justice Lawrence wants to deliver is between him and his conscience."

Sean set down the pendant and just shook his head mournfully.

"It won't be enough, Clara," Nelson said, eying Artemis. "We could have the entire thing on video tape, and he still wouldn't believe us. Lawrence isn't looking for a fight with the werewolves. He isn't even looking for revenge. He's looking for control. He didn't control the vampires, and it got his daughter killed. He didn't control the werewolves, and it got his wife killed. That's why he wanted your pack's names. That's why he's keeping the Boston Boys and Jericho around. He's trying to make this city his city again, and everyone is going along with it because if they aren't with him, then they're against him."

"If Lawrence wants to try to set himself up as a dictator, then that's a problem that *will* be addressed at a later date. However, at this very moment, I don't care what grief-fueled delusions of grandeur your vampire dandy has," Clara said in a low growl as she switched her glare from Nelson to Sean. "Right now, my main concern is that there are over a dozen new werewolves circling the city right now. They've been here, in these streets. They've killed and are looking to kill again, and I doubt they care who it is they're sinking their fangs into as long as they get to do it."

Such a harsh truth did not sit well with any at the table. Nelson cursed, Artemis paled, and Penny looked away from the table, unable to meet anyone's gaze. All Sean did was get more frustrated.

"I told you, I can't convince Lawrence to do anything, much less trust his wife's murderer to people he suspects *are* her murderers!"

"Then don't convince him, just stall! I don't want or need his permission. I just want him to understand that we're trying to protect the peace that his wife fought for. If every vampire in the city armed themselves to the teeth and charged into the forest, you'd still never catch them. Werewolves can smell silver and vampires from two miles away. The Howlers would just run away and return to pick off vampires when they wanted to. That's how a hunt works."

Nelson looked up at her questioningly. "So, you need werewolves to catch werewolves. That's why you want to go now. You're afraid they'll get away and then you can't prove your innocence."

Clara nodded.

"Werewolves and vampires may hate one another—were created to hate one another, it seems—but that doesn't mean that everyone who lives in this city wants a war. We never asked to be cursed, and we do our best not to let it own us," Clara said. She'd pulled the blanket so tight around her she thought she'd meld with it, but it gave her comfort and strength. "Leon might not target us directly, but what he's doing is going to get someone in my pack, someone in my *family*, killed. But we can stop him. We can catch him. But there won't be any point in doing so if we're just going to catch a silver bullet in the back for our trouble."

Sean slammed his fist down, causing the pendant to bounce into the air.

"Lawrence doesn't give a shit about being fair right now. If I go to him, all he'll want is your name so he can track you down." Anger made Sean's voice brittle and tight.

Clara snatched the golden pendant back. Then she reached for Sean's hand, turning it upward. With a smile full of confidence she didn't feel, she pressed the pendant and the proof of the true murderer into Sean's hand.

"I'll risk it. What I'm fighting for is worth it. I never intended to keep our secret forever, Sean." Clara stared at the others in the room.

"Babe, please just listen. . . ."

Leaning forward, Clara interrupted Sean by kissing him briefly.

"I've got to do what I've got to do, Sean. Trust me. Just like I'm going to trust in you." They weren't going to agree, but she didn't have time to try to persuade him, either. She had to act soon. "Do what you can to make Lawrence see reason. Make Thomas help. I'm going to try and make my pack see the same thing and hopefully, when we regroup back here, it'll be in a city that isn't about to tear itself apart."

179

Without another word, Clara turned and headed into the night, shedding the blanket as she released the wolf within once more.

Helpless, Sean watched her go. She heard him mumble to himself as she rocketed up the stairs. "I can't do this."

Sometimes you did things because you had to, not because you could. Clara wished more than anything she didn't have to risk herself, that she and Sean could just be happy together. But Leon's actions had changed everything for them. There was only one way forward now.

Sean was just going to have to find the resolve to talk to Lawrence. Her pack, and her own life, depended on it.

INTERLUDES

"I don't like it. Don't smell right."

"Shuddup. We gotta find out who offed Schmitt. Wasn't vampires. Look around; no ticks want to be away from people to snack on. So no blood suckers, no silver. Whatcha care?"

"'Cuz Schmitt is dead you idiot! And Boyd said we need to watch it. Boyd's got an eye for these things. Even told Leon to watch himself."

"Are you two Howlers or whelps? Because if you aren't Howlers, then I'll rip out your throats right here," Violet growled.

Finally, they stopped bickering, giving her long glances. She refused to meet their gazes and returned to inspecting the creepy shop in this near-abandoned section of the city. The Trouble and Toil building seemed to repel visitors and graffiti, but there didn't appear to be anything special about it. Her skin itched as if silver were present, but Dirk and Kale had said it'd felt like this last time, too. The only seemingly dangerous things here were herself and maybe Dirk and Kale if they'd stop arguing with each other. At least they didn't try to bring her into their spat. Neither of the two male Howlers would have wanted to tangle with Violet on a good day and, as of right now, she was having a very bad night.

The Howlers had always had a bad habit of collecting strays. Leon didn't much care if the wolves he picked up could play nice with others, so long as they offered him their wholehearted devotion. How they acted toward each other was a different story.

Violet and her sister Rose were the only two female members of the pack. They had to act extra tough and prickly to ward off the unwelcome passes made at them by most of the pack members.

Perhaps that was why Violet had taken Schmitt's death so hard; he'd been the only werewolf to restrain himself from making any sort of advance. He never made a lewd comment or lunged at either of the sisters. That had bought him a certain amount of leniency in her eyes and perhaps a measure of fondness that could have become something more given enough time.

That was no longer the case. Schmitt had been dumped in the woods after his death.

"We aren't running, Violet. We're Howlers, you know that," Kale, the primary complainer, replied with a huff. "Just thinking of what Boyd said was all."

"Well Boyd isn't here, is he you mewling little whelp? So you better get ready to bare fang, got it?" Violet snarled. She then pointed to the back of the ratty jeep that they had driven from their makeshift hideout in the forest. "Now get the gear together. We're wasting moonlight."

Kale and Dirk didn't bother to complain; the combination of being demeaned and threatened was the only type of motivation they had known their entire lives. Even before they joined the Howlers, the two of them had been delinquents, bouncing in and out of jail as long as they could remember. Dirk particularly liked to boast about his five-year stretch in prison for arson.

An art he still had a passion for.

Opening up the back of the jeep, Dirk got to work, muttering to himself about his Green Priest Special. Because of his constant stories and explanations, Violet knew more about explosives and fire than she ever wanted to know. The Green Priest Special was an explosive recipe he said was taught to him by an Irish militant who had been his cellmate for a few years. He claimed it was slightly more sophisticated than the average Molotov cocktail; the cocktail being a gasoline and carbonated water mixture in a glass bottle, duct taped to a tin can of lighter fluid that was rigged to a handheld taser.

With only a few strips of tape the stun gun trigger would be held down, letting it spark freely. Then all he had to do was hurl the entire bomb through a window. The glass bottle was too thick to shatter but would crack, releasing the gasoline fumes at a high pressure thanks to the carbonation. The fumes would hit the sparks, ignite, and then the lighter fluid would be caught in the blast, going off like a proper bomb.

The Green Priest Special was Dirk's favorite because it didn't explode immediately nor did it have any quick means of being doused before being set off, like det-cord or a flaming rag sticking out of the top of it. In those precious few moments after being thrown, between the time the gasoline fumes met the stun gun sparks, the bomber could turn and run.

Or in this particular instance, the Howlers would have the have time to get in position and catch anyone running from the burning building.

"Alright, I'll kick open the door, toss in the hot stuff," Dirk said after he added the last little tweak to the makeshift bomb. "You two clean up like we planned, as quick as possible. Leon don't want us to be starting too much fun until he gets a proper feel for the city."

Violet turned her head toward the pudgy werewolf, her lips peeling back to reveal a mouth full of canine fangs. "I want to feast on the heart of whoever murdered Schmitt."

Dirk glanced over at Kale for support.

"Um, we gotta do this quick-like or Leon's gonna be mad," Kale said, reaching into the jeep and pulling out a scoped .223 caliber rifle—its previous owner was in a group of unfortunate hunters who had taken a shot at one of the Howlers during a full moon. "'Sides, this place smells so bad that being a wolf might not be the best idea."

Stomping over to Kale, who did his best not to whimper, Violet looked as if she were about to strike him. Instead, she turned towards Dirk and tore the bomb from his grasp.

No matter how much she cared for Schmitt, she cared for her own throat a lot more, which was exactly what Leon would tear out if she screwed up any of his plans.

"Fine! But I want to see the face of whoever is inside as they burn," she snarled. "I'll go in and drop the bomb. So help me, if I find out that either of you missed a shot and let someone escape, I'll neuter you."

"Wait," Dirk said hastily and did his best not to shrink away from her stare. "If you gotta drop that in yourself, let me adjust it so you don't get caught up in it."

******

If it wasn't for the rage of the wolf within and the emotional confusion of Schmitt's death, Violet might have found herself unable to take more than a few steps into the insanity of the shop after kicking open the door.

The confusing reek of foreign substances made her stomach turn and her sinuses burn. In addition, the entire place seemed cramped and cluttered, and her skin burned from silver stashed somewhere in this dump. Darkness usually wasn't a problem for her, but for whatever reason, Violet's keen eyes were having trouble piercing the gloom, as if the darkness itself was somehow resisting dispersion, even after her inhuman eyes adjusted.

Even the monster inside her was uncomfortable being within this maddening shop, and, for a moment, Violet thought about just hurling the bomb and then fleeing.

But no, she owed it to Schmitt to see his killer die.

Violet moved deeper into the shop, getting right up to the counter before a dry voice scraped through the darkness.

"Fair is foul, and foul is fair; hover through the fog and filthy air. Many of your curse don't make it this far into my little hovel after I've set the wards. Amazing what a little wolfsbane does in a candle, isn't it my lovely pup?"

A low, rumbling growl issued from her throat as Violet turned in a slow circle. She couldn't find the source of the voice, and a fear she hadn't experienced in decades paralyzed her breath. The wolf inside howled, and she transformed claws enough to pierce the skin of her empty fist.

"Are you the one who killed Schmitt?" Violet snarled, nearly dropping the makeshift explosive in her hand when she located a figure standing behind the shop's counter.

"If you are speaking of that thief, I did not end his cursed life, but I did administer a bit of poison and hex to chase away a starving coyote. Just a handful of powder to drive home a warning to you and your kin. It is unfortunate it was not heeded."

"You killed him, and the death of a Howler is a death sentence for you, you old freak."

"Had I the means to kill a werewolf, why ever would I allow you to stand before me instead of striking you down?" the crazed occultist asked, her voice eerily reasonable. "Perhaps I created an opportunity for his death, but I did not murder. So you must ask yourself, who did?"

Her words cut through Violet's haze of anger and she licked her lips. The speaker sounded ancient, decrepit. An old bat wouldn't be able to kill Schmitt. The bruises along the former Howler's body looked like the effects of a harsh beating. But if not the witch, then who?

"She didn't kill anyone. The Crone hasn't left this property since you were a twinkle in your granddad's eye," a British accent cut through the darkness. "She calls to us through our dreams because she cannot defend herself."

What were Kale and Dirk doing? They were supposed to be guarding the shop in case someone tried to escape. Wouldn't it have been natural to keep others from coming in, too?

The figure behind the counter, the Crone, huffed as a burly British man maneuvered through her shop. "I was hoping it would be Deva or Donald who answered my summons, not an ungrateful git like you. How horrid are the fates to send you to me, Bertrand?"

"It's just Bert now, thank you, love."

Violet spun around, trying to identify Bert. The foreign smells in the room were so heavy it was hard to differentiate if his scent from the myriad vials and potions littering the shelves. But the man had left open the door, and a breeze shifted through the room and brought in a coppery tang of blood and a musty wolf stench.

A werewolf.

Thin light from the open door revealed a tall man with his hands soaked in blood up to his wrist, staining his trench coat sleeves, and his nails were like blackened arrowheads.

"Your man out front was pretty careless; he was smoking a cigarette and didn't see me coming. Didn't smell me neither." With a wince, Bert made the claws retract and resume their human form. "And I wouldn't be putting my faith in the man out back either . . ."

Raising his voice, Bert finished his sentence. ". . . isn't that right, Bostonian?"

A low creaking noise was followed by a waft of more blood, vile rotting flesh, and sunscreen.

A vampire.

When a glint of silver caught her eye, Violet almost instinctively hurled the bomb in its direction and ran, but her body froze instead.

Both exits were blocked. If she threw the bomb now, would she be able to get past the vampire with the silver strangle-wire or shoulder past the werewolf?

"My, my. I was hoping to call heroes to my side, but instead I get two killers and a scared pup," the Crone grumbled as if having a bomb-wielding werewolf in her shop was a common occurrence. "What cruel fates conspire against a poor old woman."

"Everyone back away," Violet shouted as she raised the bomb overhead, trying to regain control. "Or I'll—"

"Kill us all?" Bert cut her off.

Violet turned her head, looking at the British man with a disgusted sneer. Had this man been a real werewolf, he would have known it would take more than a bit of fire to end someone with lycanthropy.

Tink tink tink.

Violet turned her head, watching the vampire emptying something out of his pocket.

Metallic beads clattered on the floor, rolling toward her . . . No, not beads.

Buckshot made from . . . silver?

"Your friends were packing silver weapons. You have to wonder why, don't you? When there was only one werewolf they knew of in this place," Bert continued. "And I bet you anything that the bomb you've got there has at least one silver cartridge attached to it. You throw that, and we're all going to be catching silver ball bearings in our faces and then get swallowed up by whatever hellish fumes that mad old woman has brewed up around here."

The Crone cackled madly.

"You're lying," Violet sputtered, the bomb feeling a lot heavier than it did moments before. If silver had been in the bomb, she'd have felt it, right? "You're just scared. Weak."

Bert sighed. "Call me what you like but I'm telling you, that bomb has bloody silver in it. The question you have to ask yourself is why? Why would your pack mates not care if you caught a bit of silver, hmm? Or what would they have done with that silver if they hadn't strapped it to the back of a bomb?"

Raising his fingers, Bert mimed a gun and shot himself in the temple.

"Maybe your pack mates were scared that you might have found out something they would have rather left secret?" he pressed. "Something that might not paint them in the best light?"

Violet shook her head, beads of sweat beginning to break out across her brow. The silver itch from when she approached the Toil and Trouble. Her two mates had said the place felt like silver was near that last time they were here, too, but what if it was because of the silver they were packing? They'd lied to her.

"I've been bouncing through this city for days now, keeping one step ahead of my lovely, pale shadow over there," Bert said, nodding toward the vampire. "Specifically looking for unusual suspects, like a trio of bumbling werewolves shaking down every drug dealer in town."

The vampire made a disapproving sound in his throat though his expression didn't change.

"Oh, what's the matter, James? If I didn't know any better, I'd say you were eager to get that silver garrote of yours around my throat. You aren't still sore over our last little tumble in New York, are you?" Bert clutched both hands to his heart as if he'd just been stabbed. "That's a long time to begrudge someone for simply defending himself. If I recall correctly, we both walked away from the incident."

"Quit your babble, you filthy mongrel, and start talking some sense," Violet screeched, trembling with fury. "You said you were following three werewolves. What happened to Schmitt? Tell me or I'll shatter this right at your feet!"

That threat seemed to have worked because Bert exhaled, finally growing serious.

"Your pack mates were easy to follow, honest. I wanted some answers and kept pace. When they split up, I followed the one I suspect you call Schmitt. He came right to this shop, which isn't any surprise because, as I said, the resident occultist is sending out some pretty harsh vibes to those who are attuned to it. Your friend broke into the shop and probably got a face full of wolfsbane, hemlock, and mercury: a combination that interrupts a werewolf's regeneration but is only temporary, unlike silver."

Violet shook her head, seeing where this story was going. "No. You lie."

"The truth isn't always sweet, wolfie. The two goons you arrived with were the ones that I saw leaving Trouble and Toil with this Schmitt of yours. They ignored his complaints for help and tried to get him to spill the information of where a blood junkie stash was. It's probably how they got the silver buckshot. They must have roughed him up without realizing his regeneration was suppressed and killed the poor lad."

Tears were welling up in the corner of Violet's eyes as she tried to find some argument to such a preposterous claim.

"They were going to do you in too. Probably scared you'd figure it out if you spoke with the Crone here. The fact they were packing silver weapons tells you that they found the blood junkie,"

Bert said softly. "This isn't a proper pack you're running with. These Howlers will end up getting you killed, love."

"Don't call me that," Violet shrieked, her pupils becoming slits as the wolf within struggled to take control and rip out the throat of this pompous fool. "You don't know anything about us or our pack. Everything you said is a lie. You don't know anything about us. We are family."

Bert held out a hand, in a gesture of receiving.

"I could have taken you down or let that noose-carrying lunatic over there kill you the moment you stepped out of that jeep. But we didn't. In fact, we're the ones trying to save your life, honest." He spoke nice and slow. "Your pack has done more damage to this city than you can possibly imagine. But you can change that. You can help us. Just answer a few questions and you can restore a hard-earned peace that was broken by the arrival of the Howlers.

"Then you can join a real pack, one that isn't looking for cheap thrills and willing to murder one another over petty squabbles. Put the bomb down and let's have a proper chat, shall we?"

Violet's heart hammered in her chest as she glared at his outstretched hand. To think that Dirk and Kale murdered Schmitt . . . but that made sense, didn't it? They had been acting so strange ever since they returned to camp. They had even agreed to go back into the city with her to help find this place.

"No, you're trying to trick me. You're working with this witch and this tick." Violet shook her head to clear her doubts. "You're a coward. Burn in Hell!"

Bert and James were in motion before the words left her lips.

The Crone just sighed.

The sound was not loud enough to be heard over the breaking glass and the wicked explosion that followed.

Violet only had a moment to appreciate the truth of Bert's words after a silver-coated piece of buckshot tore through her right lung.

****

"Are you really going to throw a fledgling to the curb like that?" Thomas asked, his voice rising steadily as his anger grew. "If you would just look at the facts—"

"Facts? The fact is one of the vampires in *my city* is dating a werewolf. Do you honestly think that woulda gone well for anyone? Maybe if you ain't so fond of your human pets, you'd realize that some dogs need be puttin' down."

Lawrence's response came through a very heavy and uncultivated slur that was so uncharacteristic for him. Heavy wasn't even close to describing the amount of drinking he'd been doing lately. Thomas had to take on half a dozen new blood donors just to keep the bar stocked for paying customers looking for some red lightning moonshine.

"Pull yourself together, Lawrence. Nelson has put just as much effort into saving lives here as I have. Without us, you wouldn't be able to afford trying to stir up a war that everyone knows is a mistake. Hell, Lawrence, even the Boston Boys are getting sick of your shit."

Thomas hated speaking to Lawrence like this. After all, Lawrence had been his boss, a leader in the supernatural community, his mentor, and the father of the woman he'd loved. Each role that Lawrence represented was something Thomas had respected and even admired, but now?

Now Thomas felt as if he were speaking with a dying man.

"You leave Bob outta this. He and his boys've backed me up longer than you could imagine. They know the score; werewolves and vampires don't mix." Lawrence paused, leaning back in his seat so he could slug the last dregs of red moonshine from the bottle he'd been nursing. "In fact, I don't think vampires mix well with anyone right now."

Thomas slammed his fist into the desk. "Because you're whipping them up for another war."

"It's a war of survival."

"I think I heard Ernest say the same thing." The words slipped past Thomas's lips before he had a chance to bite them back, and he immediately regretted them. There was only one person who could feel more hatred for Ernest than Thomas, and that was Lawrence.

"Don't. You. Ever." Lawrence's voice trembled with a rage that made the entire room grow cold. The bottle shattered in his hand as he clenched it into his fist. *"Speak to me like that again!"*

Thomas's guilt was short lived. He pressed harder.

"Because the truth stings, Lawrence? Is that it? You've already cost us a medic and a vampire who really needed our help. Not to mention a chance to restore peace. A peace that your wife created," Thomas shouted. "What is this about, huh? What is this really about? Because you damn well know that a pack of werewolves would be the best to track down your wife's killer! Sean and his girlfriend practically offered you the monster in a gift-wrapped package, and what do you do? You cast Sean out!"

"Because werewolves can't be trusted. It's a trick, a filthy trick to try and cover up that they murdered my wife and are now scared of the repercussions." Lawrence stumbled to his feet and stared down at Thomas with bloodshot eyes.

Thomas shook his head, battling sorrow with disgust.

"I can't believe I stood up for you. I can't believe I told Sean you would be reasonable. He was right. We could have video evidence and it still wouldn't be enough for you. You know, Lawrence, I hurt, too. Your friends hurt. I miss Julia every hour of every day."

Ernest had killed Julia, Lawrence's only daughter. Thomas wasn't sure if it was the right thing to bring up, but he couldn't think of any other way to get through to the man he once respected. He had to make him understand.

"Don't you dare—"

"But I'm still here, doing what I can and living how I think she'd want me to live. Because she showed me it's important to cherish every moment we can. If you're so determined to destroy yourself, I won't stop you from chugging a gallon of holy water. But you will not take this city down with you. I won't let you."

Lawrence blinked in surprise and a heavy atmosphere filled the room. The air was charged with a vibrant energy. It carried with it the potential for change.

That potential disappeared when the door to Lawrence's office flew open. Boston Bob stepped in, his ugly face harder than granite as he moved toward the desk. Lawrence shook his head, muttered something under his breath and sat back down. Thomas' heart sank when he realized that the chance for Lawrence to change his mind had just been missed.

"Well?" Lawrence demanded.

"I'm the last Boston Boy," Bob said, his voice brimming with sorrow. "Just thought you'd want to know."

Thomas sank into the nearest chair.

Lawrence was just as unsettled.

Without invitation, Boston Bob stepped over and reached behind Lawrence's desk to pull a bottle of whisky from a shelf. He bit down on the bottle's neck, shattering the glass and spitting out the shards before taking a long swig.

The first of the Boston Boys to die was Albert, who had been another casualty of the war with Ernest and his blood junkies. Over the course of the vampire war that ravaged the city, he'd been caught in several explosions, stabbed twice, and nearly gunned down by machine gun fire.

Thomas had patched him up each time.

In the end, Al wasn't so lucky.

"I figured I'd outlast Al, or at least, until he quit this work. Killing was something he was good at, not something he wanted to do. But I never thought I'd be the last of our trio."

"What happened to James?" Lawrence pressed, his voice less angry and more urgent. "What's goin' on, Bob?"

Three more quick gulps from the whiskey bottle drained it, and the ugly vampire wiped his mouth with his free hand.

"That's a good question and one I can't really figure out. Since Jericho was attacked, I had James working the city border, figuring that the guilty werewolf would be at least smart enough to try and flee once he realized that every vampire in the city was gunning for him," Boston Bob said, sounding a little angry at himself for giving the order. "That's when James caught sight of a mongrel coming into the city. A bloke named Bert Ashworth who was kinda like us, taking jobs with a lot of folks in the supernatural community. He and James had almost killed one another in New York, several years back. Odd that he would turn up now, don't you think?"

This was all news to both Thomas and Lawrence. Thomas had been too busy with trying to tend to Sean and running the business side of the Red Lightning Pub to pay too much attention to the war effort that the Boston Boys had been putting in. Lawrence trusted in the expertise of his vampiric hitmen to know their business, which was why he was comfortable spending most of his time locked in his office, grieving over the loss of his wife and child with bottle after bottle of moonshine.

"Yes, that's odd, ain't it?" Lawrence hissed, shooting a harsh glance at Thomas. "Almost as if they were gatherin' re-enforcements for a war."

"Give me a break, Lawrence," Thomas began to retort when the argument was ended by Boston Bob.

"It ain't logical, and that's the problem," he growled, silencing the other two in the room. "Bert is a weak-kneed Limey who is little better than a bloodhound for hire. If he's sniffing around, it's because someone called him in to snoop around."

Thomas and Lawrence both started to speak, but Boston Bob cut them off with a raised hand.

"As far as I can tell, James stuck as close to Bert as possible, only losing him a few times. James didn't pass along everything. Well, you know how he is—was—more stalk than talk. When he reported in, he said how Bert was keeping around a poor part of town, staking out a place called the Trouble and Toil." Boston Bob shook his head, as if the last meeting with James had been even more unsettling than usual. "James said that place had an ugly feel behind it and when he was near it, he had a hard time focusing . . . kept daydreaming about nonsense."

After a moment of thought, Lawrence frowned. "The Crone."

Thomas and Boston Bob were both silent, waiting for him to continue.

"An occultist, maybe a true witch. She never left that shop, so no one bothered her. Sara tried to bring her into the accord meetings every now and then, but the Crone was only interested in trying to sell her weak charms and snake oil. She must have been consorting with the enemy."

"The enemy?" Thomas asked, growing more irritated with Lawrence's every word. "You don't even know who the enemy is."

"Well the Crone isn't an enemy," Boston Bob butted in. "Because she ain't much more than cinders now."

Thomas and Lawrence stopped their bickering and looked up at him, startled.

"Her place was burnt to the ground. When James didn't report in last night, I checked it out. The place was still

195

smoldering." The remaining Boston Boy frowned. "It was a mess . . . I found . . . well, what was left of James . . ."

Reaching into his pocket delicately, Boston Bob pulled out a burnt silver cord wrapped in cloth.

"Everything there was a mess. Four corpses inside, including James and what was mostly a blackened skeleton which might have been this witch. The other two were definitely werewolves, as some of their burns had tried to heal themselves but failed. Maybe silver wards or something," Boston Bob said. "There was also a corpse in the back alleyway, James' work. Stuffed in the back of an old jeep across the street of the place was another body, missing its' throat, heart, and a good chunk of the right lung as well."

Having spent so many hours operating on the supernatural physique of the vampires, Thomas had come to understand that the destruction of the major organs was a surefire way to take the fight out of an inhuman opponent. A vampire could recover from grave wounds rather quickly but reknitting muscle and skin together was a lot easier than trying to regrow or heal complex organs.

The removal of enough of those organs was sufficient to push the unnatural rejuvenation of a supernatural creature beyond its impressive limits.

"Four werewolves and a witch?" Lawrence asked, equally horrified and puzzled. "James tried to take down all of them? On their home turf?"

Boston Bob looked angry for a moment, as if his friend had just insulted his late partner.

"James was too smart to try anything like that, Lawrence," he snapped. "And the body in the jeep wasn't his work anyways."

"So what does this all mean?" Lawrence shot back. "And how does the witch fit into all of this?"

"I don't know," Boston Bob replied. "And that's going to kill us all; we don't know anything."

"That's not true; we know who killed Sara. An outsider werewolf and his gang who call themselves Howlers," Thomas said hastily, hoping to gain an ally in Boston Bob.

"What?" This news cut even through the ugly vampire's grief.

"No, we don't!" Lawrence shouted, slamming his fist so hard onto his desk it sent cracks along the oak top. "These fledglings have been associating with a werewolf, who is clearly trying to pin the murder on a patsy in hopes of fooling us so we don't put a silver bullet between each of their yellow eyes!"

Thomas threw his hands in the air in pure frustration. "Bob, talk some sense into him. Lawrence would rather start a war with the werewolves than have a little faith in us."

"The last time I had some faith in someone, they drove a stake through my daughter's heart," Lawrence bellowed, standing up so fast his chair hurled behind him and shattered against the wall.

Lawrence's explosion of fury was so unexpected that Thomas found himself calling upon his vampiric strength just in case he needed to defend himself. Boston Bob seemed to have been caught off guard as well, as he'd drawn a hidden knife out of reflex.

"I've lost my family, but I will *not* lose my city. And if you ain't gonna help me keep this city under my control, then you're against me, got it? Now, where do you stand?"

Thomas's fists curled into fists as Lawrence glared at him.

"By every Saint and his mother, Lawrence," Boston Bob grunted, slipping the knife back into the sheath at his belt. "We're all Red Lightning vampires. Of course we're going to help you keep this city safe. Right, sawbones?"

The ugly vampire turned his head toward Thomas.

Thomas just looked from Boston Bob to Lawrence.

"No, I'm not. Not like you want me to," Thomas said, turning around and walking toward the door. "I'm tired of piecing everyone I love back together, and I'm not going to leave my friends behind again."

"Thomas! Thomas! Get back here, boy," Lawrence roared. "You owe me your life. This is your family."

"Maybe so," Thomas said. "But they were my family first."

15 DATE NIGHT DISTRACTION

Nothing.

Clara had rushed to the Den in search of Donald, but he wasn't there. None of the pack leaders were there, and no one was answering her frantic phone calls or urgent text messages. They were just gone.

She wanted to scream in utter frustration. She couldn't warn her pack or organize them to strike the Howlers if she couldn't find anyone. The wolf picked up on her irritation and fed on it. She had to calm down or she'd lose it.

Before Sean's turning, Clara wouldn't have felt too worried about the inability to reach one of her pack mates; after all it was well past midnight by the time she'd arrived at the Den and nearly one o'clock in the morning when she'd given up searching for her pack members and started calling them. Not even Chelsea was picking up, and she usually stayed up later than Clara partying and playing video games. But with a pack of rabid werewolves surrounding the forest and a vampire leader itching for a war stirring up trouble in the Colesbrooke metroplex, she was beyond worried.

Any failure of communication now seemed sinister, and her mind was a playground where all sorts of paranoia were tromping about.

That paranoia led Clara back to Artemis' apartment where they were supposed to regroup. After she'd left a message for Benjamin at the ranger's station, as well as leaving separate voicemails on both Izzy and Vic's cell phones, she'd stopped at her own place just long enough to grab an overnight bag.

When Clara opened the door at Artemis' apartment, she found an atmosphere so grim she wanted to retreat. Artemis was working hard to combat it with double chocolate chip cookies, milk with chilled peppermint leaves, and a flickering frankincense candle, but her efforts weren't helping.

Clara stepped inside cautiously, unsure what to do. No one had seemed this grim when she'd revealed her werewolf status earlier or when Sean was still getting his vampiric legs under him.

Nelson stood fuming at Artemis' small table. "Less than a month ago I literally reached inside that man's chest cavity to remove a bent nail from a blood junkie pipe bomb lodged in his right lymphatic duct. And Lawrence still had the guts to call me a worthless parasite? That's rich coming from an actual blood sucker! Er, no offense."

Shit. Thomas and Sean's talk with Lawrence must have gone sour, though what had happened to destroy even Artemis' cheery nature or Penny's ability to brush everything off was beyond Clara.

"None taken," Thomas and Sean said in unison, their tones listless.

Clara needed to say something. No one had even looked at her as she opened the door and entered the room. What if she'd been the enemy? A Howler? This strange group of humans and vampires needed to wake up. Being apathetic would get them killed.

"Bad news," Clara said, instantly regretting the direction she was taking. "I can't find anyone in the pack. They're all missing and no one is responding to my calls or texts."

"At least you have a pack," Thomas grumbled.

What?

Sean nodded, sinking into his chair. "Lawrence kicked us out. Well, Thomas decided to leave on his own, too after we got kicked out."

Nelson cursed the pub and called Lawrence a long list of names from both the English and Spanish languages.

Now it was all on them, and hopefully Clara's pack, to stop the Howlers. But she hadn't been able to find her pack.

Artemis checked the oven timer and then pulled Clara through the front door and up the metal stairs.

"Clara, they need time."

"We don't have time, Artemis. I couldn't find my pack. No one is protecting this city right now."

Artemis rubbed her eyes, bags under her eyes that hadn't been there earlier in the night. "Please, Clara. They've given everything to the Red Lightning Pub and the vampires there, and now they've been banished. All three of them are hurting and scrambling to figure out what to do next. And yes, Nelson isn't a vampire, but he gave his all while doubting his very beliefs in science and nature. He sewed up monsters and assisted with a war he didn't believe in."

The pain in Artemis' voice revealed she was hurting, too.

If Clara's pack disowned her, she'd be a mess. But at least she'd have Sean. Sean and his weird group of friends. That's what she'd have to be for them now.

"Thanks for the heads up, Artemis."

Penny stuck her head out the door. "Art, the oven is beeping."

Artemis gasped and flew back down the stairs, and Clara wanted to laugh. She knew she shouldn't, but it seemed so strange. They were deep in the trenches of an approaching war, and Artemis was worried about burning cookies.

Walking back down the stairs, Clara steeled herself. She would be Sean's flock if needed. But they still needed to deal with the Howlers.

The aroma of cocoa was extra heavy as she opened the front door, and Clara caught herself salivating. Maybe Artemis was smarter than Clara thought. Maybe Sean's little sister was the one keeping everyone together because of the chocolate chip cookies.

"I'm sorry, Nelson. Sean. Thomas. I didn't realize that this plan would get you guys thrown out of your pack . . . er, flock," Clara said as she walked inside and closed the door.

Penny groaned. "Don't blame yourself. Lawrence was in a downward spiral before you turned up. Another dead vampire didn't help either. We'll figure this all out. The last little while has been difficult for everyone, and I think we all need to take a breather and regroup."

"Wait, another dead vampire?"

"James? I think it was Jugular James." Penny stifled a yawn. "Thomas found out when Lawrence was disowning him."

Clara swore. The Howlers were already causing more trouble. She needed to find her pack.

Artemis served a fresh plate of hot cookies. "I'm sure once Lawrence calms down we can try talking some sense into him, and hopefully start returning this city back to normal."

For a moment, Thomas looked as if he was about to speak up, and by the look on his face, whatever he had to say was not going to be positive. Artemis shot him a pleading glance, and he stayed silent.

"No offense, Art," said Sean, taking advantage of the silence and grabbing a warm cookie, "But these are definitely not your best."

"What are you talking about?" Artemis gave the almost empty plate a significant glance. "You've had like six and just grabbed another. If you don't like them, why're you eating them?"

He shrugged. "Stress eating."

"I think they're great," said Penny, dunking hers in a glass of milk.

Were they really fighting over cookies right now? It just seemed so . . . out of place.

"I don't know, I think Sean's right," Thomas said, his voice flat. "I can smell how delicious and chocolatey they are, but something's just not translating in my mouth."

"That's totally it," Sean agreed. "In fact, the last few things I've eaten that you've cooked have kind of been like that. Disappointingly bland. Maybe your spices are just old?"

"I beg your pardon," said Artemis stiffly. "My spices? Old? Penny, please tell these nimrods about the last time you went spice shopping with me."

"Two days ago," said Penny promptly. "We hit up the farmer's market and she spent an hour sniffing the poor spice gal's wares."

"This is real cocoa powder," Artemis added. "Like ground from real cacao beans, not that processed crap you buy from the grocery store."

Sean and Artemis began bickering about the quality of her cocoa powder until Clara, unable to listen any longer, finally spoke up. This wasn't how she imagined being there for Sean.

"You might both be right."

The Butler siblings' heads swiveled her way.

"Artemis, I'm sure that your spices are just as fresh as you say they are," Clara placated. Then to Sean she said, "And I'm sure they taste just as disappointing as you say they are."

"They can't both be right," Penny said.

Clara looked at Sean, at a loss for words. As a lover of food herself, she really didn't want to be the bearer of this particularly depressing bit of news.

"Foxe—sorry, Lawrence—didn't mention anything about how the taste buds of a vampire work, did he?"

"No," said Sean.

"Should he have?"

"Obviously I'm kind of new to the ins and outs of what vampires can and can't do, but werewolves can't taste normal foods well. Maybe it's a condition of both species."

"What?" Sean and Thomas shouted together, looking aghast. It was good to see Thomas looking less pale, but this wasn't how Clara wanted him to perk up.

"It's very possible that Artemis' cooking is as good as ever, and you two just can't appreciate it. It doesn't happen immediately. You lose it over the course of a year or so, and then everything tastes more bland except for the supernatural diet you crave. Thomas probably didn't notice at first because he was so focused on the war."

"How could Lawrence not tell us something like that?" Sean demanded.

Thomas looked shattered by disappointment. His eyes were hollow as he remembered something, and while Clara wanted to know what he was struggling with, she didn't want to ask. Something had probably happened during the war that was food related, maybe something involving Julia. Artemis had warned Clara that Julia was a forbidden subject with him.

A muscle twitched in Thomas's jaw. When he spoke, his voice was barely above a whisper. "Is there anything else we should know about?"

"I don't know, but we should figure out how to deal with the Howlers."

"No," Penny interrupted her. "Tomorrow, we'll figure out what to do with the werewolves and vampires tomorrow. It's late. Or early. We need rest."

All eyes turned to Penny.

"Don't give me that look, just hear me out," Penny said, holding up her hands. "We're all stressed, worn out, and no good to anybody in this state. We've done what we can for a day and working ourselves into a depression isn't going to help anyone."

"You're absolutely right," Artemis agreed, following her best friend's lead. "And just because you supernaturals don't need as much sleep, some of us are exhausted."

"So how about we forget all of this nonsense, at least for the night?" Penny was working hard to keep an upbeat tone to her words, but her hands were clammy.

After several heavy heartbeats, Nelson spoke up as he pulled out his cell phone. "Yeah, you're right. You know what? I'm going to call Gabby."

Penny leaned toward Clara and whispered loudly. "Nelson's a real serial flirt. Gabby's a resident at the hospital who is giving him a run for his money."

"Yeah, yeah. Zip it," Nelson muttered, ignoring Sean's chuckle as he fired off a text message. "I've been disowned by one group. You can be a little nicer to me. There's got to be some luck for me out there in the universe."

Sean snorted. "Yeah, you'll need all the luck you can get, buddy. Gabby is smoking. Outta your league, tough guy. And it's late."

Nelson arched an eyebrow at the friendly barb thrown his way.

"First, I happen to know she's free tonight, and she's still up. And it's kinda hard to take criticism from a guy who's living proof that women make bad choices," Nelson shot back with his own cocky smile, turning to Clara and giving her a wink. "Honestly, you can do a lot better than Sean. Maybe trade up for a mannequin with a bunch of knock-knock jokes scribbled over it. It'll be a lot more handsome and a lot funnier."

She couldn't help but giggle and feel glad Nelson had something to get him out of his funk. "True, but I've already gone through so much trouble to keep Sean around as it is."

"Yeah, so . . . wait, what?" Sean brushed crumbs from his face.

Even Thomas was brought out of his bad mood enough to laugh over that. Before he could add to the friendly banter, Nelson's phone chirped.

Glancing at his screen, Nelson grinned and stood up, making his way toward the door.

"Hey, come back in the morning so we can figure out the Howlers," Penny shouted.

"Maybe after a hot breakfast," Nelson said as he stepped out the door.

"Oh wait, Nelson, you forgot your—" Artemis called after him, but the door had already closed. "Gloves. Oh no . . ."

"He'll be fine," Sean said. "It's not even that chilly."

"But now they're going to clutter up my table."

Glove clutter didn't seem terribly important, and Clara knew they needed sleep. "Sean's told me about your wild sleepovers. Tonight we may need to skip to the sleeping part."

Sean snorted. "Let the humans sleep. I'm going to destroy Thomas through the video game of his choice."

******

The smell of popcorn, heavy in the air, was one of the first things Clara became aware of when she woke up. Not too far from the air mattress, Penny and Artemis were back-to-back on Artemis' bed, both breathing the rhythmic breath of sleep and looking peaceful.

Thomas, settled deep within the beanbag chair, also looked peaceful as he slept, though Clara wasn't sure how. He was using the flipped bowl of popcorn as a pillow.

She suppressed a yawn and wiggled a little, trying to get comfortable. Artemis' air mattress was extra thick and was plugged in to stay inflated, but it was still an air mattress. Her shoulder dug into the compressed air, and it was starting to ache.

They'd played video games until Thomas finally beat Sean at a new racing game.

"I missed this."

The soft whisper teased the back of her neck and caused an involuntary shiver. Clara smiled, leaning back against Sean's chest.

"You better be talking about me in your arms," Clara whispered back in a playful tone, "And not where you've got your hands."

There was a soft chuckle.

"Why can't it be both?" he asked as he drew up closer to her body. "I love you, Clara. You're the best part of my life."

Her heart fluttered as a rush of happiness and contentment warmed her.

"That was beautiful, buddy."

Sean groaned. "Seriously, Thomas? If you were half as good at changing minds as you were at killing moods, we wouldn't have been disowned yesterday."

Sitting up, Thomas glared at Sean then smirked.

"Sorry, I can't help that I have such good ears. Besides, Clara's heart is pounding so hard it's making me hungry."

"What?" Clara said, her face heating up as she rolled off the air mattress, "You can hear my heart?"

Sean chucked. "Hell yeah. But not like in an 'I vant to suck your blood' kind of way. More like, 'Hey, I'm a heart and I'm pumping blood, here I am!'"

"Sean," Thomas said, but he didn't get to finish.

A chorus of yawns cut him off as everyone else started rolling up and onto their feet. Artemis offered to make breakfast, but everyone opted for coffee first.

Penny turned off the air mattress and sat beside Clara to quicken its deflation. She fingered through her bedhead as she sleepily gazed around the apartment. Thanks to Artemis having sealed up the windows with several layers of dark cloth, it was still gloomy and disorientating.

"Anyone know what time it is?" Penny asked.

"Let's see," Clara said, reaching into her pocket and pulling out her phone. "Shit, we really overslept. It's almost three in the afternoon."

Penny, the only member of the group who was on a regular schedule, gave a defeated sigh.

"Three?" Sean said and then added slyly. "Well, it seems Nelson was luckier than I thought."

Thomas started to comment, but stopped after noticing a disapproving glance from Penny. He quieted down to a snicker.

Hiding a smile, Clara saw she had several missed calls on her phone. Immediately the small moment of comfort burst, and she remembered Lawrence and the Howlers. Hopefully one of the voicemails was from Izzy, Vic, or the Von Grimmel brothers, who would at least provide some help in getting in touch with Donald. Once that rigmarole was completed, they could start planning their confrontation with the Howlers.

Excusing herself and stepping outside into the bright sun, Clara raised her phone to her ear, beginning to listen to her messages.

"*Crrrkt. Clara, it's . . . sssshhhhnttt . . . me.*" Benjamin's voice was laced with static.

Even if you excluded the static, the sound quality of the message was terrible, with an obnoxious echo to it. However, Clara was used to this kind of message; it came from an old satellite phone that Benjamin and his forest ranger buddies carried when they were still roughing it out in the woods. The phone was useless the majority of the time, but if one was willing to climb a tree or hike up a big hill, a ranger could manage to get a call to connect after three or four attempts.

"The station . . . radio our squad . . . hhhhsttt . . . said you left a letter frrrrr! Me. Then said . . . Izzy's car . . . abandoned . . . trashed near station. She said . . . borrowed it. . . . Call station as soon . . . pfft . . . possible. If not . . . coming home . . . night . . ."

Izzy's car!

Clara released a frustrated sigh. She'd completely spaced it, trying to get as far away from the Howler freaks as possible. Luckily she didn't leave anything of value in it, but it seemed that the boys at the station had recognized it as she borrowed it from Izzy frequently. They probably already called the cops to get the abandoned car towed, but not before giving her brother just enough information to make him freak out.

Well, after Benjamin got back to Colesbrooke to see what a fine mess had been made of the local politics, Izzy's car was going to be the least of her worries.

Making a mental note to call the ranger station so one of the forest service guys could pass along to her brother that she was just fine, Clara hit the button to play the next message. This one a lot clearer.

"Ms. Warren, this is Jerry Smith from the Villa Housing Agency. We are contacting you about an incident last night at your apartment; your neighbor called us about damage to your front door. We reviewed our security cameras and believe there may have been a possible break-in. We have contacted the police—"

Icy fingers of dread began to twist themselves into Clara's stomach. Benjamin calling her about Izzy's car and her apartment complex reporting a forced entry in the same night might be connected.

Leaving the car in the woods had been dangerous. If the Howlers found it, they could have tracked her scent from her clothes to her front door.

"No, no, no, no . . ." Panic crushed her lungs, and she found it difficult to breath.

What all could they find?

She had pictures, her computer, her books from university . . . every aspect of her life was there, ripe for the picking.

All things that the Howlers could use to gather intel on her. Information concerning the city, her pack, her family . . .

. . . her friends.

"Sean! Sean!" Clara choked, hurrying back into Artemis' apartment.

Everyone stopped chatting and waited, concern etched into their eyes and frowns.

Sean spoke first. "What is it?"

"I think that the Howlers have found my apartment."

"What?"

She shook her head, unsure how to reply. Tears welled in her eyes as her fear and panic took control.

Her phone beeped, alerting her that she'd received a text message.

She had to tell the pack. Everyone was compromised. Looking at her screen, Clara felt as if she'd just been punched in the stomach.

Keep the pendant, Clara. I found a better trophy.

Attached was a picture of Nelson sprawled, unconscious on the floor, a nasty gash across his forehead.

16 RANSOM CALL

"Hello?"

Clara's grip was tight on her phone. If she had the same strength the vampires did in her human form, she would have cracked it for sure.

Minutes after receiving the text with Nelson's picture, Leon had called her. He still hadn't spoken, but Clara could almost feel his presence through the phone.

"I must say, I'm surprised by the company you keep."

Even though she'd been prepared for the sound of Leon's voice, Clara shuddered as it slithered into her ears. Artemis and Penny were watching with baited breath from Artemis's bed. Sean was sprawled on a giant beanbag chair, looking green. Thomas paced nearby, not making eye contact with anyone.

"Where's Nelson? What have you done with him?" Clara shouted into the phone.

"Careful, you wouldn't want to release the wolf," Leon purred. "Your friend is fine, for now. He's moaning a bit, but he'll heal up."

Clara bit back the urge to swear, waiting to speak until she was calm enough to avoid intentionally provoking the Howler.

"What do you want?"

"I'm more interested in what you want," Leon said. "What is it you want? Why would a wolf with a pack pretend to be a loner and take one of my prize trophies for her own?"

Clara's blood ran cold. How had they known? Had they really found everything?

"You can tell me later. I don't mind," Leon continued. "You can tell me all about your pack, too."

"Later?"

"When you come to pick up your friend, here. You don't think I'm going to keep him until the full moon, do you? Anyway, I trust you'll be able to find me. I'll be waiting, Clara."

"Wait, no don't hang up," Clara cried.

"Oh, and it would be best if you came alone."

Clara's stomach dropped as the sound cut out.

Four pairs of eyes stared at her.

"Well?" Thomas asked. His tone was deadly.

"He wants me to come and find him," she whispered. "He wants information on the pack."

"What will we do?" Artemis' voice trembled. "What can we do?"

Thomas walked over to Sean and pulled him to his feet.

"Come on. We're going."

"Where?" Sean asked.

"To Lawrence," Thomas replied.

"What? There's no way—"

"Wait, Tom!" Artemis called.

"We should really be planning something here," Penny added, jumping to her feet.

"Sean, come back!"

Their pleas fell on deaf ears. Thomas had already dragged Sean outside, pulling the door closed behind them.

213

A brief sliver of sunlight illuminated the floor as they exited the apartment. Silence followed in their wake as the three women stared at the closed door in darkness.

"I hope the sunscreen hasn't worn off," Artemis said quietly.

Clara didn't respond. She had to get moving. If Thomas and Sean were going to try to salvage their resources, then she would pull on hers. She had no doubt why Leon had not given her a location. Werewolves could find other werewolves. It was just a matter of time. Luckily, Clara knew the best in the business.

She needed to find the Von Grimmel brothers.

"I'm off," she said, rushing out the door.

She was going to have to brave the potent scents of *Das Gemütlichkeit Biergarten,* a bar that been opened by a first-generation German immigrant nearly eighty years ago in the hopes of bringing a taste of his homeland to this city. He'd vowed that his pub would be a place where anyone from the Mother land would be welcome and never feel like a stranger.

The Von Grimmel brothers had taken an immediate liking to the place as soon as they had both agreed to join the local pack of Colesbrooke. Of course, Alban and Albert both agreed that the third-generation barkeep had become too Americanized and even had the audacity to write "The Peace of Mind Beer Garden" in English underneath the original sign.

Despite their grumblings over the Americanization of their favorite pub and the fact that there was even talk of the newest barkeep offering to sell ice-cold beer, the beer garden was the only place the werewolf brothers felt at home.

The potent aroma of sauerkraut might have been endearing to human senses, but to Clara's keen nose, it was like shoving a rotting cabbage up each nostril.

"Excuse me," Clara said as she approached the counter at the far end of the bar.

Most of the chairs in the pub were still stacked up on the tables, it being far too early to get the place ready for the patrons who were looking for a nice drink after a long day. But there were still a few customers looking to grab an authentic German meal for a late lunch.

The most prominent person enjoying the pub's fare was the heavyset barkeep behind the counter.

"Hello there, *Fräulein*. How can I be of service?" asked the barkeep with a big, friendly grin that only those who truly enjoyed the service industry could manage.

Returning the smile the best she could, Clara quickly said, "I'm fine, thank you. I'm looking for the Von Grimmel brothers. It's important."

She already knew they were here. Their mangy scents were too prominent for them to be anywhere else, but she still had to play the game.

Unfortunately, the barkeep's smile evaporated and was replaced with suspicion. "Oh? The Von Grimmels you say?"

Clara nodded. "Yes. Alban and Albert? I've heard they're here a lot."

"Is that what they say?" the barkeep asked, drumming his heavy fingers across the countertop. "Are you sure you have the right bar?"

Clara drew a deep breath. She couldn't lose control here. The wolf was watching.

"Look, can you get in contact with them or not? If you won't help me, I'll just head over to the Church of Saint Wilgefortis and start asking there," she said impatiently, folding her arms across her chest. The church was their other hideout, their private space.

"How do you know about the church?" the barkeep asked, his eyes narrowing. "Only their oldest and closest—"

"I can assure you that I have known the Von Grimmels a lot longer than you have. Now either tell me what I need to know, or stop wasting my time. I need to talk to them immediately."

The barkeep rubbed his chin, looking her up and down. Finally he muttered something and shrugged.

"Alright, if you know about the church of Saint Wilgefortis, I guess you really are friends," he said, taking a few steps back away from the counter and raising a heavy booted foot. "Sorry, I don't mean to be rough, but they asked me not to let anyone know they were here."

He slammed his boot three times against the floorboards and then stepped back toward the bar. He crossed back over to the counter and gave Clara a sheepish smile.

"You gotta understand that Alban and Albert are local legends here in this neighborhood. Not everyone was that fond of us Germanic folk after the World Wars. But the Von Grimmel family has always been there, helping out the community. My grandfather even has a story of a Von Grimmel saving this very bar from burning down back in the fifties."

Clara would love to see the look on the barkeep's face when he realized that the family that this community so highly regarded was actually the same two brothers. Keeping a low profile was second nature to the supernatural, so it was only reasonable that the barkeep and probably the entire neighborhood just assumed that the Von Grimmel brothers were the grandsons of the folk heroes they always talked about.

But it was not her place to break the news. Instead, she just nodded and waited. She didn't have to wait long.

From behind the counter, a door opened and revealed a staircase leading down to the cellar and an exhausted Alban standing at the threshold.

"It's Clara," Alban called down the stairs, relief relaxing his entire posture.

216

A moment later he was joined by Albert. Saying something in German as they passed the barkeep, the chubby man nodded and headed out back for a smoke. Soon Clara, Alban, and Albert were seated around a table.

"So you're still in the city, hmm?" Alban said. "I thought for sure Benjamin would have talked you into splitting."

"Benjamin is off on a forest service project. He'll be home in a few days," Clara replied, doing her best to keep calm. "Why would I leave the city? Never mind, listen. Something big has happened."

"We know," Albert and Alban said at the same time.

Clara frowned, blinking in surprise. "You know about the Howlers?"

The twins glanced at one another. Then they both turned and looked at Clara in confusion.

"The Howlers? What are those?" Alban asked.

Albert let out a small curse and then said, "Wait, you don't know?"

She didn't have time for this. Every second wasted was a second Nelson crept closer to death.

Clara growled, "If you don't know about the Howlers then what are you talking about?"

The Von Grimmel brothers were silent for a moment. Then as one, the twins let out a grim sigh.

"Bert is dead," Alban whispered.

Clara leaned back in her seat, feeling numb. Bert dead? She hadn't thought it was possible.

"So is the Crone," Albert added. "Her entire shop was burned to the ground along with her entire stock of potions. There's nothing left to keep us human."

****

Clara's head rested against the cold stone wall of the *Das Gemütlichkeit Biergarten* as she doubled over, shoulders shaking as she heaved. The nervous knots in her belly loosened somewhat as she expelled the bile left in her stomach.

The Von Grimmel brothers stood a respectful distance away, having followed Clara out into the alleyway.

As much older werewolves, both Alban and Albert had plenty of experience in having to obey the terrible burden of their curse and had slain many vampires in their day. For them, the loss of the potion was tragic, but they were no strangers to life without it. The handful of years Clara spent without the potion were still her nightmares.

"The news traveled fast. It's been pure chaos ever since. A lot of the pack are getting out of town, trying to prepare for a new hunt. No one has heard from Izzy and Vic, but odds are they fled town as soon as they heard. Donald is doing his best to keep everyone calm, but with the peace between the blood suckers gone, it's only a matter of time before someone lets the inner wolf take over and a vamp gets their throat torn out," Alban said in a jaded voice. "It took a while, but the curse has caught up. It always does."

"No peace for the likes of us or the vampires," Albert added. "Not that we're not trying to figure something out. Deva has already left town and is going to try and get in contact with the Pack fathers and see if any nearby area has a blood junkie problem that we might be able to solve. Buy us some time at least."

Blood junkies. Sure, they were the preferable targets, but murder was murder. And if she was ever too close to Sean during a full moon . . .

"Bert," she croaked, wiping away the mess around her mouth with the back of her hand. "What happened?"

"No one knows. He'd been asking around, like Donald had asked him to do. Stuck to the area of the Trouble and Toil because . . . well, we don't know why. Deva said something about the Crone calling for help. She tried to use . . . um, otto-mancy or something?" Alban replied, glancing at his twin brother.

"Oneiromancy. Dream magic or something like that," Albert said without missing a beat. "Deva said that it's really weak magic, little better than a Tarot card reading. She probably didn't even control it that well. She only managed to give a lot of people around the city bad dreams. The Crone probably didn't even know what she was really doing."

Clara felt faint. Bad dreams? Like the ones that she'd been having lately? Clara turned and heaved again.

Albert ignored it as he continued.

"Apparently Bert knew enough about magic to figure out what it was the Crone was worried about and that something bad was on the rise. Best guess is he waited around for the trouble to show up and it did. He was killed in the shop with the Crone and three other werewolves that no one recognized. Certainly not members of the local pack. There was another one . . . a vampire . . ."

The Von Grimmel brothers both whispered his name, as if worried that speaking too loudly would somehow invoke an angry spirit.

". . . Jugular James."

Clara looked up at the brothers. A vampire hitman with a silver garrote wire, an occultist with a temporary fix for the brunt of the werewolf curse, good old Bert, and three Howlers, all being killed? Each one of those targets would have been incredibly tough to handle one-on-one, but to have them all die under such mysterious circumstances?

"Listen, that's not why I came. I can't deal with that right now. I have another problem that I need you guys to help me with.

It can't wait," Clara said. "Those werewolves killed with Bert? They're probably from an invading pack that followed the blood junkies to Colesbrooke. They call themselves the Howlers."

The Von Grimmel brothers glanced at each other, uneasy.

"They're the ones I ran into during the full moon. I ran into them again in the forest. They are bad news. They've totally given into the wolf within. I think . . . I *know* they're the ones responsible for killing Sara Foxe. And I wouldn't be surprised if they were responsible for the Crone's and Bert's deaths as well." She was talking so fast that she was almost winding herself to get as much information out as possible. "They wanted me to join them on a hunt and I lied and got away, but they must have followed me. They took one of my friends. If I don't find him fast . . . Please, I need your help."

The Von Grimmel brothers were silent for a long moment. Even though they had been pack mates with Clara and her brother for decades, now was a time of caution and no one was more cautious than the Von Grimmels.

"If there is a rabid pack around here, we need to find Donald first," Alban said. "It'll take some time to gather up a few people to send these mongrels running . . ."

Clara shook her head. "I'm not asking you to fight them, just find them. You tell me where my friend is, and I'll take care of the rest."

The doubt was clearly drawn on the twins' features.

"Please."

The Von Grimmel brothers looked at one another, not too keen on what Clara was asking them to do. There was already too much going on, and if the local werewolves were going to survive the silver bullet wielding vampires, the turmoil brought on by the death of the Crone, *and* an invading pack of rabid lycanthropes, they would have to be both careful and lucky.

Alban and Albert sighed as one.

"Alright, we'll track down your friend—" Albert began.

"—but right after we're going to find Donald. Better to let him know what's going on." Alban finished.

Clara leaped forward, throwing an arm around both twins and hugging them.

"Thank you," she cried. With these two on the case, Nelson was as good as found.

"Now, do you have anything that we can use?"

"Yes, I brought this . . ." Reaching into her pocket, Clara pulled out the pair of gloves Nelson had left at Artemis' house.

Each grabbing a glove, the twins turned and began walking away from Clara, heading toward a more secluded area behind the beer garden. They each glanced over their shoulders, their eyes turning a deep yellow color as they began their transformation.

"We'll find your friend, Clara," Alban promised as his blond hair began to transform into thick fur and his ears started to mutate.

"And if we don't hear from you by tomorrow," Albert added as his face began to twist, a muzzle beginning to form. "Then we'll hunt down the Howlers."

17 FINDING NELSON

Outside of Artemis' apartment, Clara lay spread out on her back in the cool grass. The setting sun wasn't warm anymore, and a chilly breeze prickled her skin. But the breeze was welcome, for it helped blow away whatever monstrosity Artemis was cooking inside.

After watching the Von Grimmel brothers take off, she'd returned to Artemis' apartment to wait for news. She didn't want to wait alone at her own place, and she was anxious to see how Sean fared after talking with Lawrence. But she'd never made it down the stairs without her eyes watering and the wolf howling inside.

It was better to wait outside with the breeze. Hopefully Sean would be back quickly with good news.

Just as the red sun began to disappear behind the Colesbrooke skyline, the breeze brought a new scent, the sting of stale death and sunscreen. Clara perked up, propping herself up with her elbows, and listened for footsteps.

She didn't have to wait long. Two sets of pounding steps grew louder until Thomas and Sean turned the corner down the path into the backyard and began slowing down.

Sean was trembling as he ran, and he refused to look at Clara when he stopped running. Thomas was right behind him, his own expression grim.

Dammit.

"Clara," Thomas said, steel in his voice as he stopped before her. "They still won't listen, and they're armed and ready. The entire pub is on lockdown, complex, too."

Sean couldn't hold in his anger any longer. "Lawrence is effed up. Going old school, according to Jericho. Packin' Bob's old Thomson machine gun, and Jericho got weird when we accused them of drive-by shootings. Lawrence's gonna be the next Ernest."

Clara wasn't sure there was a curse word that embodied the anger and frustration she felt.

"We couldn't get anyone to help us find Nelson, not even Jericho," Thomas said flatly. "And Nelson saved Jericho's life numerous times. But he's sticking with Lawrence, and Lawrence is set on eliminating every threat. He's going to pick off every werewolf he can."

"Aha!" Artemis' shout from her apartment startled Clara. She twitched, twisting to see around Sean.

The metal stairs rattled and Artemis appeared, her curly hair sticking to her face and bouncing with each heavy breath. She was holding a large paintball gun in one hand and a bulging water balloon in the other.

"It's finished," Artemis informed them as Penny followed her up the stairs. Clara wasn't sure how the paintball gun, let alone the water balloon, would help.

"Okay, but what did you finish?" Sean asked sourly, regarding the monstrosity in Artemis's hands with suspicion.

"Something that's going to give anyone that tries to mess with our friends second thoughts, no matter who or what they are." She tapped her creation. "I think I'm gonna call it the Glob Lobber. Or maybe the Problem Solver."

Penny groaned. "Go with the second one."

"Great. Nelson's missing, and my sister's lost her mind," Sean said bitterly.

Artemis threw the water balloon, and it splattered yellow paint between Sean's feet, covering his shoes.

Immediately Clara, Sean, and Thomas began to gag, each holding their hands to their faces and moving away from the splattered paint. The smell that had kept her from the apartment was destroying her senses in full force, making her lose control of the wolf.

"I've got more of that in some empty paintball shells I ordered to put holy water in, too. It's a brewed mixture of belladonna, wolfsbane, and garlic oil. I mixed in paint so we could see if it hit our target or now. That's what I was doing while you were out talking to people," Artemis said smugly.

To the heightened senses of the non-humans, the smell of the some paints was enough to make their eyes water. Clara was suffering between a mix of coughing and gagging while trying to fight back the raging wolf inside. On her hands and knees in the grass, she couldn't concentrate enough to see if Sean and Thomas were still reacting.

"Great. If we need to make anyone smell worse than a skunk, we can count on you," Sean said, his voice sounding as if he were plugging his nose.

"It's not just that." Artemis cracked a wicked smile. "I've added a bit of silver sulfadiazine in all of them. It isn't much silver, but it was all I had on short notice."

"Silver?!" her brother cried out, taking an instinctive leap back from the paint.

"It's a cream that's sometimes used for burns," Thomas said. "I wonder if it's pure enough to actually cause some of us a problem."

224

"Oh, it is," Clara cried between gagging fits. "I can feel it from here."

Penny cleaned up the paint with a rag and ran it inside the apartment. The stink still remained even if it wasn't as strong, but the wolf was a bit more manageable. Clara could have kissed Penny.

"That was what I was hoping for," Artemis said. "We can get you a paintball gun, too, and then—"

"Whoa, whoa, whoa," Sean said, cutting off his sister. "You don't think you're actually joining us, right?"

"Hell yeah," Penny shouted as metal clanging announced her approach.

Artemis nodded vigorously. "Nelson is our friend, too."

"We're going up against werewolves," Sean warned. "We can't have you two tagging along. It's going to be hard enough keeping ourselves alive without throwing you gals in the mix."

Clara understood Artemis' and Penny's desires, but they were humans. Fragile. Sean and Thomas had a point, but maybe the gun could work.

Thomas sighed. "It might be safer if you two stayed here."

"No, it won't." Artemis said. "Werewolves don't have any trouble crossing thresholds. We'll be safer if we stick together. Besides, I have the Problem Solver, remember?"

"Yeah, I don't think that name's going to work for me," Penny said, frowning at the gun in Artemis's hands.

Sean rolled his eyes. "Seriously, Penny? Like that matters right now?"

"Calm down, Sean," Artemis said. "Things are bad enough without you freaking out."

"Calm down?" Sean cried, throwing his hands in the air. "Nelson could be dead. You want to throw yourself at raging werewolves. And you want me to calm down?"

Clara's phone buzzed, and she checked it as her coughing and gagging fit slowed. There was a text message from the Von Grimmel brothers. An address. She cleared her throat, though it really just sounded like more gagging.

"Whoever's coming along for the rescue, decide now because it's go time," she coughed. "The Von Grimmel brothers have found Nelson."

Without hesitating, Penny pulled her keys out of her pocket and stalked down the cement pathway. "I'll drive. And unless you want to hoof it, I suggest you all hurry up."

"We're going to get killed," Sean muttered as he offered his hand to Clara. "All of us."

She took his hand and pulled herself to her feet. "At least we'll be together."

****

Blazing lights illuminated the night streets as Penny navigated the metroplex maze. Neon business signs flashed, streetlamps burned wide beams into streets, white headlights blinded while reds glowed in a steady stream before them, and a hundred different windows of businesses, apartments, and houses illuminated the air. Yet as they drove, the lights dimmed, and as they reached the outer rim of the metroplex, there were dim or even darkened areas sucked away the life of the city.

The address that the Von Grimmel brothers had sent Clara was deep in a dark outskirt town at a lone squared spire of cement and brick atop an asphalt island, surrounded by a chain link fence that was more for show than any practical purpose. The warehouse had a realtor sign that, at one point, might have read the words "For Sale," but it had long ago been scrawled out with graffiti.

This entire property was nothing but a wasteland of a forgotten industry that had been streamlined by machines, now nothing more than the stomping grounds of things that polite and modern society liked to forget.

Clara hated it immediately, probably because she'd caught the raw and unclean scent of sweat and grime-covered clothing on the wind. It was the same sour scent of unwashed bodies she'd breathed in the Howler's tent camp.

"I don't see anyone," Sean whispered. "Are you sure this is the place?"

"The Howlers are definitely here." Clara crinkled her nose. "I can smell them. And if Nelson isn't here, well . . ."

Her fingers tingled as they teetered on the edge of transforming into claws.

". . . we can make the Howlers tell us where they are."

Sean laughed nervously. "Remind me never to piss you off once we survive this."

She smirked. "I do. You just never listen."

There was a crunch of gravel on asphalt. In a moment, Sean and Clara were joined by Thomas, who crouched alongside them as they all took cover behind a rusted-out bulldozer.

"Alright, Penny and Artemis are just down the street," Thomas said. "We can get Nelson to them, and they'll drive off while we take care of business here."

They hadn't wanted the noise of the car engine to alert any attentive werewolves, though Clara had thought the precaution was unnecessary as werewolves would smell the vampires easily.

"I don't like them being so close," Sean said, glancing over his shoulder. "I mean, what if a Howler comes up behind them?"

Thomas smiled. "Artemis already thought of that. She's popped a few of those paintballs open in the car. If anyone tries to get inside, they're going to be hacking up a lung."

Thank god they were upwind of the car. Clara didn't think she'd be able to concentrate through Artemis' foul paintballs.

Nodding, Sean took a deep breath and looked toward the warehouse. "We're going to hate the ride home. Let's do this."

With Clara in the lead, the three of them began to creep toward the warehouse, each moving as quickly and as quietly as possible.

Her heart pounded so hard in her chest it made her ears ring, but she couldn't calm it with deep breathing. Leon could be in the building, and she did *not* want to fight him. Though something told her he wasn't the type to sit around with some hostages. Leon was a man of action.

If he was inside, this was going to be more deadly than they'd planned on.

"If you were going to hold hostages, where would you hold them?" Sean whispered as the three of them drew into the shadow of the warehouse.

"Top floor," Thomas said, examining the three-story building. "They would have a longer way to run to get free."

"And anyone coming to the rescue would have a longer way to go to get to them," Clara agreed, looking up as well. "Or at least, a rescue mission would have to work from the ground floor up if they weren't . . ."

"Inhumanly strong?" Thomas finished as he took a few steps back, eying the wall of the warehouse.

The only windows in the warehouse were large square panes right below the roof itself, slanted slightly to let as much sunlight into the building as possible during work hours. With just a sheer wall nearly twenty feet high, it would have been a difficult climb for anyone to do it safely and quickly. At least, it would have been difficult for someone who wasn't suffering from either the lycanthropic or vampiric curse.

Thomas charged forward, kicking off a jutting brick and scurried up the wall and swung himself though a broken-out windowpane.

"Wait," he hissed.

His elbows poked in and out of the window, but at her angle, Clara couldn't see inside the building. Tension knotted in her shoulders. She didn't like waiting, and she wasn't sure she liked Thomas acting like he was in charge.

A makeshift rope of Thomas' coat, shirt, and belt flew out of the window. It dangled, thumping against the wall, and only reached about halfway down. Clara nearly rolled her eyes through her skull.

"Dammit," Thomas sighed.

Clara wanted to mocked him, but Sean fell into a crouch and then leapt straight into the air, kicking off of the wall and grasping the belt. He quickly scampered up into the window next to Thomas. His feet had barely hit the floor before Clara was in through the window after him.

She hadn't needed the rope.

"That was so cool," Sean said in wonder, marveling at his own hands. He hadn't tested his powers yet. "Why couldn't I have had this body in high school?"

Clara rolled her eyes. She would help him later figure out his strength after they'd saved Nelson and stopped the Howlers and Lightning Pub Vampires from destroying her pack and relationship. "Focus. I smelled at least one werewolf around here."

"Won't they be able to smell us, too?" Thomas asked as he pulled on his shirt.

"Yes," Clara said, making a face. "But they knew we were coming in the beginning. Nothing's changed."

The trio began to move toward the exit of the room. The top floor of the warehouse seemed to have been where the business had been taken care of, being designed like an office floor. Hallways, a few doors leading to offices, and a carpet that was more mold and dirt than fabric and fiber at this point.

While the dark didn't bother her, the musky scent of the old office and her still painfully accelerated pulse made Clara feel completely stripped of her senses. The wolf growled in agitation, demanding that she transform so she could hunt and track better than her ill-suited human form.

She was doing her best to focus on her surroundings and mentally block out her lycanthropic curse when Sean's hand shot out, grabbing her by the shoulder. She tensed as her boyfriend pulled her over through a doorway, the wolf howling at the surprise, and Thomas followed them.

It was only after they all froze in the darkness of another office space that Clara detected the sound of movement. The werewolf she'd smelled wasn't any closer, but the heavy mold and dust made it hard to know what species was approaching. She swallowed nervously, and the three of them spread out, preparing to pounce.

A shadowy figure passed in front of the doorway in the gloom. A human. Clara started to warn Thomas, but moving faster than a human eye could follow, he'd lunged forward and took hold of it.

The sudden shouting must have taken Thomas by surprise as he then caught an elbow to the eye.

Cursing, Thomas released the struggling figure, throwing up his hands. "Nelson, it's me."

"Thomas?" Nelson asked, equally confused.

Even if his eyes had been as well adjusted to the darkness as a vampire's, it was possible Nelson might not have been able to tell who Thomas was. His right eye was swollen completely shut and his shirt was covered in dried blood from a split lip and a broken nose.

"Nelson! Oh, man, are you okay?" Sean asked.

Nelson winced as he tried to stand. "Of course I'm not okay. I feel like ground beef. Probably look it, too."

"I'm so sorry," Clara blurted. "It's all my fault . . . I . . ."

"Hey, no worries, right?" Nelson said with the ghost of a smile. "If I didn't get caught up in your mess, it would have been one of Sean's."

"Hey!"

Nelson shrugged. "I already lived through the Thomas debacle."

"What about Gabby?" Thomas asked. "Did they get her too?"

"I never even made it to her," Nelson said, shaking his head.

"Alright, let's get out of here then," Thomas said, motioning Sean over to help him lift Nelson to his feet.

"Hurry," Clara hissed. "Their smell is getting stronger."

The wolf stench was heavy, and Clara wondered if there was more than one werewolf coming.

Sean groaned. "Yeah, let's not run into the crazed werewolves if we can help it."

"Oh, I'm afraid it's too late for that."

Spinning around, Thomas, Clara, and Sean found themselves looking at two very angry Howlers.

"Take a look at this, Clive. Ticks, humans, and a werewolf all workin' together like one big, happy family," a Howler with a green mohawk chuckled. "No wonder the others got all done in. This entire city is workin' against us."

A grizzled-looking man turned his head and spat out the toothpick he'd been chewing on.

"That true, lil' lady?" Clive asked. "You helping these ticks? Or do you just like playing with your food before you eat it?"

Sean and Thomas tensed, both about to make a move, but Clara placed a hand on each of their shoulders, stepping forward. She blinked and her eyes became golden discs that nearly lit up the gloom as her fingernails twisted into blackened claws.

"Oh, I'm done playing," Clara growled at the Howlers as she tossed aside her jacket and removed her shoes. "In fact, I think I'm going to get some work in by taking care of some strays."

18 JOINING FORCES

The sound of cloth tearing could not blot out the terrible sound of bones re-sculpting themselves, joints popping to accommodate a new skeletal structure and flesh being warped in ways that nature had never intended.

As Clara finished transforming, she began growling, adding her own guttural warnings to the thunderous growls of the other two fully transformed werewolves. The floor vibrated beneath her paws, and for once the wolf inside didn't fight for control.

Just as they had been in their human form, both Clive and Mohawk retained their brutish, large forms as werewolves. Both stood larger than any prized mastiff, with claws like curled knives and spittle-soaked fangs, and there was a disconcerting gleam in their eyes that spoke of a wild and savage hunger.

That wasn't to say that Clara wasn't impressive in her own lupine form. Where the Howlers were bulky and fierce looking, more akin to junkyard dogs who'd been allowed to feed and indulge in their aggressiveness, Clara was sleek and possessed the grace, even majesty, of a true apex predator who had realized long ago there was more to being a successful hunter than just a hard bite. Her golden eyes gleamed with both an animalistic brutality and human-like intelligence—both her bestial and human form were working in perfect concert to ensure they would make it out of this fight alive.

With a lifetime of violence behind them and a lycanthropic curse assuring them that this fight would end in victory, Mohawk and Clive both roared as they charged forward, their heavy claws scarring the flooring as they set upon their target like the dogs they were.

"Clara," Sean shouted, snapping out of his stupor.

The moment the two Howlers had opened their fang-filled maws to roar, Clara lowered her center of gravity and fell into a crouch, her sleek, yet deceptively powerful, muscles tensing. Both Clive and Mohawk had barely gone three paces forward when she launched herself through the air with all the speed, power, and precision of a warrior's spear.

As she sailed over the two surprised Howlers, Clara bit one of their backs and twisted her body in midair, rotating in almost a lazy motion so her hindquarters swung about. She released the matt of fur and flesh from her jaw and landed facing the two werewolves she'd just leaped over, immediately coiling up to spring once more.

The two Howlers scrambled to turn around to face their opponent, foolishly playing right into Clara's plan.

The moment Mohawk turned, Clara lunged again. This time right at her opponent, slamming into his side, her claws finding purchase on his ribs and her teeth sinking into the back of his neck like ivory daggers.

A roar of surprise, agony, and sheer fury erupted from the injured Howler, who immediately tried to shake off his attacker. Clara held on firm. Her fangs sank in deeper as her claws began to work furiously, gouging out great swaths of fur and flesh from her opponent's side. Panicking, Mohawk began to thrash about, doing everything he could to dislodge her incredibly powerful fangs from the back of his neck.

As Clara hung on, she heard Clive howl. She eyed him, watching him prepare to spring forward and join the fray. She needed to finish Mohawk quickly before Clive took her out.

Then Clive slammed into the ground from a blow to his back, accompanied by the sound of splintering wood. He issued a low growl and started to scramble back to his paws.

"That was supposed to be more effective," Sean said meekly, the ruins of an old chair crumbling in his hands.

No. Clara would not let Clive kill Sean. She dug deeper into Mohawk, ripping more flesh from his body. But he wouldn't go down.

Clive turned and reared back opening its massive jaw as wide as possible, towering over his would-be snack as if he were looking to remove Sean's head in a single bite. Clara started to let go of Mohawk, but Thomas slammed his shoulder into Clive's chest with enough force to collapse the werewolf's ribs.

Thomas could hold his own, and Clara hardened her bite to keep hold of Mohawk.

Unfortunately, Thomas' shove sent Clive flying into Nelson, and the force of the hit sent the weaker human stumbling backwards. With a sickening crunch, he landed on top of a desk before falling to the floor.

"Nelson!" Sean and Thomas's voices rang out as one. Clara growled but kept hold of Mohawk. They seemed at a stalemate, but she knew she couldn't let go. Thomas and Sean were going to have to handle Clive on their own.

"Sean, get Nelson," Thomas shouted.

"No, wait, if we both hit him, maybe he'll stay down longer."

"Sean—"

"No time! I'm going in! Follow me!"

There was a mix of howling, scratching, and shouting, but Mohawk had spun Clara around and she couldn't see the other fight anymore. Instead, she focused on keeping hold of her purchase as her hindlegs swung with Mohawk's jerking turns. Dammit, he wasn't going to throw her off.

Someone crashed into the wall, and the layer of dust shook and stung Clara's nose. Mohawk was howling now, trying to snap at her over his shoulder. She had to scramble her back paws to keep her side and hindquarters out of his reach.

"Nice," Sean crowed in delight.

"Don't celebrate just yet," Thomas said grimly. "Come on, we need to get Nelson out."

Clive must have been down. Her jaws ached, and she needed to release Mohawk to be able to run another attack. She was more willing to let go now that there was only one werewolf standing, only one left to attack Sean.

She released Mohawk, and he tumbled from her jaws into the wall as she was no longer pulling against his strength. Before he could stand straight, she rammed him again. Bones cracked, and Mohawk released an earsplitting roar.

She'd broken his leg. Stepping back, she surveyed the damage. Mohawk whimpered as he reared back and released another low howl that was so primal it raised her hackles.

The fight was dragging on for too long. The wolf inside of her was slowly gaining ground, its delight making it forget it needed to work with her human mind. It craved more control with every passing second, and if she didn't end this fast, she might lose it.

Mohawk lunged forward, jaws snapping. The look in his eyes was wild and fierce, and Clara was momentarily cowed by his ferocity, but the wolf within reared its head, pushing her toward her opponent.

She hadn't reached him before his howl turned into a wet, horrid gurgle as a jagged piece of wood nearly a foot long lodged in his throat.

Mohawk's entire body began to convulse as he frantically clawed at the projectile that was now piercing both the front and the back of his throat. The intensity of the pain was enough to drive the wolf within back, the lycanthropic part of his psyche instinctively fleeing the pain and allowing the human half of the mind to suffer.

Soon the werewolf was reduced to nothing but a filthy, naked man, weakly grasping at a wooden spike that was too slick with blood to pull free.

Whoever had wielded the wood, Sean or Thomas, had good aim. Clara changed back into her human form before her wolf and grabbed another piece of the chair. Her body only had a few angry red scratches on it, and those were quickly fading as her regeneration was kicked into overdrive.

Clive was wheezing by the wall where he'd fallen. Clara watched the two Howlers without sympathy, deciding if she needed to stab them another time or not.

"If you boys are done playing, I think it's time for us to go," Clara said as she moved toward Mohawk, who had managed to finally get a solid grip on the wooden spike in his throat.

"Yeah, I think we're done here," Sean said as he watched the horrifying performance that was Clive's body trying to mend lethal levels of spinal injury. If Sean was going to be a supernatural being, he'd have to get used to heavy gore quickly.

"Good. Sean, could you be a sweetie and fetch me my jacket and shoes?" Clara asked in a calm and collected voice as she stood in front of Mohawk.

Issuing another gurgling growl, the Howler began to tug the wooden spike free from his throat, staring daggers at Clara as she locked eyes with him.

Raising the wooden chair leg, Clara drove it down, right behind Mohawk's right collarbone.

"Sure, okay." Sean stumbled over to the window and grabbed her jacket.

The light jacket did little to cover her, but she slipped it on anyway and reached into the inside pocket. She kept neatly bundled leggings in all her jackets just in case.

As Mohawk writhed on the ground, Clara casually slipped on her pants and zipped up her jacket, giving her enough cover to at least avoid a ticket for public indecency.

"We should hurry," Thomas warned. "I can't do much more for Nelson's arm in here."

Clara nodded and tucked her hands into her pocket after slipping on her shoes. Her fingers brushed against a cold chain, and she remembered the pendant. When she withdrew it, the wolf grew excited at her ache for revenge.

Raising a foot, she stomped down on Mohawk's chest, pinning him to the floor.

"Listen here and listen good, Howler," she said, her eyes becoming just as gold as Sara Foxe's pendant. "Tell Leon he came to the wrong city. If the vampires don't put a silver bullet between his eyes first, my pack will find him and give him a much slower death."

"My, my, Clara. I thought I told you to come alone."

Clara froze. Leon.

As she turned, Clara saw the Howler's Alpha wasn't the only new arrival. Other forms were lurking in the dark of the warehouse, waiting on tenterhooks for one word from their leader.

"Leon," Clara said stiffly. "You were quick."

"You didn't think it would be so easy to walk out, did you?" Leon asked, tilting his head to the side. He glanced down at Mohawk and Clive dispassionately. "You've been hurting my family, I see. You know how I feel about that, Clara. I'm afraid this will require some disciplining."

Sean's cold hand slip into hers. Unfortunately, Leon had noticed.

"And who is this?" he asked, looking Sean up and down. "Your affection toward your meal is a little unusual. Or are these ticks the pack you've been hiding? Is this what you meant by being a lone wolf?"

Clara glanced briefly at Sean. His face was pale and his hand was growing clammy. Thomas was standing guard over Nelson, looking fierce.

"Why do you think I have a pack?" Clara asked. Her eyes scanned the warehouse.

There were almost fifteen Howlers now and no clear exits. They were going to have to jump. She wasn't sure Nelson would be able to handle it.

"I'm not stupid, Clara," Leon said.

He walked toward her, eyes fixed on the pendant in her hand.

"You were running with a whole pack the first night I saw you. I wasn't sure you belonged to them at the time, but now I'm convinced of it. But to think you are in with the ticks, too," Leon shook his head in wonderment. "You amaze me."

"Yeah, you're pretty amazing yourself," Sean muttered.

Leon turned his gaze toward the vampire, a steely look in his eye.

"I wonder how long you can keep this up, Clara," Leon said without looking away from Sean. "I doubt a relationship between a vampire and a werewolf could last. If you don't want to be the one burdened with his death, I could help you out."

Clara growled and stepped between Sean and Leon.

"Touch him, and I will end you," she snarled.

Leon tore his gaze away from Sean.

"A compelling argument," he said coolly. "But you see, you've lied to me, made a fool of me, and now you've hurt my family. I'd like to return the favor."

As one, the Howlers began to close the circle around them. Even though they were all still in their human forms, their teeth were bared and saliva dripped from their mouths. Clara tensed. She would have to transform again. So much for this pair of leggings and shoes.

"Get ready to run on my count," Clara said under her breath.

"Wait," Thomas replied, his voice barely audible.

"One."

"I said wait. Someone's coming."

"Two—"

Clara stopped. Now she could hear the footsteps, too. Someone was approaching. The reek of the Howlers was masking their smell. She wasn't sure who or what they might be. She and Thomas exchanged wary glances. It was about to get complicated.

"Well, well, this is a fine mess you've gotten your mug into, ain't it, kid?"

Clara was sure her heart had stopped. As she watched, Lawrence Foxe emerged from the gloom, along with Eternal Jericho. They were followed by one or two of the other vampires from the Red Lightning Pub and behind them was—

"Benjamin!"

She couldn't help but cry out when she saw her brother, followed by any of the local pack who was still in town. Donald was there, as were Deva, the Von Grimmel brothers, and Chelsea.

"How are you—? Why are you—?"

"I was worried about you abandoning Izzy's car," Benjamin said, overtaking Lawrence with ease and striding casually through the circle of werewolves. "Looks like I was right to be worried."

240

"Now, as I recall, you were sayin' somethin' real interestin' about family just now, weren't you, mutt?" Lawrence said, walking up to Leon.

"Yeah, something about hurting ours?" Donald added, joining Lawrence in front of the Alpha of the Howlers.

Leon smiled. "The leaders of the packs, I presume?"

"You presume nothin' but my foot up your ass," Lawrence growled, leaning in close. "Jericho? You said those mongrels with Sean's girlfriend ain't among the ones who attacked my Sara. What about these scumbags?"

Jericho stared Leon down and nodded.

Lawrence broke into a nasty smile.

"Well then, I'd say we have a problem."

19 FOR SARA

Clara's mind was reeling. How and why Donald and Lawrence had shown up together was beyond her. Even now with both of them staring down the same opponent, the tension was thick enough to cut.

Jericho and Benjamin joined Clara, both ignoring their leaders.

"Are you ok?" Benjamin asked Clara, recognizing her spare clothing.

Clara nodded. "But, how?"

"The Von Grimmel brothers," Benjamin said, answering her question before she could finish it. "They weren't comfortable with what you were doing. They rounded us up."

"And you?" Thomas asked Jericho.

Jericho shrugged. His lopsided arms made the gesture almost comical, but none of them felt like laughing. "Like you said. I owe you and Nelson my life. Lawrence knew that, too. Just took some reminding."

Thomas smiled at the giant vampire. "You're a brave man."

"Yeah, but how'd you get Lawrence to leave Clara's pack alone?" Sean asked.

"They're not the killers," Jericho said simply.

"Where's Bob?" Thomas asked.

"Out back. He's instructin' your human friends."

"What?" Thomas and Sean said together.

Jericho shrugged again. "We're gonna need all the help we can get."

Across the room, Leon shrugged on his jacket, which jingled with all of the trophies from his past kills. Boyd wasn't that far off, looking more glum than usual as he chewed noisily.

Other than the leaders, the Howlers were in a frantic motion around the warehouse, having lost their bravado when Donald and Lawrence showed up.

Lawrence didn't take his eyes off of Leon as he spat on the floor. "Well then, should we get down to business?"

****

A bright quarter moon illuminated the night, a few stars glistening despite the distant metroplex lights. Boston Bob perched atop a neighboring store from the warehouse where Nelson was kept, and he pointed at the dark building as he explained tactics to Penny, who eagerly listened. She was excited to help—she hadn't been a fan of being dead weight during the vampire turf war.

"And tell them to concentrate fire, got it? Once their job to put down a wolf is complete, we'll put a silver round in them to keep them from getting back up again," Boston Bob said. "And reload in turns. Blast both barrels, then sidestep to reload as your friend takes the ledge."

"Got it," Penny said, taking the rifle from the massive vampire.

Crouching low, she watched the building and hoped no one saw her. She was supposed to be the surprise backup, which she was fine with. She'd rather shoot at the enemy than tussle with werewolf or vampire.

Artemis should be back by now. She'd ran downstairs to grab a box of smelly water balloons from the car's trunk.

"I hope these mutts can fight half as good as they say," Boston Bob grumbled. "Otherwise this might get messy."

"Trust me, their abilities will surprise you," Penny said. She hadn't seen them fight, but Clara had been confident. And if werewolves were designed to take down vampires, they should do okay against other werewolves. She hoped. "And speaking of trust, how much faith do you have in Lawrence to let him go inside like that? I'm not so sure he's going to draw them out like he's supposed to. He's a bit unstable right now."

Boston Bob shook his head. "It wasn't my call."

Penny sighed, adjusting her ponytail to ensure it kept her hair out of her face. "This isn't going to go well. I can feel it."

"Cheer up, Pen," Artemis said as she emerged from the roof access, the small box in her arms brimming with water balloons. "It'll be fine. Thomas and Clara will take care of things on their end. And Sean's there, too!"

Penny snickered. "That's a lot of confidence you've got in your brother there."

"Sean's always been physical and strong. He'll enjoy his vampire strength, I think. Plus, I've still got the Glob Lobber and its companion water balloons," Artemis said brightly.

"Glob Lobber?" Bob asked, wrinkling his nose.

"That name isn't any better," Penny rolled her eyes.

"I don't know." Artemis set down the box, the balloons jiggling, and picked up the paintball gun affectionately. "I thought it gave it character."

"Just keep your eyes forward," Boston Bob sighed. "This bad egg is going to break wide open any second now."

"Just trying to lighten the mood," Penny said, aiming the rifle. It'd been a while since she handled a weapon. Her dad was a hunting fan, and she'd kept a gifted shotgun locked away at her apartment since she'd left for college. It was still there, untouched and probably needing to be cleaned after years of disuse. Hopefully she could shoot half as well as she could back in high school. She was going to need her old aim.

****

No one moved inside the warehouse. The howlers had calmed, picking up on the dangerous aura emitted by the others, and Lawrence and Donald were still glaring into Leon's face.

"A problem, you say?" Leon asked, lazily taking in Lawrence's dapper appearance and jaunty hat. "The only problem I see is a pack of ticks who've gotten ahead of themselves. Don't forget where you fall in this world."

"You there, werewolf," Lawrence snapped at Clara without taking his eyes off of Leon. "Where'd you get that pendant?"

Clara's grip tightened on the pendant. She'd forgotten how sharp a vampire's sight was.

"She stole it from my jacket, the little thief," Leon said before Clara could answer.

He met Clara's gaze with the intensity of a volcano in his eyes. Despite the heat of his hatred, Clara could not help but feel cold. She shivered.

"I was looking for answers," Clara said.

"Looks like you got 'em," Lawrence growled.

"I'm sorry." Clara's voice was barely audible to her own ears, but she saw Lawrence's hand twitch as she spoke. He'd heard.

"Why were you wearing the pendant on your jacket?" Donald asked, his voice level.

Lawrence took a step forward, but Donald put his hand out to stop him.

"I always take trophies from worthy kills," Leon breathed. "Especially ones so beautiful."

An animal growl escaped Lawrence's throat, Donald's fist closed on the vampire's suit, his muscles bulging from the effort of holding the man back.

"Steady," Donald said quietly.

"Steady my ass," Lawrence snarled. "That man killed my wife."

"She was your wife?" Leon asked, his voice raising with interest. "Then by all means, let me help you join her."

Donald now had both his arms wrapped around Lawrence.

"Like I said," Donald grunted as he tried to keep Lawrence from leaping onto Leon's throat. "That's not how we do things here. Now I can give you a head start, but I can't hold the vampires back. You've killed one of their own and they are looking for revenge, but if you head toward the edge of town—"

"You think we want to leave?" Leon asked, his laugh sounding hollow. "After what you've done to my family? I don't think so. We like it here, don't we, Howlers?"

Fifteen howls ripped through the air, making Clara's blood run cold anew.

The smallest mistake now would result in an explosion.

"Now, come on," Donald said, still trying to bring reason back into the conversation. "You say you're keeping an eye out for your family, and so are we. You can't just come in here and make a mess of things and expect to get off without consequences."

"I'm not trying to avoid consequences," Leon replied. "By all means, attack us. You'd be a nice whetting stone for my pack's claws."

"Leon."

A wheezing voice cut through the air as the leaders of three supernatural factions stared each other down. Donald and Lawrence were momentarily distracted. They along with everyone else in the warehouse, save Leon, searched for the source of the voice.

Clara saw him first. Her heart twinged with guilt as her eyes fell upon the pitiful form of Mohawk crawling across the floor toward his alpha. He'd managed to dislodge the spike in his throat but had only loosened the one in his shoulder from the floor, freeing him enough to move. His throat was raw and oozing blood as his supernatural regeneration raced to heal him.

"Leon," Mohawk wheezed again. "Please. Help me."

Mohawk raised a trembling hand to tug ineffectively on the stake protruding from his shoulder.

"Ah," Leon said, lowering his gaze as Mohawk drew close enough to cling to his pant leg.

"Please, help me."

"Weren't you and Clive to watch the boy?" Leon asked.

The hairs on the back of her neck raised at the icy tone in Leon's voice. This wasn't going to end well.

"Come on, now," Lawrence sneered. "Why don't you help out your family? His whining is getting a bit pathetic."

Leon stared dispassionately at the man sniveling at his feet.

"He is pathetic, isn't he?"

Then, with a swift motion that made half the observers in the room jump, Leon lifted his foot and slammed it into the stake protruding from Mohawks's shoulder. The force of the kick drove the stake clean through his flesh, accompanied by a sickening crunch as it broke bone. Mohawk whimpered as he collapsed onto Leon's foot and was kicked backward.

The Howlers shrank away from Leon, wincing in fear. Donald had noticed. Clara could see the same look of dawning understanding that she'd experienced when she saw his treatment of the pack in the forest.

"Now, what were you saying?" Leon asked, turning back to Donald as if nothing had happened.

"You shouldn't have done that," Donald said quietly.

"You see what kinda scum he is?" Lawrence snarled. "Now take your filthy paws off of me, mutt, and let me kill that bastard."

Leon smiled in amusement. "Don't tell me I've offended you? Discipline is necessary in any family. You should know that very well. If an individual let's down the family, they have to be punished. Didn't the tick cut off his little protégées? So we understand each other."

Donald's face grew dark, and he didn't reply. Instead, he released his grip on Lawrence. The vampire leaped toward Leon, screaming at the top of his lungs. But before Lawrence could reach him, Leon was in his wolf form. The rest of the Howlers howled and followed suit.

"Clara!"

Clara sought Sean's face. His eyes were wide with terror, and his grip on her hand would have broken it had she been a human. He'd done okay with the first spat with Clive and Mohawk, but this was a battle.

With a swift flick of her wrist, she pulled free. No time for sentiment now.

The war had begun.

****

"I can't see a thing," Artemis complained, lowering her paintball gun. "It's so dark. What's going on in there?"

The repeated werewolf howling from inside the warehouse only increased her anxiety. Something was happening in there, but she didn't know what.

"The fighting's just started," Boston Bob replied, remaining focused.

"How are we supposed to snipe the werewolves if we can't see?" Penny grumbled.

"Just give them a minute," Bob said. "Lawrence will draw them out. We've lived through a lot of wars. This one will be no different."

Sure enough, as he spoke, a figure burst through the glass of an upstairs window. Within seconds, several more followed of their own accord. After them, more figures flooded through the lower level into the vast parking lot. Here, bathed in the sickly yellow light of the streetlamps, Penny could make out a few of the individuals. If only the lamps weren't so sparse.

"How are we supposed to tell which are our werewolves and which are the good guys?" Artemis asked, her voice quivering.

"Does it matter?" Bob asked.

Penny glared at him.

"Aren't you the one that was complaining about how little ammo we had to spare?" she snapped.

"Just watch for signals," Boston Bob said, ignoring Penny's question. "My pack will be pointing them out to you."

Artemis shifted as she edged to the ledge. "Seems a little shaky to me. I sure hope this works."

A loud whistle pierced the air.

"It will," Bob said and he fired off the first shot.

****

Clara was in wolf form again. She'd had never shifted this many times in one day, and it was taking its toll. The wolf's craving for blood was growing stronger with every beat of her heart, and the confusions of smell made it more anxious. With so many vampires and werewolves in close quarters, she could only differentiate the smell of someone if they were immediately in front of her nose. The adrenaline coursing through her veins wasn't helping either, and watching Lawrence throw Leon through the window had been enough of a thrill to intensity the wolf's bloodlust to a barely controllable level. It didn't help that the wolf naturally wanted to attack the vampires, and she had to keep careful tabs on who her target was.

Some of the fighters had chosen to follow Leon through the window, including a majority of the Howlers. But Clara had taken the stairs as a guard for Thomas as he carried Nelson, and the delay had her frothing at the mouth, just itching to sink her teeth into someone.

Her craving was satisfied as she rushed out of the warehouse into the night.

The wolf she'd bitten into howled and tried to throw her off, snapping. Clara clenched her jaw, holding on with all her might. The Howler swiped at her with its back legs and she felt its claws dig into her flank.

She let go in surprise. Without wasting a second, the Howler was upon her. Clara's lips peeled back in a snarl and she kicked at her opponent, throwing them off. She scrambled after it, aiming for the throat, and for the second time, her jaws met their target.

Blood pooled in Clara's mouth, making her feel dizzy from the pleasure. She had to focus. If she didn't fight to keep hold of the wolf, she would lose herself, endangering her friends.

With a ferocious yank, Clara ripped flesh from the wolf's throat, leaving it incapacitated as it tried to heal. Clara trotted back, chewing on her spoils. As she was backing away, a vampire approached the fallen wolf, exciting her wolf. The vampire placed two fingers in his mouth and whistled.

Clara watched him, her human curiosity momentarily winning out against her bloodlust. The vampire was waving at the building across the street and pointing at the Howler Clara had incapacitated.

A shot exploded from a neighboring roof and struck the Howler, the sting of burnt cordite burning her nose.

After a second whiff, Clara reeled backward. Fear and instinct from her inner wolf nearly overwhelmed her as she began to itch. It took every ounce of control she had to keep herself from running away.

That gun was firing silver.

Managing to contain her desire to flee, Clara turned to find another target. All around her, small groups were locked in fearsome combat. A small movement near the back of the crowd caught her eye. One of the Howlers had maintained her human form, and she was carting a box filled with red cylinders from the warehouse.

Clara sniffed the air. The presence of gunpowder hadn't been there earlier, and there was a strange mix of acrid chemicals she didn't recognize either. There was no time to find out. Clara raced toward the woman, who was reaching into the box and withdrawing the first of her weapons and a lighter. Clara increased her speed, pushed on by urgency. She couldn't let the woman light that thing. She couldn't.

The flame caught the end of the cylinder, and Clara watched in horror as the night was engulfed in flaming light.

****

"Flares," Boston Bob spat the word like a curse as he shielded his eyes. "They're trying to throw us off."

Werewolves howled in the distance as the ground burst with another flash or red. If the flares were blinding to Artemis, she couldn't imagine the pain they were bringing to the vampires and werewolves.

Another blast, but this time they missed it as they were still rubbing their eyes from the last one. Boston Bob grumbled a string of curses and tried to aim again, but he didn't squeeze the trigger. The smoke, lightning and commotion must have been too much.

"What are you doing? Why'd you stop?" Artemis asked.

"Might not look like much to you, but vampires have got sensitive eyes," Bob snapped, rubbing his eyes again. "I can't take aim like this."

"We've got to do something," Penny said as she concentrated through her scope. She wasn't firing either. "Isn't there anything we can do?"

"I'm thinking," Boston Bob said, pulling away from the edge.

There wasn't time for thinking. Artemis grabbed one of her water balloons and tossed it into the fray below. If the Howlers were using flares to confuse sight, she could use special smelling paint to confuse smell. Though with its small arc, she wasn't sure if the balloon had flown far enough.

Boston Bob rubbed his nose. "What's in those things?"

"A mixture that smells bad enough to confuse werewolves. I tried it at home and it worked," Artemis said.

"Good enough for me," Bob shouted and threw one himself. The arc was higher and the balloon flew faster. Vampires had better aim, or at least some did. Artemis smirked as she remembered how much Thomas hadn't improved at pool despite gaining better physical powers.

"Art," Penny asked. "Do you have more in the car?"

Artemis threw another one. "No, just these. I only had about a dozen balloons left from last summer."

"Then let's make these count!"

****

"What the hell," Benjamin shouted in frustration. He and the Von Grimmel brothers had momentarily shifted back to their human forms in the confusion produced by the sudden field of smoke and red light and were pressed up against the side of a van. "Why the hell'd they let off those flares? How the hell does that help anything? And who is throwing those awful paint bombs?"

Garlic, wolfsbane, and paint mixed in with the heavy smoke and burned his nose.

"They're blinding the vampires," Alban groaned. "So they can fight by scent and sound. I'm not sure who is messing with the scent though."

Benjamin growled. "That's not playing fair."

"No one ever said we had to play fair," Albert said, looking up at the car.

Alban smirked. "A bit much, don't you think?"

"Not at all," Albert said. "Time to shake up the battlefield, I think."

"Wanna let me in on the big plan?" Benjamin normally didn't mind being left out, but now lives were on the line.

"We'll need a couple of ticks," Alban said, ignoring Benjamin.

"I see a few. HEY!"

Benjamin watched in confusion as the Von Grimmel brothers flagged down two of the vampires and beckoned them toward the van. The vampires quickly sent the Howler they had been fighting flying into the chaos of the battle and trotted toward the three werewolves.

"You called?" one of the vampires asked, a jaunty grin plastered on his lips.

The Von Grimmel brothers nodded toward the van, and the vampires looked it up and down.

"What do you think, Thomas? Think we can do it?"

Thomas shrugged. "Let's give it a shot." Then, turning toward the werewolves he said, "You'll want to be out of the way when Sean and I get this thing in the air."

"We've gotta move fast. We've got Howlers at six o'clock."

Benjamin's heart leapt in his chest. "Sean? Sean Butler?"

But the Von Grimmel brothers were already dragging him away. All he could do was watch, as the vampire his sister loved picked up one side of a van and threw it into a small pack of approaching Howlers.

****

In his century-long life, and in all the battles he'd lived through during those many decades, Jericho had never doubted his own power. He knew his limits, both physical and mental. When he pushed those limits, he'd learned to catalogue his body's aches so he better understood how they might affect his performance. He'd learned how to respond when the vampiric part of his mind, the predatory part, thirsted for human blood. When you had lived as long as he had, all you had to do was remember past experience to know the outcome of your future.

That was why Jericho knew he was going to die.

More of the Howlers had fallen back to help the female hurling flares out onto the battlefield. The sharp light burned Jericho's eyes, and the smoke was so thick it swirled about like fog. He knew the flares must have been wreaking havoc on his opponents, too, but the werewolves' sense of smell was more powerful than his own and would be able to sift through the fog better. Not only that, they worked as a pack, each growl, yip, and bark acting as some sort of signal for the others.

That was the only explanation Jericho could come up with on how the Howlers were able to keep avoiding him. The tides had turned fast.

Jericho lunged forward, bringing his hatchet down on a lupine shape in the acrid fog only to find that the attack had done nothing but disturb the smoke. Experience told Jericho to expect a counterattack, so he spun on his heel after missing, swinging with a backhanded strike.

The attacking Howler already in midair in his blindside, committed to the attack, so it had no time dodge. It felt the full strength of Jericho's strike.

Bone crunched as the blunt back of the hatchet connected, and a pained whine filled the air.

Experience also told Jericho the blow he'd landed was nothing but a temporary inconvenience for the Howler. The werewolf's monstrous regenerative abilities would see it back in the fight in no time. Why werewolves had to heal faster than vampires, he didn't know.

Smoke swirled and Jericho heard the scraping of claws against pavement.

Experience told him that he needed to accept his fate, for it was too late for him to bring his weapon to bear against the other Howler attacking his blind spot. Still, he turned his head, determined to look his killer in the eye.

How fortunate for Jericho that experience was wrong.

A Howler's maw opened wide, looking to sink into his throat, and then another werewolf collided with the first in midair, sending both of them into a rolling tumble.

The local pack was making good on their temporary truce, the truce they formed to save the stray members of the Red Lightning Pub and their new werewolf friend. It had been confusing at first, but the longer he spent in the fight, the easier it was getting to distinguish who was who. With the exception of

Leon, who was still locked in combat with Lawrence, the Howlers were mangy and weedy. The members of the local pack, not so much. But, the smoke and flares were making it difficult again.

Jericho watched apprehensively the spot in the fog where the werewolves had disappeared. Any second now, one of them would reappear.

A wolf emerged from the fog, limping heavily on one foot. It was still growling, glaring at him with resigned aggression. Jericho raised his hatchet, but something made him hesitate.

A second wolf burst from the fog, jaws open wide. Jericho swung.

There was a wet crunch, a gurgled whine, and slowly the werewolf with the hatchet buried in its breastbone morphed back into a tattooed and grizzled human.

Definitely a Howler.

The werewolf who had saved him looked up, maw bloodied with the atrial spillage of the Howler it had fought and bowed its head low, as if in thanks.

Then the werewolf leapt back into the surrounding fog, still limping.

Jericho hurried to retrieve his hatchet, pulling it free. Everywhere he looked, there were shadowy figures of werewolves fighting werewolves.

This should have been unsettling, but experience told Jericho exactly what he needed to do.

He just needed to bury the axe into any werewolf that was going to try and take a bite out of him.

******

"You're doing great. Just great. Keep it up," Boston Bob muttered in Penny's ear. "Just get the ones on the edge like you've been doing."

Penny took another shot. She missed.

"No problem, just go again."

"How can you tell I missed?" Penny asked grumpily. "You can't even see through the flares."

"Experience, my dear. Now take the shot again."

Penny obeyed, and this time she made her mark.

"Well done."

Artemis was proud of Penny. Her best friend's aim was better than her own, so she was mostly watching the swirling smoke, looking for the right moment to throw one of her last water balloons. There were only three left, and she didn't know if she'd need them to disorient more Howlers later.

Glob Lopper was at her side, ready to fire. But since she couldn't see as well, she didn't want to misfire. Hitting one of Clara's pack on accident would be heartbreaking.

"Is there a trick I'm missing?" Artemis asked. She didn't like not doing anything, not when lives were in danger. "I can't see anything with the smoke."

"I'm just hitting the ones on the edge," Penny shrugged, raising her gun again.

She shot again. Another hit.

Penny flashed a small smile. She was enjoying this.

The smoke was starting to clear up in a few places, making it easier to see. Artemis readied Glob Lopper, looking for a good Howler target to smash with her smelly shells. She was going to need to make more of the mixture for the future, just in case.

A shaggy werewolf that looked almost boar-like due to its broad shoulders and stumpy tail caught a charging Howler by the back of the neck and shook him like a rag doll. After the broad werewolf discarded it for another foe, Artemis aimed at the Howler. It was still twitching, and she wanted it to stay down.

She fired. The kickback was minimal, and the paintball shell almost hit its target. The lack of recoil was worth the lack of aim precision, but the shell smelled bad enough she didn't need to hit her target. She just had to get close enough.

Penny fired, too, and clicked her tongue.

"You're pulling to the right," Boston Bob said. "You need to fix that."

"You're not even watching."

"Experience."

"The hell you know that from experience."

"Shit."

Artemis paused looking for another target and glanced at the vampire. He was cursing as he aimed his rifle at a target closer to the store. The roof was only one story up, but it was high enough that they were safe from the werewolves on the ground. Yet when Artemis looked for Boston Bob's target, she saw a frumpy werewolf crouching low and glaring at them.

Bob fired and swore. He'd missed as the werewolf leaped into the air, achieving a height Bob had assured wouldn't be possible, and landed on the ledge, its back legs dangling over the side and clawing at the mortar.

Boston Bob was aiming again, but he was also right in the werewolf's path. It was going to tear through him like a Thanksgiving turkey.

Clara grabbed one of the last three water balloons and chucked it at the werewolf. It smashed into its nose, splattering paint and the glob mixture she was proud of across its face and fur coat.

Immediately the powerful wolfsbane-mixed-with-paint smell overwhelmed both Bob and the werewolf.

The Howler let out a painful yip and shook its head furiously, as if trying to shake free the sticky mess mercilessly stinging it. The silver had been an excellent addition.

Boston Bob recovered first, his sense of smell not as strong as a werewolf's though still better than a human's. He lined up a shot and squeezed the trigger, putting the Howler out of its misery.

Penny scrambled to her feet and shoved the wolf corpse off of the roof.

"What exactly did you put in that?" Boston Bob shouted, wiping away tears.

"Wolfsbane. Garlic. Belladonna. Extra potent paint."

"You're a force to be reckoned with, kid," Bob said.

Another flare launched up in a lazy arc. Only one flare was being launched at a time now. It arced but did not gain the altitude a flare gun would have given it. These flares were also burning for an incredibly long time. Road flares?

"Here," Boston Bob said, handing Penny more silver bullets. "Load! Don't bother with the scope. Trust in your instincts. Artemis, keep firing your globs. Try to hit the werewolf throwing the flares."

They both obeyed.

Boston Bob manually lined Penny and Artemis' shots up for them and then took his place between them, raising his own rifle. "Wait for the glow. Wait for it . . ."

An orange–red glow fizzled to life in the shadow of the warehouse.

"Fire!"

As one, two rifles cracked, and the Glob Lobber hissed.

The glowing flare continued to sputter but it didn't get any higher. Instead, it dropped to the ground.

Presumably, so did the Howler who had been holding it.

Boston Bob smiled and clapped Penny on the back.

"See? You fix that right pull and your aim is on the nose."

Penny smiled back, looking pleased with herself.

"And Artemis, good work on that mixture. Any way we can order a supply from you?"

****

The very ground seemed to tremble with Leon's low growl. His gray fur blended perfectly with the fog-like smoke, making him seem more like some vengeful apparition than a massive wolf.

Undeterred, Lawrence stared into those golden lupine eyes as he raised his sawed-off shotgun and squeezed the trigger.

The discharge of gunpowder and the muzzle flash made the surrounding area light up in a manner Lawrence hadn't been expecting. In that split second of disorientating illumination, the Howlers' Alpha vanished. Since his ringing ears weren't detecting the pain-laced howling, Lawrence knew his shot had missed. He had to move.

Falling to a crouch, Lawrence sprang forward, right at the space that Leon had been occupying. It was the only place he could be certain he wouldn't run immediately into a set of fangs. Letting his momentum carry him into a roll, he came to a halt and raised his firearm, pointing right at the spot he'd just been standing.

His instincts were correct as powerful jaws snapped down in empty air and another frustrated growl rumbled through the gloom.

Lawrence had a clear shot.

Leon turned a glowing golden eye to the side, snarling at Lawrence just as the vampire squeezed the trigger.

Another bright flash, and Lawrence missed his target again. This was getting ridiculous.

Had he been interested in wasting his breath, Lawrence would have issued a curse that would have made a sailor blush. The fog was throwing off his aim. He'd aimed for the neck of the Howlers' Alpha, knowing it was the broadest target provided for him. Yet instead of catching muscle, his slug had just skimmed fur, leaving no more evidence of its passage than a swirl in the smoke.

His barrel was empty now. He would have to reload and he was out of silver slugs. All he had left was a single shell of buckshot dipped in low quality silver. It would be a miracle if he got a chance to actually load it.

Leon didn't miss a beat, as if he could sense his opponent's weakness. Flinging spittle, the alpha charged forward, snapping at his prey.

Lawrence called on all of his inhuman agility and was still just barely able to keep those wicked fangs from tearing into him. He sidestepped and pulled his right hand back in the same instant, and the wolf's fangs shredded the sleeve of his shirt instead of removing his hand. He jumped backwards to avoid another bite aimed for his knee.

His shoes had barely hit the ground before he narrowly avoided claws looking to shred his face.

He would never be able to reload like this. He needed a distraction.

As if answering his call, a small ball of what looked like paint burst open on the ground next to him. Leon tracked the ball's fall with his eyes, giving Lawrence the opportunity he needed to kick the beast away.

But before he could load, Lawrence smelled the rank odor he couldn't identify.

He wrinkled his nose.

"If that ain't the most demonic smell I've ever had the misfortune of happenin' upon," he muttered, stumbling away from the paint.

Leon must have had the same idea, for Lawrence ran into the stumbling wolf a few feet from where the paint had fallen, pawing at his nose.

"Well, well, well," Lawrence said, cracking a grin. "Looks like you got a nose full of that stench. Doesn't agree with you?"

Leon snarled and lunged at Lawrence, snapping. Lawrence cursed as he felt his weight suddenly shift as loose gravel gave way under his foot, throwing his balance off for just a heartbeat.

That heartbeat was all Leon needed. He opened his mouth wide and twisted his head to the side as he lunged forward, it was the perfect angle to rip out Lawrence's throat.

It was impossible to tell who was more surprised when a sleek werewolf emerged from the fog and slammed right into the Howlers' alpha, fangs biting down on the back of his neck.

Despite the undeniable power in the second werewolf's attack, Leon was simply too big to knock over. Worse yet, the incredibly dense muscle of the massive lycanthrope's neck provided ample protection to his delicate vertebrae, the target of the sleek werewolf's fangs.

Lawrence recovered immediately. Combining his speed and inhuman dexterity, he drew out the last silver ammunition he had, broke open the barrel from the stock, ejected the spent shells, and reloaded in the space of two heartbeats.

He lined up his shot. Since the buckshot had a spread, he could easily blast both werewolves at this range with silver, hopefully ending them both.

Lawrence hesitated.

He could hear Thomas's chiding voice. This new werewolf had saved his life. It would be a poor show indeed to repay it with buckshot.

Lawrence spat and raised his sawed-off shotgun, lining up both of the werewolves' heads down his barrel.

"Move, you stupid beast," he shouted.

Lawrence told himself that the only reason he gave the warning was because he knew that buckshot had plenty of stopping power but lacked the penetrating force of a slug. That meant if he wanted to put the Howlers' Alpha down, he would need as many silver-dipped bearings to strike him as possible.

He muttered under his breath. He knew he was lying to himself. That wasn't why he'd warned the mutt. If Thomas found out he'd shot at a wolf that saved his life, he'd never hear the end of it.

The sleek werewolf must have heard his shout, for it released its hold on Leon and shoved off the ground to move.

Too enraged by the attack of the lesser werewolf to even notice the vampire, Leon snarled and bit down on the werewolf's forepaw and yanked, whipping the sleek wolf around.

Lawrence had already squeezed the trigger.

The buckshot grouped nicely, nearly half a dozen silver pellets slamming right into Leon's face, shredding his muzzle. The seventh pellet ruptured his right eye. Amazingly, he was able to keep his feet for several more seconds, emitting one last snarl before collapsing and slowly transforming back into the large human form of Leon.

The sleek werewolf wasn't as resilient.

A single pellet of silver went wide, and with its paw in the jaws of the Howler, the second wolf hadn't been able to pull free. The silver slammed right into its ribs, breaking skin and piercing flesh.

Lawrence watched in horror as the sleek werewolf stumbled into the fog, slowly shifting back into the lithe figure of a young woman.

He didn't even have time to shout a warning before another lupine figure emerged from the fog and slammed into her.

20 THE SILVER BULLET

A warning rang above the shouts and howls of the battle as Clara tugged at Leon's neck with her jaws. Instinct took over as she released him and dove away. He was too massive to take down, and she needed a better angle anyway. Moments before she could get clear, she felt Leon's fangs rip into her flesh, applying enough force to cause her bones to crack as he tugged on her foreleg and swung her back.

That pain was bliss compared to the agony she felt now.

Her mind had barely registered the impact of something slamming into her torso, something so small it couldn't possibly compare to the pain of the fangs sunk deep into her wrist. That all changed as soon as that same, small object broke the skin.

The pain was so pure it could rival the silver now poisoning her veins. It left her mind reeling and her body convulsing. Instinctively trying to shy away from the pain, the wolf within withdrew from Clara's psyche, banished by the hurt and sent to the furthest and darkest parts of her mind, transforming her back into a human.

More out of instinct than reason, Clara found herself trying to move, as if this kind of suffering was something she could crawl away from, despite knowing full well that it was pointless. She was as good as dead.

What was she going to tell Sean? She'd done everything she could so they could stay together and to protect her pack. But as white hot needles of agony continued to spread from her chest, she quickly forgot her regret and wanted nothing more than to die and be spared from her torture.

Clara felt herself lurch and for a moment, she was confused as to how she could be falling sideways for such a distance. Nothing was making sense. Only after she hit the ground did she realize she hadn't fallen but had been tackled by something big.

So this was the end. Ripped to shreds by a werewolf while silver stopped her lycanthropic regeneration.

****

"Clara! Clara!"

Benjamin was screaming himself hoarse over the limp form of his sister. He'd changed in mid-leap back to his human form, scooping Clara in his arms and carrying her as fast as his human legs could carry him away from the battle.

But it was pointless.

Clara was on the ground, bleeding from a wound in her side, each one of her gurgling breaths forcing more of her lifeblood from the wound. Already an ugly bruise was spreading across her ribcage, a spider web of green, black, and blue hues visible even on her dark skin. Her body was being poisoned and destroyed by the silver lodged inside her flesh.

Hands trembling, Benjamin tried remove the bullet, but his joints locked up and his mind reeled so suddenly it made him dizzy.

The wolf inside was roaring in instinctive fury and fear for Benjamin to stop. He fought his lycanthropic nature and again, tried to force his unsteady hands so he could save the life of the only family he had left.

The wolf would have none of it. Here before him was the monster's one weakness, and the wolf was nothing if not good at protecting itself.

Try as he might, Benjamin couldn't even fight for enough control to put his hands on the wound to staunch the bleeding.

"Clara?!"

Benjamin snarled, turning away from his injured sister, his eyes glowing gold as his fingers twisted into dangerous claws.

If Sean had noticed Benjamin's dangerous posture, he didn't show it or didn't really care as he ran over to Clara's side.

"I—I saw from the back of the lot. I—what do we do?"

Benjamin's heart leapt as he saw a single ray of hope shining through the gloom.

"Silver. A silver bullet. In her ribs. Take it out," he yelled, forcing out the words as quickly as he could.

"But I'm not a doctor . . ." Sean said in a distracted sort of way and looked back down the street. "I'll get Thomas . . ."

Benjamin grabbed Sean by the shoulder, forcing him to his knees beside Clara.

"A silver bullet can kill a werewolf in sixty seconds," Benjamin seethed. "Get it out of her *now!* I can't touch it."

Sean's hands trembled as they hovered above Clara's heaving chest.

"If you don't do this, Clara will die!"

****

Heart hammering in his chest, Sean inhaled sharply and his pupils narrowed. He pulled back a hand and raised it high, letting his vampire senses come to the forefront of his mind. He'd never done this before, had never called purposefully on his curse, but it came easier than he'd expected. It was like it was waiting for him to rely on it.

He could see it now, the way Clara's body moved, the location of the bruising. He could hear as well, the sound of her leaking side. The bullet was lodged in her lung. Sean swallowed nervously.

What if he pulled out the bullet only to rupture a lung? Could she heal from that? What if her regenerative properties were suppressed or . . .

"Sean," Benjamin cried.

Sean sucked in a breath and gritted his teeth. No time for doubts. His hand became a blur.

Clara let out a scream that made Sean flinch.

"I'm sorry, babe. I'm sorry, just hold on."

His fingertips pushed through the wound in her side, digging deep. His stomach churned at the feeling of wet flesh and warm blood. This was Thomas' specialty, not his. What if he couldn't find the bullet? A sudden burn singed his fingertips, as if he was touching a hot stove. That must have been the silver bullet. It stung, but it wasn't lethal on contact.

He gritted his teeth, his index and middle finger taking hold of the silver bullet between them. He tugged as hard as he dared, pulling out the silver-coated projectile. As his hand exited the wound, blood spurted out, creating a pool where Clara lay.

Sean dropped the silver bullet immediately. Ripping off his shirt, he pressed it into her bleeding hole.

Clara gasped, trembling, still in agony. But the bruise spreading across her body had stopped. He couldn't tell, but he hoped it might even begin to recede as her regenerative lycanthropic nature returned.

But he just didn't know.

Instead, Sean kept putting pressure on her chest, mumbling wordless comforts as she shivered and twitched.

Benjamin leapt from the ground, issuing a low growl. By the time his feet landed, he'd phased into a werewolf and shot back into the fray. Fear shivered over Sean as he realized how powerful Clara's brother was, how powerful she was.

With her death, none of the Howlers would escape that night.

****

With the flares no longer being hurled out into the battlefield the smokescreen began to fade. Artemis set down Glob Lopper and sighed. Her arms were sore and she was out of water balloons.

The battlefield was utter chaos, werewolves tearing at one another, their savagery only matched by their ability to heal even the most grievous wounds with horrifying speed. A few vampires still fought to change the tide, but some Howlers were keeping them separated from the main fight. The battle was in a deadlock.

It was impossible to tell friend from foe, and therefore impossible to pick a target.

Boston Bob twitched next to her, his eyes steady on the battlefield. He could easily turn the tide of this whole fight, but he probably didn't know who to shoot, either. Even Penny had complained, setting down her rifle and rubbing her shoulders.

In the middle of the blood-soaked grounds, one werewolf was being torn apart, piece by piece, by two others who appeared to be identical copies of the same beast. The two werewolves tore at their target in perfect unison, one lunging forward to claw or bite, and as soon as the victim turned to retaliate, the other one would attack its blindside.

"Miserable little curs," Boston Bob growled, raising his rifle and taking aim.

"Wait," Penny said. "They could be on our side."

"They're just mongrels," Boston Bob said, something in his voice wavering as if he was uncertain. Did that mean he was feeling for the Colesbrooke werewolf pack?

"The kid is right."

Artemis spun around, grabbing for Glob Lopper. Lawrence clambered over the far edge of the roof. There was a low grunt and a fist clutching a bloodied hatchet cleared the rooftop. A moment later, Eternal Jericho pulled his massive bulk onto the roof as well.

Boston Bob lowered his rifle. "If you want to have a werewolf-free city, now is the time to do it."

No. Artemis held up Glob Lopper, aiming it at Boston Bob. She knew he could kill her, but she wasn't going to let them destroy all Sean and Clara were working for.

"You can't," she shouted.

Penny spun her rifle around, too, and aimed at Lawrence. "If you tell Bob to shoot, I'll shoot first."

Lawrence shook his head and then held something up.

In his hand was a golden pendant.

"No. It's time to wake up, I reckon. All this was . . . all this was done by outsiders," he spat. "Sara kept the peace, fought for Colesbrooke, and right now, those mongr—werewolves—are fighting for the very same thing."

Penny and Artemis glanced at each other as they lowered their weapons. Perhaps Thomas had been right to trust his mentor after all, though Artemis still felt weary.

Boston Bob didn't look convinced. He stared down at the battlefield where the ferocious battle was still raging.

"It's impossible to tell who's winning," Bob said. "If these werewolves on our side don't pull this off, we could get butchered easily."

"That won't happen," Artemis said with more confidence then she felt.

Boston Bob gave her a doubtful look.

"Again, the kid is right," Lawrence said with a bitter smile. "I just filled their Alpha with silver buckshot."

****

Pain throbbed in unison with Clara's slow heartbeat. Each throb made her temples ache as if a hammer was slamming into them in a steady rhythm.

She released a whimper, which only reminded her that she was incredibly thirsty. Her wordless sounds had scratched against her parched throat like sandpaper, and she coughed reflexively, which reinvigorated the pounding in her temples.

The tears welled in her eyes from coughing made it a little easier for them to open, and when she did, her watery, blurred vision found nothing but gloom. After a moment her eyes adjusted enough to spot a glass of water next to her, resting on a nightstand.

The initial confusion of where she was or how she came here was washed away by her body's desperate need for that water.

Her hand felt as if it weighed as much as a cannonball and was just as nimble. The effort of lifting her arm made beads of sweat break out across her forehead, and her clumsy grab for the glass of water resulted in her knuckles slamming against it, sending it clattering to the ground.

The glass shattered, and she nearly shrieked from the sharp ringing in her ears.

"Clara?"

The voice was soft and gentle, if a little urgent.

The sound of her name acted like a mental trigger, and Clara suddenly found herself drowning in a chaotic flood of memories, each so potent that the anxiety and urgency she'd been experiencing in those moments rushed back to her.

The battle!

The Howlers were everywhere. Acrid fog burned the nose and stung the eyes. Wafts of vampires and werewolves mixed with Artemis' nasty paint bombs. Leon! His fangs had sunk into her wrist and then the artificial thunder of gunpowder and . . . and . . .

Silver. Silver had pierced her. It was rotting her flesh, turning her blood into poison.

"Clara!"

The voice sounded alarmed and was much closer as Clara began to flail, panic seizing her as she tried to find the strength to sit up and tear the silver from her body with her own hands.

Large hands felt cool against the fevered skin on her bare shoulders. She could finally make out a face of the person calling her name.

Sean's deathly features were etched with concern.

"Sean?" she croaked.

"It's me," Sean said, his face relaxing as he fell to a knee beside her. "I'm here."

Her boyfriend reached over to the nightstand and grabbed something. Weakly she turned her head to see he'd put his hand in a bowl and withdraw a wet washcloth.

Clara's hands shot out, ignoring the cloth and grabbing the bowl. Sean helped her sit up awkwardly and drink as much water as she could from the bowl, anything to soothe her throat.

In her haste, she spilled a lot of water down her chin and onto the sheet wrapped around her, but she still didn't stop until the bowl was completely empty. Then she collapsed back down onto the mattress.

"I take it that means you're feeling a bit better," Sean said with a wan smile.

It took her several heartbeats to find the energy to speak. "What happened?"

He picked up the wet washcloth and dabbed at her forehead. She must be running a fever. For a moment the washcloth felt cool, and then the next, it felt warm.

"How about we start with the good news? We won. We put them down for good. Thanks to you, we managed to take down their Alpha and a good chunk of the others. Only one or two gave us the slip, but I doubt they'll stop running until they hit the ocean, and even then, they'll start swimming for safety." Sean delicately wiped the beads of sweat from her brow.

Clara wheezed. "The . . . bad news . . . is?"

Sean swallowed nervously.

"That all happened three days ago. You caught a piece of silver buckshot when you were fighting with Leon. It's been touch and go for a while, and you've been fading in and out of consciousness for nearly seventy-five hours. This is about the third time I've explained this."

He smiled sadly and then brushed his fingers through her hair.

"I don't mind."

Clara tried to smile, but she couldn't really feel much of anything other than her pounding headache, so she wasn't sure if she managed the right expression.

"I must be some sort of werecat."

"Werecat?" Sean asked, frowning.

"Because I've got nine lives." Clara's weak laughed was more of a whimper. "No way could I have survived a silver bullet as a werewolf."

A shadow of emotion flitted across Sean's face and he cleared his throat nervously.

"Well, about that . . . see . . ." Sean's brow furrowed in concentration, as if he was having a hard time trying to select the right words.

"Oh, god. If you tell me you turned me into a vampire . . ." Clara moaned, closing her eyes.

"No, no, no. It's nothing like that," Sean assured her, waving his hands as if to clear away the misunderstanding. "I don't even know if that's possible. Is that possible?"

"Sean."

"Right. I was the one who had to pull out the silver," Sean said. "Benjamin couldn't touch it."

Clara nodded. Of course Benjamin hadn't been able to touch it.

"And . . . and Thomas wasn't around . . ." Sean continued. An emotion Clara didn't recognize stained his voice. "I must have done something wrong because you're not healing like you need to. The silver isn't a problem, but it's slowed down your regeneration and there's an infection and you're . . ."

Putting on a brave smile, Clara managed to lift her hand and touch Sean's face.

"I'm alive because of you," she whispered. "You saved me, Sean."

"But you're sick and it's my fault. If only I had . . ."

"I'm going to be fine." She closed her eyes. "I'm going to be fine, Sean . . . don't . . . you . . . worry . . ."

"Yeah, I'll do my best," Sean said, trying to steady his voice.

"How's Nelson?"

"Nelson?" Sean said in surprise. "Oh. He's fine. A little freaked out, but he has every right to be."

"He's not hurt?"

"His arm, a little," Sean said. "But he'll be fine."

His cool hands were heavy against her own, but they seemed distant with each breath. How could she make him not worry? The thought was slow, tedious. And after a minute, she couldn't remember the thought at all, only the pain.

21 NEW RESOLVE

Even the pleasant and vitalizing smell of coffee did little to erase Lawrence's sour expression when he stepped out of the car. Though he had no personal vendetta against this place in its current reincarnation, the location used to belong to a real pain in the neck who had stuck her nose in the business of the supernatural community more often than not.

Yet that particular annoyance had skipped out of the city nearly thirty years ago, so Lawrence decided it was probably safe to assume the building was just that: a building. Even if it still had the faintest hint of sorcery hanging about it, tickling the nose like the rich roast of coffee beans.

"The Café Compendium. Pheft! They didn't even try to hide that it used to be a hovel for spell-flingers or warlocks or what have you," Lawrence said bitterly to his companion, turning his eyes from the large sign. "But the kid vouches for it, so I guess that makes it neutral territory."

Jericho nodded in his usual silent, brooding manner, though it was easy to tell what he was thinking about. His hand kept running to his hip, reaching for an item that wasn't there. The giant vampire's look of annoyance at finding the item missing was something that Lawrence understood—he was feeling much the same way. His jacket was far too light, the reassuring weight of a revolver gone. It left behind a feeling of uncomfortable vulnerability.

Lawrence couldn't remember a time when he hadn't carried a weapon on his person, and he was hoping he wouldn't regret that decision.

Shaking his head and offering one last grumble of complaint, Lawrence stepped forward, ignoring the closed sign on the café's door, and reached for the handle. It was unlocked, just as the werewolf-lovin' kid had said it would be.

Pulling the door open, the two vampires stepped inside the bookstore, ignoring the rows of shelves stuffed full of books and heading straight to the tables in the café section.

Two interlopers seeking neutral territory, just like the vampires were, had already taken a seat at a table in the cramped little coffee nook.

"Welcome! Take a seat. I've brewed a pot o' joe, and hopefully this little gab fest of ours doesn't take long enough that I got to brew a second, aye?" the mongrel leader of the Colesbrooke werewolf pack, Donald, said as he raised his coffee mug in salute as if he were in a pub.

The statuesque woman seated next to Donald gave a shake of her head and turned her nose up at the untouched mug in front of her, making the vibrant colored beads on her headdress clatter.

"It's a terrible brew. People these days throw around the word 'artisan' as if they've forgotten the very definition of the word," Deva huffed as if the coffee's low quality brew was a personal offense to her.

Lawrence wasn't sure how much he and the werewolf woman had in common, but at least they could both agree that the cheap blend of milk, sugar, and coffee that most coffee houses

275

whipped up was nothing but a pale imitation of the bitter brew that was so popular in days gone by.

"Oh, it's not all bad," assured Donald, though he might have just been defending the brew because he'd been the one to make the pot of coffee.

There was no real hostility in their voices. The constant stream of arguments and disagreements the two undoubtedly shared sounded commonplace or, perhaps, even some sort of flirtatious ritual between them.

Sara could be like that at times, having been at Lawrence's side long enough to know exactly what buttons to push to make him nearly shake with anger one minute and then double over laughing the next.

A twinge of sorrow knifed through him, and he did his best to banish it with a scowl.

This was not the time to be distracted.

Moving forward, he took a seat opposite of Donald, but Jericho stepped around the table entirely and began to pour himself a mug of the coffee. Either he didn't much care about the quality of the coffee, or he thought it best to remain standing until some of the tension was bled from the air.

After all, the Howlers might have been driven out of the city, but so had the peace his Sara had worked so hard to foster between the supernatural communities.

Perhaps that would change tonight. Or perhaps not.

"So, where do we begin?" Lawrence asked. It was best to cut straight into the matter at hand.

There was a difference between being someone's ally and being someone's friend, and while he could see himself as an ally to a werewolf, he'd rather eat a stake of hawthorn before he'd ever let anyone call him a friend to the beasts cursed to hunt his kind.

"How about you start with a formal apology for doing everything you could to drive my kindred into hiding and turning this entire city into your personal kingdom?" Deva asked. Unlike her snide comment with Donald, her words now were vitriolic.

Lawrence's lips peeled back into a sneer, intentionally revealing his elongated fangs. He was about to give his own acidic retort, but Donald raised a hand.

"Please, let's not start with the bickering. We're all here to address the issues of the future not slights of the past," the werewolf said. "And it *is* the future of this city that is at risk. We all know it. Changes must be made and the faster we put 'em in place, the better it'll be for everyone."

Lawrence managed to swallow his bitter words and replace the sneer on his face with a flat, fake grin.

"But of course, let's discuss the future of the city, one that'll be undoubtedly pleasant to your kin," Lawrence said with false sincerity. "So, what're these changes you propose? Dividing up my territory? A tithe? Or a monthly sacrifice?"

Donald frowned, folding his arms and leaning back in his chair. His counterpart seemed about to spit on the table.

A noisy slurping sound cut through the air.

"It's good," Jericho said as he took another sip of the coffee. "Thanks."

All eyes turned to Jericho as he inhaled the coffee aroma. Lawrence's hostility evaporated and he sighed, rubbing his eyes.

"Don't be stupid, old boy," he said. "You can barely even taste it."

"Don't you think we've been fighting long enough?" Donald asked. "Most of my pack has deserted this city . . . and before you ask, no. They will not be returning, either. There is nothing left for them here. We've both lost our packs. The time for power plays has long since gone."

Lawrence eyed Jericho's cup of coffee. "Why won't they return? They ain't got nothin' to fear from the Howlers anymore, and they ain't got nothin' to fear from the Red Lightning Pub,"

Lawrence said. "You gotta understand I find it hard to believe that I'm lucky enough that the biggest threat to my people suffered some misfortune when I'm at my weakest . . ."

His eyes narrowed as he looked at Deva.

". . . especially as they ain't the ones bein' hunted for sport like my flock was."

Deva blinked and her brown eyes turned gold, a subtle threat that prodding at a werewolf was a bad idea.

Donald seemed oblivious to Lawrence's blatant suspicion and instead explained in earnest. "It's true the Howlers didn't seek us out to do us harm like they hunted you. Well, I hate to say this but they've done more damage to my pack than they have your flock."

Rage flowed through Lawrence, and his fingertips ached.

Donald hastily drove on. "And I say that in knowing of your terrible loss, but I stand by my claim. You see, while the Howlers claimed the lives of your family members, they've poisoned the souls of my pack."

Lawrence's hand curled into a fist.

"How do you mean?" Jericho asked, setting his coffee mug down as he sat down at the table. "How'd the Howlers hurt you?"

"If the answer could bite you, both of you would lack throats," Deva snarled. "The Howlers have wronged more than just you. They were the ones responsible for the death and destruction of the Trouble and Toil."

Where Jugular James died.

"We lost someone there, too," Jericho said. "But what's that got to do with anything? How're the souls of your pack getting poisoned cuz of that?"

Donald let out a defeated sigh. "The reason my pack even bothered staying at this city was because we were able to be human. Or at least as human as we could be. I don't have to remind you that my people's curse is to hunt your own people . . ."

Lawrence gave a bitter laugh, and Deva's eyes narrowed dangerously.

"Well, then perhaps we *should* remind you that despite this curse, our pack hasn't gone about killing your clan," she growled. "Nor do we bear the consequences of sparing your lives. We haven't been trapped in our bestial states by showing you mercy."

Jericho's eyes widened. "The witch! She broke your curse?"

For a moment, Lawrence's breath caught in his throat. Was that even possible?

Donald shook his head.

"No, the Crone wasn't able to cure us. In fact, even if she could have, I doubt she would have. She had some sort of vile brew, a potion of sorts that satisfied our curse's demands." Donald explained. "We slaved for these potions, you see, giving her all the coin she could ever want. We paid her, and on a night of a full moon, we would consume the draught. Then we could hunt and feast on a beast's heart and still transform back into humans."

A sudden sickening feeling twisted in Lawrence's stomach.

"We didn't need to kill your clan," Deva said angrily, "because we could cheat our curse of its due. But now, we don't have that benefit because the Howlers have slain the Crone."

"And you need to hunt vampires again," Jericho said.

Donald nodded. "Yes. This city allowed us to keep our humanity and freed us of the obligation to murder every month— that was the foundation of our pack. All of my pack that settled here were kindred spirits who did not want any more blood on their hands. But now that's no longer the case. Now each and every member of my pack is going to have to decide on whether to be a murderer or to be a permanent wolf, and there is nothing we can do about that."

Lawrence was silent for a moment and then said, "So that's it then? If you can't control your pack during a full moon, there's no hope for peace is there? You'll be compelled to hunt my people. My flock."

Donald stayed quiet.

"I have spent years traveling and searching for an alternative to the Crone's methods, but none have presented themselves," Deva said, finally breaking the silence. "I doubt we will discover a cure for lycanthropy before the next full moon."

"You have to understand, we want peace. . . . We truly do," Donald said. "We will take every precaution we can to make sure we don't harm any vampire who refuses to drink straight from humans. But we've been placating the wolf within for a long, long, time. We don't know what'll happen to us when we suffer through a full moon without the potions. It's only fair to warn you."

Lawrence stayed quiet for several heartbeats. "I believe you, wolf. Thanks for the warning."

Donald, Deva, and Jericho all stared at Lawrence. The vampire boss himself was surprised to hear the words leave his lips. One hand ran down to his wrist where he began to toy with his golden cufflinks imprinted with the symbol for the Red Lightning Pub. It was the symbol he and Sara had designed, the symbol representing a bootlegger vampire who had the gall to believe that neither prohibition nor his curse would rule him.

"As I see it, we've been fightin' long enough," he said. "I'm plumb tuckered out. A bit of a breather would be mighty welcome, but seein' as that ain't gonna happen, we better plan for the future."

"Well, I'm glad we're thinking along the same lines," Donald said and then frowned a bit. "But I'm at a loss as to where to go from here."

Lawrence frowned, too. With the numbers of the local werewolves and vampires in shambles, their resources nearly tapped, what could they possibly do? Was all this talk just a waste of time, making the fact that they'd one day meet as enemies, as the hunter and the hunted, that much more bitter?

Once more Jericho noisily sipped his coffee before speaking. "I've an idea. What were those twins of yours called again? The Von Grimmels?"

****

Boyd gave the stolen prescription bottle cap a twist and then tossed the white lid to the filthy ground. He tipped his head back and opened his mouth, letting the little white pills land on his tongue. Each brought with it a faint sour taste.

Ignoring this sourness, he crunched the pills into a disgusting paste with his teeth then raised his liquor bottle and took a long pull from it.

The taste of the stolen painkillers was washed away in a flood of sweet rum, rushing down his empty gullet and bringing with it a soothing warmth.

Much, much better.

"More of them showed up than what I thought," Clive said, leaning against the brick wall of an alleyway as Boyd approached. "A lot more actually. Not many believed the whole werewolf thing until I tore someone's throat out."

A nod was Boyd's only reply. He was paying far too much attention to the chemical transformation happening within his own body. The burning liquor was thinning his blood and making it easier for the opiates to ride the crimson river through his system until his brain was finally hit by them.

Then he would feel . . . funny. His limbs would tingle pleasantly and the entire world around him would just get a light, bubbly feel to it. It wasn't necessarily pleasant, but it was one of the few things that Boyd could actually feel since becoming a werewolf.

Not even his lycanthropic ability to heal could repair the damage to gray matter that years of hard drugs and harder living had done before his turning. However, his lifestyle had the perk of helping him get ahold of the much-needed pills he constantly desired.

That was the only reason why Boyd was bothering to stop in a little town, far away from the one that the Howlers had been slaughtered in.

Boyd had wondered if he and Clive were the only survivors of that massacre. He didn't hate Leon for letting his stupid ego get the best of him, nor did he blame any of the victors for his most recent blight. Leon died and that was that. The only thing Boyd really cared about was staving off the numbness lurking behind every corner of his mind. His constant fight to feel was the only reason why he was even bothering to put up with Clive at all.

The big brute of a werewolf wanted to rustle up a new gang, becoming the Alpha he so desperately wanted to be. He didn't know how to lead, though, so Boyd wondered if Clive would pull off his idea for a good initiation ritual. He wanted new recruits to return to the city that had nearly been their deaths and get revenge on those who had destroyed the Howlers.

So, Clive was recruiting in a particular fashion. He was going around to local gangs and using his lycanthropic curse as an advantage to transform the humans who thought themselves the leaders of their gangs. The plan was simple: get a good number of people, pass along the curse, then head back to the vampire's city on the night of the full moon and let their newest recruits run wild.

The bloodbath that would follow would be utter chaos, spreading the lycanthropic curse even further, allowing Clive to gain a massive new pack, end his enemies, and reap the benefits of a beaten city in one fell swoop.

Naturally, Boyd approved of the idea because, in part, it had originally been his. Clive wasn't really a thinker. He just wanted to wield the same kind of brutality that Leon had wielded, so Boyd had devised a plan that was so evil and so simple that even his new partner couldn't screw it up. Adrenaline was the best cure for numbness.

It was also a good way to get more meds. The gangs were loaded with them.

Besides, if things began to go south, Boyd was confident in his ability to slip through danger's grasp and get to safety. That was what he'd always done before. He'd managed to dodge bullets in Vietnam, managed to avoid a heroin overdose thanks to becoming a werewolf, and then even managed to avoid a silver bullet when the Howlers had rushed in to tear down the gang of vampires and werewolves.

If Boyd could feel anything like pride anymore, he decided he might've been proud of the fact he was a survivor.

"How many?" he asked Clive, holding up his hands and opening and shutting them, savoring the sensation of each digit buzzing.

"If those idiots down by the docks know what's good for them and show up, we can probably get a good thirty people total," Clive said with a twisted grin. "Then just a single bite and alls we gotta do is wait for a full moon. When the dust settles, we'll be top dogs."

Boyd nodded, his eyelids drooping. They popped open when his ears began to ring, and Clive gave him a horrified look as his mouth opened and shut wordlessly.

Boyd frowned, trying to concentrate on what Clive was saying. The burned-out werewolf didn't think it was his ears that were making Clive mute. The other werewolf just couldn't speak well because blood was gushing out of a hole punched in his chest.

Boyd glanced around, nonplussed, trying to cut through his drug haze to figure out what was happening. The ringing noise in his ears went up a tone as something else thudded through the air. He turned around to ask Clive what was going on but the werewolf had collapsed, the upper portion of his skull missing.

Frowning, Boyd wondered why Clive's skin wasn't already trying to reknit itself. Even the blood wasn't slowing its flow out of Clive's body, which never really happened to werewolves unless deadly silver or wolfsbane was introduced into their system.

That was odd.

"You should've believed us from the very start," one voice echoed down the alleyway.

"Nothing can give us the slip when we want to find it," came another voice.

A third voice rumbled so loudly that Boyd's bones rattled.

"Bah! Luck, I say. Pure luck. If Al and James were around, I'd have found these guys in half the time. But no! I'm stuck with you two miserable Krauts."

Boyd turned around and through his drug haze, he began to feel something. Fear? It was hard to tell with the alcohol and stimulants rushing through his body.

A trio was approaching. Two of the three were dressed identically, making them appear as a mirror image of one another. Between them was a stocky and horribly ugly vampire who clutched a massive revolver in each hand.

Boyd glanced back down at Clive's corpse and then up at the trio.

A sudden spurt of understanding cut through his drug-addled mind, and Boyd realized that he was in danger.

He turned to run when another thunderous roar cut through the air. Boyd didn't feel any pain, but suddenly his right leg wouldn't support him and he collapsed to the ground, falling straight onto Clive's corpse. Struggling, Boyd began to crawl over the obstacle and pull himself down the street.

He didn't get too far before a heavy weight slammed into his shoulder, flipping him over.

"Alright, tough guy, listen up," said the ugly vampire as the twin werewolves hovered around behind him. "The gun in my right hand has hollow points. The gun in my left hand has silver tipped rounds."

Boyd swallowed nervously as he felt two barrels press down, one into each shoulder.

"Now I'm going to be squeezing one of these triggers no matter what," the vampire said with a wicked grin. "But which trigger? Well, that depends on your answer, got it?"

Instinctual fear and adrenaline were doing a good job of sobering Boyd up, so he nodded quickly to show he understood.

"What do you want to know?" he asked.

The vampire didn't answer immediately. Instead, he used his thumbs to draw back the hammer of the revolvers.

"Apparently you Howlers . . . or should I say, former Howlers, were pretty good at finding nests of blood junkies," he said. "Well, as it turns out, a few of my associates are in need of knowing where some blood junkie warrens are."

Boyd looked beyond the vampire and over to the two werewolf twins. It didn't seem like they were going to help him.

"Better answer him, we're on a tight schedule," one of the werewolves said.

"It's true," the other said. "We've got to play superhero, butcher, and chef before the next full moon."

Boyd cleared his throat nervously. "So, did you guys ever hear about the vamps backing the drug cartels in Texas?"

22 TO THE FUTURE

"Are you sure you don't need anything?"

"I'm positive."

"Well I mean, I have water, some juice. . . . How about I put on some soup?"

"No thanks, I'm fine."

"It'll just take a second."

Clara had to concentrate on keeping her smile on her face as she looked at her brother.

Benjamin meant well, but he wasn't really the best nurse. He didn't put much stock in werewolves eating human food, but he knew that it was something that soothed Clara, so he'd gone out of his way to bring home groceries more suited for a victim of the flu. He was somewhat aggressive in his caretaking, needing to do something or else he'd feel like he was somehow failing her.

Not that Clara was really convinced that she needed a caretaker, anyway. Though it had been touch and go for nearly a week as a wicked infection ravaged her body, her body was slowly recovering more and more of its strength and lycanthropic regeneration. If Sean hadn't removed the silver from her body, she wouldn't have even had a chance to recover.

Thomas theorized that the infection spread from the silver bullet's penetration had likely suppressed her lycanthropic regeneration despite the bullet's removal. Or perhaps, her regeneration was combating internal injuries and infections, which was why Clara felt so drained until recently.

No matter how much she wished Thomas to be correct, Clara had a feeling that he was wrong. The reason Clara was growing stronger was because the curse was growing stronger with each passing night as the full moon approached.

That little suspicion was driving Clara nearly sick with worry, almost as much as her brother's pesky presence was driving her nuts.

"Okay, well . . . I'll be back in a bit," Benjamin said, catching onto her annoyance. "If you need anything just call."

"Alright, I will," Clara promised from her little fortress of recovery that had once been Benjamin's couch.

Benjamin nodded and headed for the door. But before he opened it, he stopped, his face knotting into a scowl. The scent of vampire and sunscreen was suddenly heavy in the room. Clara noted the hint of clove. Sean was here.

When Benjamin opened the door, he did it with a sneer.

"Hey there, Benny boy," Sean said with a smile, a box of chocolates tucked under one arm. He seemed unfazed by Benjamin's contempt. "Is Clara awake? Can you let me in?"

Benjamin's sneer dropped into a frown. He hated the familiar terms Sean kept coming up with. Clara almost snickered. Benji hated her nickname for him, too.

Her brother had promised her not to let his personal opinions of vampires influence how he saw Sean, but he'd quickly discovered over the last week of constant visits that his opinion of Sean was pretty low even without factoring in the whole blood drinking thing. Clara knew he couldn't stand how Sean joked around, always ready for a quip. However, it gave Benjamin a chance to poke his own fun with the *punk* dating his sister.

"Hmm, sure. I might do that if you . . . jump up and down on one leg," Benjamin said seriously, folding his arms across his chest.

Sean rolled his eyes. "Ah, c'mon. Don't be a jerk."

"Hey, the door is open. It's the threshold that's keeping you out." Benjamin smirked. "And I'm sure with a little ritual of the one leg hop, it'd lower."

Sean grumbled, moving his hands. Probably an obscene gesture, but Clara couldn't see around her brother. There was a hollow thud, and Sean hissed in pain. He probably smashed his knuckles across the invisible barrier blocking him from entering the apartment. Again.

"Is that Sean?" Clara called, giggling. She kind of liked Benjamin's and Sean's weird ritual.

"No, just some delusional insect who thinks he's actually good enough for you," Benjamin said.

"Hey, not cool. If I were delusional, why would I think of myself as an insect?"

"Sean?"

"Yes, come on. I know you know it's me. You can smell me," Sean said. "Benjamin won't invite me in. Well, or you. You could just let me in while he stands here in the doorway."

"It is true." Benjamin smirked as he took a step back. "But she didn't. C'mon, get in here."

The threshold fell and Sean strode into the apartment, a mixture of frustration and contentment spread across his face.

"I'll be back in an hour," Benjamin said loudly as a reminder to Clara. He then dropped his voice as he whispered at Sean, "She's having a good day, but don't let her move around too much, got it?"

Like whispering would keep her from hearing.

"Alright, well there goes all my plans to salsa dance her illness away," Sean said with a cheeky smile.

Benjamin muttered an obscenity and left, slamming the door behind him.

"I think he's almost tolerating me," Sean said as he approached her. "Maybe in time, he may even come to like me. I'm guessing in two, three hundred years. Four hundred tops."

Clara giggled as her boyfriend presented her the box of chocolates. A hungry gleam must have flashed through her eyes, because he started to laugh.

"A few sweets for my sweetheart. I thought you might enjoy them considering your brother has been going overboard with the chicken noodle soup."

It was about time Sean rescued her with something tastier. Even if food was blander now than when she was a human, quality foods with strong flavors still tasted delicious. It was why the werewolves loved strong coffee so much.

She ravaged the box's wrapping, eagerly searching for the perfect chocolate. The creamy texture was just the change of pace she needed from the watery soup, and the dark cocoa smelled so good that she could almost taste it. She popped a dark rectangle one it into her mouth, and the bitter chocolate melted into her tongue. Heaven.

"You're telling me. I've been eating canned soup every meal for nearly a week. I'm surprised Benjamin hasn't tried to turn it into an IV drip or something," she said, making room for Sean to sit down then sinking back into the folds of blankets on the couch. "But this is the first time I've been sick in like, fifty years. The werewolf blood usually does a really good job at keeping all sorts of illnesses away."

Sean reached down and stole a piece of chocolate for himself and chewed on it thoughtfully.

"But you're getting better."

Clara nodded. "Yeah, but . . ."

He stopped chewing. "What is it?"

"I'm only getting better because the lycanthropic curse is getting stronger, no matter what Thomas says. The full moon is bringing out the wolf within. After the new moon, the wolf starts waking up, getting stronger. It's realizing that the silver is no longer threatening it," Clara said, doing her best to try and explain. "Sean, I was very lucky to find Donald and the others of this city, to learn there is a different way from slaughtering vampires every month. But the potion from the Crone made it possible, keeping the worst of the curse away."

She set down the chocolates, staring into Sean's uncomprehensive eyes. He needed to understand.

"Without those potions, I'm going to become a killer, Sean." The words bubbled out of Clara and her eyes began to water up. "A vampire killer. The wolf is going to feed because I won't be able to stop it. I won't be able to control myself any more . . . and I don't know if I can handle that . . ."

She wiped at her eyes, trying to banish the tears she refused to let fall.

"And if I won't let myself become a killer, I have no choice but to give up being human. I'll be trapped in my wolf form," Clara said bitterly. "That means that we can't— we'll never be able to have what we fought for."

Sean reached out and placed a comforting arm around her, pulling her gently into his chest. "We still defeated the Howlers and made the city safe for everyone again. The vampires and the werewolves are going to have some hard times ahead, but at least we have the city."

She snorted. "I don't see that as much of a consolation prize. I guess I'm not as noble as you. I'm more worried about us."

He gently hooked his fingers underneath Clara's chin, raising her eyes up to meet his.

"I was saying that vampires and werewolves have gotten the best they could out of this whole mess thanks to us. Lawrence even accepted Thomas back as his barkeep, and Artemis has been hired to spruce up the pub." His voice was warm despite his cold touch. "I'm not going to let them forget all we've done for them. Now it's time for us to finally have our own happy ending, and they better be sure to help us with that."

"How?" Clara lowered her gaze, still far from reassured.

"I don't know," Sean sighed deeply, his chest rising and falling. She felt as if she were riding an ocean wave, one with a beating rhythm. "How about we find a way to become human again?"

She pushed away from him. "What? Do you think that's even possible?"

"Who knows," he said honestly, "But when I'm next to you, I feel there isn't anything we can't do. We're unstoppable."

Any disagreement Clara might have had was silenced as he pressed his lips against hers. His proposed future was a good one indeed, and for the first time in many decades, she truly wanted to be human again.

THE END

TO MY READERS

Thank you for reading *Moonlit Woods*. I loved continuing the *Children of Kaespars* series and am grateful that you've loved reading it. Thank you for picking up the second book.

Did you like the first book? Did you like the second? Want more? Authors like me survive because of readers like you. Please help us out and write a review. It doesn't have to be long, but it does need to be honest. So please, tell me what you think and let others know, too.

The third installment of the *Children of Kaespars* is on its way. Watch out for book three, *Bloodstained Theory*. For updates on its release and the rest of the books in *Children of Kaespars*, follow me on Facebook and Twitter or subscribe to my website.

Thank you for your readership and support!

Website: http://brandyitimmons.bdrqazz.com/
Newsletter: https://mailchi.mp/df6cccb961b9/brandyitimmons
Twitter: BrandyITimmons
Facebook: brandyitimmons
Instagram: brandy_i_timmons_author

ACKNOWLEDGEMENTS

First of all, I want to thank readers like you who are making it possible to continue this series. Your readership means everything to me.

Second, thank you to the wonderful writing friends I've made on Twitter. Your examples and encouragements empowered me to keep writing, to keep editing. Thank you.

ABOUT THE AUTHOR

Brandy I. Timmons is a Canadian writer obsessed with the supernatural. Captivated by the interactions of humans, vampires, werewolves, and other supernatural creatures, Brandy seeks to weave new worlds and characters that question humanity and life. She spends her non-writing time daydreaming and reading.

BOOK SUMMARY

Clara Warren has finally accepted being a werewolf. Running with her pack feels natural, and a local witch brews a potion that allows them to hunt animals at the full moon instead of vampires. Clara likes not murdering every month, though vampires are no friends of hers.

When her human boyfriend starts to stink of vampire, Clara must reveal her own supernatural identity to protect him or risk losing another happy relationship. As she steels herself to reveal everything, her boyfriend becomes the latest casualty of a vampire spat, their newest fledging.

A vampire.

In the chaos of salvaging her relationship, a drifting werewolf pack breaks the treaty among Colesbrooke's supernatural community. Old feuds are rekindled. As a new war threatens, Clara must decide whose side she's on.

The second installment of the Children of Kaespars series, *Moonlit Woods,* forges new bonds of friendships and propels the quest of humanity forward.

CHILDREN OF KAESPARS

"There's nothing wrong with wanting more. We will figure this out. Not just you. Not just me. All of us. Together. And if we don't find a cure for another fifty years, at least we'll have each other."

When Thomas Spencer is wrenched into the supernatural world, everything changes for his best friends. As they adjust to new lives, they begin to question what it means to be human.

Not everyone is satisfied. Meeting and dating new people only teaches them that the supernatural world isn't as marvelous as immortality claims. Some vampires and werewolves aren't satisfied.

The desire for a cure sets them on a journey of science, magic, and danger that forces them to question their beliefs and morals. Not every answer is ethical, and each person must decide what they're willing to sacrifice to be normal again.

Follow Thomas Spencer and Clara Warren and their friends in the *Children of Kaespars* series as they discover the price of living.

DON'T MISS THE REST OF THE SERIES

Children of the Kaespars

Book 1 – Shadows of Colesbrooke

Book 2 – Moonlit Woods

Book 3 – Bloodstained Theory

Book 4 – Quest by Candlelight

Book 5 – Severed Ties

www.ingramcontent.com/pod-product-compliance
Lightning Source LLC
Chambersburg PA
CBHW051940220626
47052CB00004B/723